REGARDING FLORIANS

REGARDING FLORIANS
Part One:
FLASHPOINT

KELLY JO PARDUE

Write My Wrongs, LLC, P.O. Box 80781 Lansing, MI 48908
United States
www.writemywrongsediting.com
Copyright © 2021 Kelly Jo Pardue

ISBN: 978-1-956932-07-2

For those who suffer in silence.

If you or someone you love is experiencing thoughts of suicide, please call the National Suicide Prevention Hotline at 1-800-273-8255. Press "1" for veterans.

CONTENTS

PROLOGUE

I t is said that our universe began with one simple event—the Big Bang. However, most don't realize that the building blocks of the cosmos have been manipulated by a special race of beings that came to be at the same time. The Beginners.

Ancient, infinitely immortal beings who can create and manipulate time, energy, and matter. They formed all of the stars, galaxies, and habitable worlds within the universe. Yet, their existence is often considered mythological, as no one living today has ever seen them.

As the universe expanded and the need for more of their kind became apparent, they evolved and began having children. This progression became the method for the reproduction of life across all of space. After a certain amount of time, some of the Beginners' children were born without their parents' abilities to create and manipulate, yet they retained immortality.

Our story follows this race of beings, the Florians.

The Florians are ancient descendants of the Beginners. When some weren't born with their parents' extraordinary abilities, they were considered defective. Instead of eliminating their flawed offspring, the Beginners decided to abandon them on the planet Rygone. These castaways are known as the First Generation, and although their parents didn't see them as worthy, the Florians were highly intelligent and very capable. They studied the world around them and formed a home to rival any other in the universe. The Florians used Rygone's resources and created a technologically advanced society to help protect and sustain themselves. Also, they built the beautiful and beyond-advanced capital, Baltica City.

Florians are an attractive species. Their appearance is similar to the humans of Earth, with the most significant difference being the paternal birthmark they all possess on the back of their neck, just below the hairline. Once the Florians began having children of their own, they were born with these red birthmarks that stayed the same throughout the paternal line. The Florians started using this as a way to determine bloodlines and accurately identify the sire of a child.

Since they're immortal, their overall growth differs from person to person. Children all grow at the same rate, but at some point, they stop. Most seem to stop aging at what would be considered their early to mid-thirties. However, some stop at what would be deemed a seven-year-old Earth child or a seventy-year-old adult.

Florian women inherited a unique adaptation from the female Beginners. They can choose when and if they want to *laval* or ovulate. If a woman isn't ready or becomes ready to have a child, she can *laval* on her own. Although this is a very specialized and coveted adaptation, Florians conceive slowly. They sometimes went a hundred years without adding a newborn to their kind, so they implemented a bold plan to increase their planet's population. At a time when they only had a few hundred of their own people, they found a way to get a message to the universe: Rygone wants refugees.

The Florians weren't prepared for the onslaught of newcomers, so they developed a method to evaluate their new residents. After a few decades, a few civil wars, and the need to establish a Florian Army to protect the innocents and themselves, they managed to make it work. Cities and villages sprung up all over the planet, and the population became vibrant and diverse. Some Florians left Baltica City and went to the outer civilizations and assimilated with the new residents living on Rygone. Many married mortals and had children of their own. Hanner, or half-Florians, aren't immortal like their Florian kin, but they possess a longer life span and are difficult to injure or kill. It didn't take long for the Hanner-Florians to outnumber their relatives. Many of these newcomers came to Baltica City and wanted to take up residence just as their parents did before them. They wanted a piece of both the life of a mortal and the coveted life of a Florian.

The strife this caused brought the residents of Rygone to the brink of war. A Second-Generation Florian named Warren Strom stepped up and made the case that they needed a formal government for the whole planet, representing all species and their needs. The citizens took up their first vote, and it was agreed that an official Rygonian parliament was to be formed. Its first task was to build two even larger and more advanced cities close to Baltica City—Baltica North and South. These would be open to all citizens of the planet. All Florian families and individuals already living in Baltica City were grandfathered in and allowed to stay if desired. Many left for the newer accommodations, but a core group of older generation Florians stayed, like the Smiths, Harlows, and Stroms. The rest of the space was committed to use by the new government, medical, and research facilities.

***

Over the next million or so years, Rygone went through ups and downs, just like all civilizations. But they were able to pull together and reestablish order and prosperity.

Until now.

You see, Florians are more than immortal; they are *invincible*. They can't be killed. They quite literally live forever. If injured—a difficult task on its own—they will quickly heal and be as good as new in no time. And this infuriates their enemies.

So, now our story begins. We start with an ancient, volatile married couple, who are trying to escape their mistakes…

iii

CHAPTER 1
FIGHT AND FLIGHT

T roy shut his eyes tight and sucked in a breath, trying not to imagine their DREX fighter slamming into the walls of the Summerset Cave. "Why couldn't we just Jump out of the atmosphere?"

"Because each Jump, no matter where the ship is, gets logged immediately, and the coordinates are sent to air corps headquarters. They'd know where we went the instant we got there." Dia glanced at her husband and continued, "I've never crashed in these caves. At least, not while I was flying with you."

Troy opened his eyes to look at her. "How reassuring."

She gave him a sarcastic grin. "I'm the best at this. I've taught all our pilots to fly in here. Nobody else in the Florian Army could get us out of this."

He knew she was right, though it would only go to her head more if he admitted it. This was the best route for them to escape. To abandon their people, their friends, and families. The ones they swore to serve and protect.

Dia turned her focus back to flying. These caves were used to train the most experienced pilots from all sectors of Rygone, but they were also incredibly treacherous. Many Florians failed. Many mortals died.

She knew they were approaching one of the most dangerous sections of the cave. Her adrenaline spiked so violently she was afraid she would make a mistake and end their escape attempt prematurely.

Quietly, her voice cool and steady, Dia said, "Hold on."

Troy watched a solid wall, with no way through, approach them at breakneck speed. He grabbed the straps on his harness tight and closed his eyes. He'd never been a big fan of flying, especially with his wife.

Without warning, the DREX went from traveling forward to shooting down into a 180-degree dive. The g-forces on their bodies would've made any other lifeform black out, but Dia and Troy were able to suppress the urge. Troy felt like they were falling forever, until another instant direction change had them traveling straight up. He reminded himself this portion of the cave would open into a giant cathedral cavern, and they would soon be on the other side of the planet.

Suddenly, there was a loud scraping sound, and the fighter shuddered violently. "Shit," Dia breathed out. "What a time to learn our new fighters don't fit in these caves."

Troy's eyes shot open, and he found his side of the craft scraping hard against the rock wall. It wasn't causing damage yet, but they both knew there was an even narrower section not far away.

Dia leaned across Troy. "Take the controls. Don't move them at all!"

Without a word, Troy obeyed and held them as steady as he could. It was hard, as Dia was now lying across his lap with her hands pressed against the canopy glass. Troy knew what she was about to do, and panic seized him.

"Dia, no! This is why we're leaving!" Troy yelled.

Again, in her cool, calm voice, she said, "Well, we won't make it any other way. Besides, the power may be useful before this is over."

The fighter lurched to the left with a loud bang. Sparks poured off the fuselage, but instead of significant damage, the energy created by the friction between the rock and the Karon steel was absorbed directly into Dia's hands. The longer they slid against the wall, the more energy siphoned into her.

Troy watched with fear and awe. First, her hands, then arms, then the rest of her body began to glow with what could only be described as a cool-green flame. When the traveling energy finally made it to her face, her brown eyes lit up the same color, like iridescent emeralds, and a pale-yellow mist streamed back over the sides of her face. Her long, brown, silken hair changed to a glowing blonde. The tips of her fingers were bright as a white star, ready to discharge her terrible new gift.

Finally, they careened into the cavern. Dia fell back into her seat with a satisfied slump and looked at him with a huge smile. She said breathlessly, "I know this power is dangerous, but it's just so euphoric."

Troy slowed the fighter down to a hover. He turned and closely examined his wife's face. But it wasn't his wife's face. It was the face of a mistake he'd made when she was in the wrong place at the wrong time. Now, what they had thought could be a potential saving grace for their people was turning into a nightmare.

"Dia, the danger is too great. We have to get out of here," he said, pleading to her.

"I know. I know the consequences. We don't have time to sit here and discuss the morality of our predicament."

Dia took back over the controls and slid her hand up the control screen, sending them shooting forward rapidly. They hurtled toward a small opening at the other side of the cavern. The rest of the way through the caves was relatively uneventful, and they were almost at the end.

Troy didn't need to look at Dia to feel the warmth and light coming off her. They'd never been able to figure out how long she could hold on to the energy before it had to be released. He was sure they'd never know now.

Dia saw the light of the cave exit coming up quickly. She slowed the fighter down significantly and engaged the cloaking drive to avoid having any of the local farmers see the damaged craft with her personal seal stamped on each side. Or, well, at least it was still on the left side.

They slowly exited the cave, and both stared out the front canopy in absolute horror. Everywhere they looked, people—their people—were being slaughtered by Coronian soldiers. Two large Coronian battle cruisers hovered high above the land, destroying buildings, bridges, and farms. It was mass chaos.

With shock filling her voice, Dia said almost to herself, "Where's my army? How did no monitoring station on the ground or orbit detect *two* battle cruisers enter our atmosphere? Were they waiting on my word to engage? *What's going on?*"

Troy flicked his eyes over to Dia. He wasn't a military man. He was a doctor and scientist who treated disease and developed inventions to make Rygone's citizens' lives better. With his lack of experience, he had no idea how to handle a situation like this. Troy watched her face closely. Even with the energy surrounding her, he could see the wheels turning in her mind. Their escape plan, he realized, had just been interrupted.

Dia slammed her hand down on the console and activated the communications system. They had turned everything off when they left in order to get away unnoticed, but that no longer mattered. They were immediately recognized by the air corps headquarters, and her position was logged. Dia, in her most commanding voice, yelled, "This is General Harlow! I'm at the north end of the Summerset Cave system, fifty tols south of the Breger Dunes. The residents are being attacked by two Coronian battle cruisers and hundreds of soldiers. There are *no* Florian resources here at all. Where are they?!"

There was no answer. It was as if they'd emerged from the cave on a different planet. Dia thought for a moment before putting her message on repeat and playing it to every outpost on Rygone, even to the station on Nexxus, one of the moons. Somebody had to hear her. She said to Troy, "We have to do something."

Troy nodded and pulled on his restraints, even though they were already as tight as they could get against his slender frame. He knew this would be a rough ride.

Dia engaged all of the weapon systems in the fighter. She had the most advanced DREX in their fleet, but Oscar and his team were still working bugs out of the system, so it hadn't been tested in the field yet. *This should be interesting*, Troy thought fearfully.

She disengaged the cloaking device and sped the fighter forward. The guidance systems determined the best possible targets to hit first, but she always trusted her instincts. If you allowed computers to do all of your work for you, what were you going to do if the computers weren't there?

She swept across the main road, heading toward the cave entrance, and fired at the ranks of Coronian soldiers advancing on a large farm on the right. Out of the corner of his eye, Troy saw a small family crawl out from under a tractor to watch them fly by. Troy wondered, *Do they think we abandoned them? Hopefully, reinforcements will come soon and get them to safety.*

Dia swept across the fields of wheat and alfalfa, taking out as many of the enemy as she could before the battle cruisers began to fire on them. She worked her way through the onslaught, but an ion cannon on top of one of the ships took a direct shot at them.

Troy could've sworn time slowed then, almost to a standstill. He watched the blast from the cannon head straight at them. His ability to react seemed nonexistent, and all he could do was witness what was happening. His eyes trailed from the incoming ion blast to Dia. She had jumped up from her seat and planted her hands firmly against the canopy, just like she did in the cave. The blast hit them, but there was no noise, no movement, nothing—nothing but a bright green light to his left. She'd absorbed the energy in an attempt to save them. She fell back into her seat, hard. This time there was no smile, no euphoria.

She felt the intense power now flowing through her veins like a living being, tickling every cell in her body. Hysterically, she screamed, "Get me out of here! I can't hold this for very long!"

Troy and Dia had been married for an exceptionally long time. Their wedding rings, per Rygonian tradition, were two rings worn on the left hand. The ring signifying love was worn on the middle finger, and a smaller ring, meaning trust, was worn on the index finger. Recently, Troy had made a new set of special rings for both of them. They looked and felt like their original pairs, only these had a secret built into them. Without her knowing, he'd exchanged Dia's one day while she was in the shower for an occasion like this.

Troy reached forward and grabbed her left hand, interlocking their fingers and making sure all four of their wedding rings touched. Though he could barely make out her features, he could see the confusion on her face.

"Troy?" Over the buzz of the power coursing through her, Dia could feel another sensation. Her head began to swim. All her memories were becoming jumbled, and she couldn't control her thoughts. She screamed, "What are you doing? Troy! Stop!"

The spinning stopped. The world went all white. Nothing was left but the power in her veins. She heard a far-off voice that she didn't recognize say, "When you feel the cool air, release all of the power inside you."

There was a rush of air over her, and she realized she was floating. *Release all of the power inside you*, the voice had said. Somehow, she knew exactly what that meant.

CHAPTER 2
TORTURE OR DEATH?

Troy didn't know if he'd been falling for five minutes or five years by the time he hit the ground.

A preconceived notion about his kind was that they didn't feel physical pain. Bullshit. Florians felt pain; it just dissipated quickly, and they healed unnaturally fast.

He groaned and rolled onto his back. It was dark out. In the distance, he could see the light of the fires. His heart sank as the events of the past few hours played through his head.

Making it through the cave only to find themselves in a nest of the enemy as they slaughtered innocents and destroyed valuable crops and property. Being the only people there to offer protection, and only by chance. What he did to Dia, his wife of almost eight hundred thousand years.

The doctor raised his left hand and looked at his rings. Locked inside were the precious memories of the only woman he ever truly loved. When or if she ever made it to a civilized world, she would have no recollection of anything. The only way she would ever get them back was if they reunited someday.

Tears flowed from his eyes, as he could no longer hold his pain in. He could feel them roll down his face to the back of his neck and drip onto the grass beneath him. He stayed like that for a few minutes before he decided he needed to find a way to get to one of the outposts nearby and figure out what the hell happened.

Troy stood and went to take a step, only to be hit on the back of his head. The pain was blinding, and he dropped to his knees. He heard two gruff male voices and one female voice. He regained enough of his composure to stand back up when he was tackled from behind and slammed to the ground. Troy felt as if he was sparring with Dia when she was in a bad mood, but she smelled a lot better than the beast of a male Coronian on him right now.

He got his bearing about him and was able to spin around, grabbing the knife in the huge creature's belt as he shoved it off. Troy stood and backed away. The beast lunged at him, but the doctor thrust the blade directly into his neck, severing the jugular vein. The male Coronian dropped like a rock and lay gasping as he bled out.

Troy was always struck by the difference between the male and female Coronians. The females were Florian-like, but the males were giant boar-like beasts. They looked more like wild animals than an intelligent species capable of the horrors they were inflicting on his planet.

The female Coronian held a torch high and eyed Troy with disdain. He could see they hadn't been expecting him to be able to defend himself. Many others had thought the same thing—to their undoing.

"Well?" Troy asked quietly.

The second male beast looked at him with confusion and shock, but the woman was undaunted. She gave a coarse laugh. "I wasn't anticipating a fight from you, but it'll definitely be fun."

Troy didn't move. He paid attention to the sounds around him to see if any others were coming up from behind. Of course, he should've done that earlier when he was ambushed.

The woman didn't move either. She just stared at him with an unsettling, toothy grin. A rustle came from behind him. Just as a large club was swung at his head, he ducked and spun on his heel. Five more male Coronians were coming up behind him. Clubby came at him again, but Troy was an agile fighter and was able to get out of the way quickly. Again, he dispatched his enemy with the blade taken from the first beast.

Unfortunately, that didn't work well in Troy's favor. The other beasts came at him all at once. He wasn't completely incapable of taking on six Coronians, but almost immediately following them was another large group.

Troy was entirely surrounded by at least thirty of his enemy. Sure, he couldn't be killed, but many enemies of the Florians had learned ways to make them suffer to the point of wishing for the mercy of a death that would never come. He knew it probably wasn't going to make a difference, but he dropped the knife, put his hands up, and said, "Well, it looks like we're at a stalemate."

He regretted that statement.

They all attacked at once like a pack of rabid dogs. Troy fought them off as best as he could, but they pinned him to the ground at the bottom of a pile of sweaty, smelly bodies. They weren't even fighting him anymore. It was almost comical.

After a few minutes of pandemonium, Troy heard a loud yell of, "Where is he? Get the fuck off him! Veronica wants him fresh!"

Troy's eyes went wide, and he thought, *Fresh? What the fuck is that supposed to mean? And who's Veronica?*

There was a commotion of bodies moving above him until, finally, he saw the light from the torches all around them. Troy was left on the ground by himself, surrounded by a large gaggle of Coronians. He felt exposed and alone, but he kept his composure.

The beast who yelled about him needing to be fresh grabbed Troy by the front of his shirt and pulled him to his feet. The rest of the audience was silent as the newest beast examined Troy up and down. Finally, he said, "Fuck me, it's really you."

Troy just stared at his captor. The beast stepped back and yelled, "At least we got one of them!"

All of the rest started cheering around him. The new beast instructed one of the others to bind Troy's hands and get him ready to return to the ship. Veronica was waiting.

***

Troy was forced to walk, hands bound and a rope around his neck, at the front of the group of triumphant Coronians. They marched him past all of the destroyed homes and farms so he could see firsthand what they'd done to his people.

Dead livestock lined the roads. Not killed in the fighting, but intentionally slaughtered and left to rot. Bodies of over a hundred Rygonians who had come out to defend their homes were strewn all over. Most of the buildings were burnt or still burning. Troy caught a glimpse of what he thought was the tractor he'd seen from the fighter. He strained to see if the family was still there. They were, and they were all dead.

Troy could see some of the survivors. The Coronians wanted him to see them. They wanted him to know they were betrayed by the leaders who promised to protect them. Troy made eye contact with everyone he could see. The Coronians herded Troy toward the worst of the damage, but instead of hiding from the devastation, he faced it head-on. He was a leader, and he knew when to take responsibility. This was one of those times.

From the left of him, Troy heard a voice call out, "Where's your wife? We saw her."

The horde stopped and fell silent. They wanted to see what Troy would say. What lies he would tell to cover Dia's cowardice.

Troy told the truth. "General Harlow was ejected from the fighter before it crashed. The angle of the trajectory makes me think she was sent out of the atmosphere. We were close enough."

People murmured in confusion and disbelief. He smiled and said, "Why don't you believe me? My head is reeling from losing her, but also from what happened to you. I would hope to figure that out, but it looks like my time here is coming to an end."

One of the Coronians behind Troy took that as an opportunity to make a statement and kicked him as hard as he could in the small of his back, sending the doctor stumbling forward onto his knees. Troy gasped and stayed there for a moment before gathering himself to stand back up, ignoring the humiliation. He glanced at some of the survivors, expecting to see contempt in their eyes. But all he saw was sadness and pity. He hoped that someone else on this damn planet knew what was happening.

They finally made it to the ramp of one of the Coronian battle cruisers. Troy was led up into the ship. He was taken to a sort of receiving area and instructed to sit and wait. He looked back to see the ramp was closing as an announcement in Coronian—which Troy knew—came over the sound system to say they were getting ready to depart. Troy tried to get a glimpse of his home as the door closed. He was quite sure he would never see it again.

CHAPTER 3
So, Who Do I Fire?

C hancellor Warren Strom shook with anger. How had this happened? Who helped the Coronians orchestrate *another* massive attack on Rygonian soil? How would they win back the trust of their people when they couldn't even find a way to protect them? And most importantly, where were Troy and Dia?

Chancellor Strom thought about Dia in particular. His daughter was one of the most revered people to ever serve in the Florian Army. His heart sank at the thought of her likely capture by the Coronians. But if she were, he was certain they'd try to ransom her back. Warren had a strong feeling their situation, at least regarding their disappearance, was Troy's doing.

Warren walked out into the hall and started down to the central control room. As he went, all the people he passed moved out of his way and saluted—an arm across their chest and slight bow, as per Rygonian tradition. This wasn't an uncommon occurrence, but the chancellor's daughter was missing, which was a big concern for the people, and even more so for her family.

The Strom family was one of the oldest Florian bloodlines on Rygone. Their ancestors were some of the first descendants of the

Beginners who left their kind on Rygone. Members of the family had served in the government in many different capacities since Warren himself founded it. Warren was usually ambassador to their allies but was also looked upon to run for chancellor on certain occasions. He'd never lost an election, and this was his 341st five-year term. Dia, in particular, was a force to be reckoned with. She was fiery, fearless, and brilliant. She was also stubborn, obnoxious, and quite unprofessional. That was actually one of the reasons she got along so well with her subordinates and was consistently looked upon to run for the office of commanding general of the Florian Army.

Warren made it to the control room and shoved open the door. "So, who do I fire?"

With that statement, the room went silent, and all eyes fell on the chancellor. He continued, "Well, now that I have everyone's attention, get me up to date."

From the head of the table, a very tall man stood up. He had long, unruly black hair and a rough, black beard to match. He had bronze-colored skin and fearsome, light-gray eyes. High Colonel Dominic Strom was the leader of the chancellor's personal guard. He was also a highly trained secret corps commander, and Dia sought his talents on many occasions. Dominic was Dia's brother and one of the chancellor's sons.

The Stroms had the whole "leading a civilization" thing down to a tee. All the positions they held were elected by the citizens of Rygone. No leading government, parliament, or military official was ever appointed unless in an emergency situation.

Dominic cleared his throat. "Well, sir, we've been going over all of the footage from the monitoring stations that would've detected the Coronians' approach and attack, and they're all completely normal. No ships, no soldiers, nothing to call attention to the situation and trigger an alarm."

The chancellor stared at the screen on the far wall. He sighed. "Someone would've had to go into the processing systems of those stations individually to upload a program that would've caused an outage like this. An outage so large that we had no idea *two* Coronian battle cruisers were attacking our people."

A voice to the chancellor's right said, "Yes, that's exactly what had to have happened. We're going to have to update the software system and institute new security protocols." *Again,* went unsaid.

Dr. Oscar Strom was the head of Research and Development. He was Warren's other son, and Dia and Dominic's brother. Oscar and Troy were best friends, and their work overlapped on occasion. Together, the two of them had developed some of the most sophisticated technology and medical advancements the galaxy had ever seen. Their work alone drove half of Rygone's economy, which was even more incentive to find Dia and her husband.

Oscar had the worst feeling about what was going on. He knew it had to be an inside job. Someone on their team had to have learned about Dr. Harlow and General Harlow's experiment. Someone in that very room could've sold out the Rygonian government for trade secrets. And now the two highest-ranking members, second only to the chancellor himself, were in the custody of their biggest enemy. Oscar knew what the two of them were working on. He could only hope the Coronians didn't get it.

Dominic said what Oscar had been thinking. "It has to be an inside job."

Warren nodded. "We must gather a team to research all of the people who have access to anything involving Dia and Troy. We also need to find out who would have the know-how to disable those stations without being discovered. Oscar, please head that up."

Oscar nodded and left to start looking for the asshole who hurt his sister and best friend.

Warren turned to Dominic. "I want you to put together a team to go out to where the attack happened. Talk to the people, find out what they need to begin putting their lives back together. And I'm going with you."

Dominic raised his eyebrows. "Are you sure? It'll be a nightmare out there. They may not take too kindly to your presence."

"That's what you're here for," Warren said. "As my protection. Right?"

Dominic chuckled. "Okay, when do you want to leave?"

"In an hour. I need to talk to your mother first."

***

Warren opened the door to the Strom family apartment and looked around for his wife. "Pam, are you here, honey?"

From the back of the apartment, she called, "Just a sec, Warren. I'll be right there."

A few moments later, Lady Pamela Strom came out of the bedroom and breezed into the living room where her husband stood. Warren could see her determination to stay strong for him, but the pain of losing Dia was wearing on her beautiful face.

She was the perfect Lady of Rygone because nobody could help but love her. Pam had long, silky black hair, large, sultry brown eyes, and smooth, tan skin. Her smile and voluptuous curves could make anyone melt. She was also his most trusted advisor, which was why he was there.

Pam's eyes were red from tears, but she smiled and kissed him gently. "What can I do for you, my love? Have you heard anything about Dia?"

Warren cleared his throat. "I'm going to the attack site. I need to see what happened and make sure there are no shortcuts taken in helping the survivors." He sighed heavily and asked, "Do you think this is a good idea?"

Pam studied her husband's face for a moment and said, "No."

The chancellor was a little taken aback, as she was usually the one who jumped in feet first to help the needy.

She continued, "I think *we* should go. I want to see what transpired as well and need to find out what happened to our daughter, to Troy."

Warren heard the desperation of a mother in her voice. Pamela loved all of her children, but Dia was a special kind of crazy that Pam cherished. She was right; they needed to go together.

"Get a jacket; I guess the weather has been difficult out there today," he said.

***

About twenty minutes later, they all met in the large hanger on the fortieth floor of Baltica City. Dominic walked up to his parents and gave them a skeptical look. "I was nervous about the chancellor going, but you as well, my Lady?" he asked.

Pam said, "Yes, Colonel. I want to see the people, but I also want to find evidence of Doctor and General Harlow's disappearance."

Dominic nodded. He knew there would be no changing their minds. If you couldn't beat them, join them.

The chancellor's personal DREX transport was almost ready to be boarded when Warren said, "No, not mine. We need to take a regular military transport. I don't want to be parading around in parliament colors to people who just lost everything."

Dominic agreed. He had the flight crew find the most suitable transport and switched their gear over. Within ten minutes, they were ready to board.

The standard troop transport was twice the size of a DREX fighter. The one they were using was a stripped-down version of the chancellor's craft. There were only benches designed to carry fifteen people on each side. There were harnesses to be strapped into, but before they even had time to fasten the buckles, they had arrived. Each craft in the Florian Army fleet was equipped with a Jump Drive, an advancement Troy had worked with Oscar to develop.

Their transport landed on the edge of the farming community. In addition to Warren, Dominic, and Pamela, there were ten regular army soldiers with them. The group started slowly on the trail leading into the center of the community. The chancellor and Lady Pam were in the center, with the high colonel out front, four soldiers on each side, and two in the rear. They were armed with thermal rifles carried on their shoulders. They were there for a humanitarian purpose, but people in duress could be capable of drastic actions.

As they approached the first farm, they were faced with a horrible scene. There was still smoke billowing out of the burnt house. All of the dead livestock had been piled in the front yard, and the only survivor, a petite Gorman girl, no more than sixteen, was getting ready to set the carcasses on fire. She watched the group with awe and apprehension as they approached.

Pam wasn't sure she knew who they were. She said, "Stop, I want to go talk to her."

Warren didn't object. "Colonel, please escort Lady Pamela," he said. "Take five of these soldiers with you, and I'll move on to the next house with the rest."

Dominic nodded and strode with his mother up to the young lady. She looked at them with wide, sad eyes. Pam felt a lump developing in her throat but managed to keep herself from crying. She smiled at the girl. "Hello. Are you the only one here? Do you need some help?"

The girl swallowed but said nothing. She just continued to gaze at them.

Pam searched her mind for the best thing to say. She felt helpless. Not knowing what else to do, she did what she would do for her family. She plainly said, "I don't know what to say to you, sweet child. Words won't do anything to help this. May I at least give you a hug?"

A tear ran down the girl's pink, soot-stained cheek. She gave Pam a slight nod, and Pam gently embraced her. The girl was shaking and cold. She probably hadn't eaten or had water in a long time. That thought kicked Pam into gear, and without letting go, she told Dominic to find food, water, and dry clothes for the girl.

Dominic knew there was a relief station being set up not far from where they were, and he sent one of the soldiers to get the items needed.

Lady Pam finally let the girl go and looked at her haggard face. She asked, "What's your name, dear?"

The girl cleared her throat and whispered, "Mary."

Pam smiled warmly. "Hello, Mary." Then she asked the tough question, "Are you the only one who survived?"

Mary nodded. "It was just me and my brother. They came up on us unawares. Bill was shot in the back before we even knew what was comin'. Their big ships hadn't even shown up yet."

The Lady of Rygone nearly became sick. The Coronians were monsters that had been plaguing Rygone for many years and had only gotten worse after the War of Breger Dunes fifty years earlier. They were known for killing innocent people and using them as shields. Hopefully, the boy didn't suffer.

Just then, the soldier came back with two sets of dry clothes, enough food for at least a week, a jug of water, and three blankets. "I dunno; I thought blankets would be good to have," he said.

Mary gave a slight smile. "Thank you."

Pam had the soldiers help with the mess of the livestock. There was a small store house behind the burnt barn that was still standing, and they made that ready for her to stay in until the recovery teams could get her settled into a better situation.

Pam gave her another hug. "We must move on, as there are others in need of assistance. Take care, sweet girl. We'll do everything we can to help you."

"Thank you, Lady Strom."

Pam was surprised that she knew who she was. "You're welcome. Goodbye, dear," she said with a warm smile.

She began to walk away when Mary called out, "Oh! I forgot!"

Pam turned around and asked, "What did you forget, dear?"

"They have him," Mary told her.

Both Dominic and Pam tensed up. "The Coronians?" Dominic asked. "Who do they have?"

"The doctor."

Pam's throat tightened. She strode back to Mary with wide eyes. "Dr. Harlow. How do you know?"

"A big group of those nasty beasts made him walk down the trail with his hands tied and a rope 'round his pretty neck. They kicked him really hard and everything. I felt bad 'cause they were the only ones who came to help."

Pam and Dominic exchanged a glance. "How did they come here?" Dominic asked.

"They were in one of those fancy DREX fighters we see coming outta the caves when they practice. She flew the shit outta that thing. Took out a bunch of those beasts until they were shot down."

Pam was shaking. She had so many mixed emotions. "Do you know where they landed? Did you see General Harlow on the ground?"

Mary shook her head. "No, ma'am, I'm sorry. I only saw him."

Dominic placed a hand on Mary's shoulder and said, "Thank you very much. This helps us a lot."

Mary nodded. "When you see them again, tell them they saved me."

Pam couldn't hold back her tears any longer. They rolled slowly down her cheeks, and all she could do was nod at Mary. She and Dominic turned together and walked back up to the road to meet up with their army escort.

Pam looked up at her son, who was also fighting back his emotions. "We know they were here, and they crashed." She paused and cleared her throat before continuing, "And they for sure have Troy."

Even though her husband was sometimes at odds with Troy, he was a dearly loved member of their family. He and Dia weren't perfect, but they were happy and loved each other unconditionally. His loss was just as great as hers.

Dominic nodded. "We need to get to the chancellor and see if he has any more information."

They quickly caught up with Warren and his guards. He was almost as excited as they were to share their information. Dominic told Warren what they learned from Mary. The chancellor was able to add to their story. Apparently, Dia and Troy circled the area, firing on the Coronian ground troops. That is, until one of the battle cruisers shot them with an ion cannon. That was where the stories started to conflict.

One man said when the round hit the DREX, it exploded on impact and the ship went down immediately.

Another claimed that right before the round hit the DREX, there was a big green light, then it crashed.

And a woman and her sister said when the round hit the DREX, there was a tremendous white light—as bright as the sun—the canopy opened, and something flew out. Then the DREX blew up.

All of the Stroms' heads were spinning. The common denominator was that the ship crashed. Dominic asked the gathered survivors, "Do you know the general direction where the DREX went down?"

They all pointed in different directions and began arguing about who was right. Warren shook his head and turned to Dominic. "Were the relief ships on the way when we left?"

"They were almost ready to leave. They should be here shortly," he answered.

Warren said, "Good. I want to get back to the carrier and fly around the area to look for the wreck." He glanced up at the sky and saw it was about to rain. "We need to hurry."

Dominic called the carrier and had the pilot bring it a little bit closer to their location. As they were about to leave, one of the survivors said. "Hey, one other thing!"

All three Stroms turned back, and Warren said, "What?

"As Dr. Harlow was being paraded past us to the ship, someone asked where his wife was. Harlow said that when the DREX crashed, she was dejected or something like that. He said she went through the atmosphere. Would that be possible?"

Knowing Troy, anything is possible, Warren thought.

"Maybe," Dominic said. "We're going to the crash site now. Hopefully, we'll find evidence of what actually happened."

Pam smiled warmly at their beleaguered citizens. "Thank you all. You've been most helpful."

As if on cue, the relief ships arrived. Three large vessels loaded with any and everything these people would need. Did Warren go a little overboard? Yes. Did he do it to win back some of their trust? Hell yes.

***

The rain was just starting when they located the crash site. Warren thought, *Damnit, please don't let the rain ruin everything!*

Once the carrier was on the ground, they exited immediately and ran to the downed DREX. There wasn't much of it left.

Dominic examined the wreck. "It came down nose-first. The impact was enormous. I can't imagine either of them being in this thing when it went down. They would still be trapped."

Warren nodded. "I agree. One of the survivors said they saw the canopy fly off." He looked closely to see if he could find their seat harnesses. Troy's was still intact, so he must have taken it off himself, but Dia's had burned in the fire. "Troy's harness is still together. He would have had to cut it off if he'd been wearing it."

Warren saw what looked like a half-burnt duffle bag in what was left of the cargo area. He leaned in and tried to pull it out, but it tore open on an exposed piece of metal, spilling what was left of the contents out on the ground. He bent down and picked up a file envelope. Inside, he found fake passage papers to travel into Deep Space, a place Dia knew very well, as she used to train pilots out there. There were account documents detailing their Universal Monetary worth but under false names. It was a substantial amount of money. Dia and Troy made significant salaries but lived very simply, so they had a large nest egg. *It's all analog. They didn't want this information in a computer where it could be easily searched for.*

Warren stared up at the wrecked DREX and said quietly, "They were leaving."

"What did you say, honey?" Pam asked.

Warren turned to his wife and repeated, "Dia and Troy were leaving Rygone. For good, it appears. All of these documents are in assumed names."

Both Pam and Dominic came over to Warren and examined the paperwork for themselves. "What the hell were they running from?" she asked.

"They must have been in some kind of trouble," Dominic mused. "And it had to have been *huge* for these two not to face it head-on." Dominic didn't want to believe Dia and Troy were cowards.

The rain began to fall harder, and the sun was setting. They would stay the night in the carrier and try to find more evidence tomorrow.

***

The next morning was clear and bright. The world didn't know the hardships of those who lived upon it.

The Stroms examined the crash again and found little evidence. The only notable exception was the canopy was within walking distance, almost a tol away, and had definitely been blown off before the crash.

As they were combing through the area, almost ready to leave, Pam called out to the others, "I found something over here." She was gagging.

Dominic and Warren joined her, and she pointed to a large indentation in the ground in front of her, then to an area about ten feet away where the bodies of two Coronians lay. "One of them definitely landed here."

Warren and Pam went to the bodies. The smell of decay was strong, the humidity making the process go faster. On the ground next to one of the bodies was a Coronian battle knife. Warren crouched and inspected the blade. At least Troy took out a couple of the bastards before getting captured.

Dominic inspected the divot in the grass, and it had to have been made by Troy. The impression was that of a tall person. Dia was tiny, and Troy was well over six feet. He shook his head and tried to imagine what his brother-in-law felt when he hit the ground. He took a deep breath. "This is where they captured him, but where did they get Dia?"

Pam looked off into the distance and said, voice quiet, "They don't have Dia. I can feel it."

CHAPTER 4
THE ENEMY IS SMARTER THAN YOU THINK, TROY

T roy had been sitting on the same metal bench for hours. He was uncomfortable, hungry, and needed to take a piss, but he didn't move. He wasn't sure he wanted to meet this Veronica just yet.

As those thoughts were going through his head, the woman from the fight on the ground walked up to him. She had a strange swagger that she didn't seem to have a handle on. She knelt in front of Troy. "Not so tough now, are ya, pretty boy?"

Troy just stared at her. No matter what he did, he knew it would provoke her into an altercation. His hands were still bound, and the rope was still around his neck. Should he fight or be tactful?

She seemed disappointed when he refused to react. She grabbed the rope and stood up, pulling him to his feet with her. Troy was quite tall, but she was just a few inches taller. She got right into his face, and he could smell her rancid breath as she whispered, "When Veronica is finished with you, maybe she'll let me have a go."

Troy looked up and met her gaze, locking eyes defiantly. "We'll just have to see, won't we?"

He decided to fight.

Troy kicked his left foot out and hooked her right leg, pulling it out from under her. As she fell back, Troy brought his bound hands down onto her arm, forcing her to let go of the rope. She landed hard on the ground and cried out. Guards seemed to appear from every corner of the ship. Troy had a very calculating mind; therefore he could process a problem incredibly fast. He used the knife on the belt of the woman to cut his bindings. He needed to get away, but at least ten male Coronians were heading straight for him, and the woman he just knocked down was gaining her bearings.

Troy was amazingly fast and agile. He was tall but thin and fit, thanks to Dia. She drilled him in all types of athletics and defensive techniques. He said a quiet thank you to his lost wife for kicking his ass in the field on a regular basis.

He pulled the rope off his neck as he ran lightning fast to the left. A loud alarm began to clang above him as he scanned the walls of the corridor he was in, looking for a place to flee to. He needed to find an escape pod. He had to at least try to get home. Maybe even try to find Dia in the vast vacuum of space and get her to a distant, safe place where nobody could find her.

The doctor saw an open door on the right side of the corridor and stopped. He looked around him, and though he couldn't see any beasts, he could hear them fast approaching. Troy dove into the room without taking any precautions, found the door control, and slammed it shut. The room was mostly dark except for a dim blue light in the corner. Breathless, he turned around to assess his situation. The light in the back of the room became much brighter, illuminating a woman sitting behind a large, elaborate desk. He slowly looked around the room and realized it wasn't decorated like anything typically seen in a Coronian ship.

His eyes locked on to the woman, and both terror and anger gripped him. She was beautiful. She had long blonde hair, deep blue eyes, a slender figure, and a perfect complexion.

She was Florian, and he knew her. He narrowed his eyes and asked, "I take it you go by Veronica now?"

She stood and walked over in front of him. She gently ran her hand down his dirty, sweaty cheek. He flinched and pulled away. She gave him a fake, pouty lip. "Yes, Troy; that's who I am now."

But he knew her as Maria.

CHAPTER 5
IMPOSSIBLE PHYSICS

Nothing. There was no way to describe it. She felt nothing. Or did she?

Dia was moving really fast. Where was she? Was this what death felt like? How did she know what death was? Why did she have a voice inside her head?

Everything was dark. Maybe she was in space. *Release all of the power inside you.*

That was the last thing she remembered. That strange voice telling her to release her energy. And she knew what *that* meant. She knew she was capable of absorbing any type of energy to use it as—what? A way to escape danger? A tool? A weapon?

She had no more energy to release and was just flying unimpeded. She had to be in space because there was no atmosphere to press against her to slow her momentum. How did she know that?

Out of nowhere, she noticed a light—and she was approaching it incredibly fast. A star. She began to panic, knowing there was no way she would make it through. *Release all of the power inside you.*

She must have been traveling faster than she thought, because the star was suddenly right in front of her. As she grew closer, the heat and light became almost unbearable.

Almost. Dia blasted directly into the star and kept traveling just as fast. Her body siphoned in the enormous energy that was pressing down on her. Intense pain shot through her; she could barely handle it. Just as her body felt as if it could hold no more, she burst out of the other side. She drew in a deep breath as the heat and light coursed within her. It felt amazing and terrifying at the same time.

As she started slowing down, she decided to release some of the energy she'd just absorbed.

She didn't even feel the impact.

***

The farmer was in his field early that day because there was a call for rain, and he wanted to get the plowing done before it hit.

He hooked up his two plow horses and got them into the field quickly. They were the best horses he'd ever had, and he knew they could get the job done.

When the farmer was about halfway through his plowing, he heard an enormous bang above his head. He fell to the ground in terror, and his horses spooked and ran off, plow and all. He got up right away and tried to chase after the animals, but he saw a streak of fire burn across the sky. His mouth dropped open as he tracked the fireball until it hit the earth. The impact was many, many miles away, but he could still see the cloud of dust and debris rising into the air.

He realized the dust cloud was moving fast, right toward him. He turned and tried to run, but there was no getting away. He was able to dive into a ditch that ran along his field to help irrigate the crops. There was a small amount of water left, which helped shield him from the worst of the blast. He crouched in that ditch with his hands over his head for what seemed like forever, but eventually, he could feel that the winds had died down.

The farmer patted down his body to make sure he wasn't injured. Once satisfied he wasn't, he peered over the edge of the ditch and couldn't believe what he saw. His entire farm was covered in a thick layer of dust and ash. He stood up and looked around. Almost everything he owned and held dear was destroyed by a fireball that landed dozens of miles away.

He felt tears well up in his eyes, and as they rolled down his cheeks, they left streaks on his dust-covered face.

Just when he thought all was completely lost, he heard a snort behind him. He turned and saw his two prized horses, unhurt and still attached to the plow. He smiled and thought about how much he could sell them for.

CHAPTER 6
CAVES, CRATERS, AND DESTRUCTION, OH MY

D ia was unconscious for a long time after hitting the ground. The impact was so hard it forced her to release the rest of the energy she'd stored from the star. Luckily, it wasn't too much, or she would have destroyed the—planet? Asteroid? Moon?—she'd landed on.

Slowly, Dia opened her eyes and saw she was lying in the fetal position at the bottom of a huge crater or cave. She looked up at the sky and found it dark and dreary. Was it night? How long had she been there?

She tentatively stood up and tried to look around, but it was too dark. Dia could feel the cool air on her skin. She had been wearing clothes when she was traveling through space, but the power of the star, or perhaps the force of the impact, destroyed everything she had on.

Not everything. She felt her left hand and could make out two rings on her middle and index fingers. Where did those come from?

Since she couldn't see anything around her and there was no energy to be absorbed, she decided to sit back down and try to think about what had happened. Dia closed her eyes and searched her mind for *anything* from before the strange voice, but she remembered nothing no matter how hard she tried. Who and what was she? Where was she from? Why did she lose her memory but still knew some of what she was experiencing? The language she was thinking in was the same as the voice, so were they someone she knew?

Her frustration got the best of her, and she felt tears fill her eyes. Dia was scared and alone and wanted answers.

She must've drifted off because she was startled awake by shouting far above her. Dia opened her eyes and looked up. The sky was still dreary but much brighter. How long had she been asleep? Hours? Days? She saw two beings at the edge of the crater. They were shouting down into the hole and must've seen her. They didn't speak the same way she thought, but they were there and would hopefully help her. She watched one of the beings throw what looked like a rope over the edge and start to climb down.

Dia jumped up with excitement, but her happiness didn't last long. What if they weren't coming to help, but to hurt her? She had absolutely nothing to defend herself with. Did she know how to protect herself?

The being zipped quickly down the rope. As it came closer, Dia began to panic. She felt exposed and wanted to run, but she had nowhere to go.

Suddenly, the being was on the ground. It looked much like her but taller and more—something. She didn't know.

The being stared at her in disbelief and asked, "How did you get down here, ma'am? And without any clothes."

Dia didn't understand the noises the being was making. Was that how it communicated? The sounds were too fast but drawn out somehow. Nothing like the voice she remembered.

She gave a slight shake of her head. He nodded and said, "Don't speak English, do you? You're a strange woman in an impact crater with no injuries or clothes; why would you?" He sighed and continued, "It's been several days since the impact, and this is the first we've been able to look down here. How long have you been here?"

Dia just stared at it.

The being unclipped itself from the rope and took off its jacket. It reached out to hand it to her. "Here, ma'am. It's cold as hell down here despite the heat caused by the impact. The first few days felt like the sun landed here! You must be freezing."

She looked at the jacket, then back at the being. She decided it didn't seem to want to hurt her, so she took the garment and put it on.

It was heavy and nearly swallowed her. The coat smelled of smoke, dirt, and something she didn't recognize, but it wasn't bad. She looked back up and stared at it with her large, odd brown eyes.

He pointed to his chest and said slowly, "My name is Paul. I'm here to help you. That meteor did a bunch of damage to the area for dozens of miles. We've been trying to get as many people as possible out of here before this cave collapses and kills even more people."

What's a Paul? Is that a people? Am I a meteor?

Paul, the people being, reached out its hand. "Okay, I need to get you hooked up. Come on over."

Dia gazed at Paul with apprehension before turning her attention to the rope and tracing it up to the top of the crater. At first, she was scared, but she reminded herself she'd flown through a star and blew this hole in the ground. Now her concern was with Paul. Would it try to hurt her?

Paul was patient and said, "I'm sure you're scared, ma'am, but I'll take care of you. I promise."

She didn't understand, but its sounds and tone seemed sincere. She also wanted to get out of the hole. Dia slowly walked toward Paul and took its hand.

Paul was nervous about touching the woman. Not only was she completely nude under his jacket, but she was incredibly beautiful. She had long, curly, light-brown hair. Large, strange brown eyes, almost like a cat. Her smooth skin was the color of a white peach. She almost looked like an angel. If his fiancée saw this lady, she would *not* be happy.

But who was she?

As she came closer, Paul had her turn around. Surprisingly, she was very warm, almost radiating her own heat. He was concerned she might have caught an infection in the cave and was running a fever as a result. He placed a second harness down in front of her. "Now put your legs through the holes," he instructed her.

She only blinked at him, though. He demonstrated what to do with his harness, and she observed curiously for a moment, then promptly stepped into hers. Paul watched as she tightened the harness around her waist. He showed her what to do with the thigh straps on his own legs, and she performed the necessary task perfectly. Paul was impressed by her ability to catch on so quickly.

The girl, on the other hand, was miserable. The material the harness was made of was digging uncomfortably into her crotch. But she was ready to go. The pain and discomfort wouldn't last forever.

He connected both of their harnesses. Then, Paul, the people being, pushed a button on a small device on its shoulder and said, "Ready. Pull us up."

Dia was amazed when the box answered back. Almost immediately, she and Paul were being pulled up toward the mouth of the cave. Dia wasn't ready at first and nearly fell forward, but Paul grabbed her and pulled her back. She gave a small laugh despite herself.

Paul smiled and said, "It's fun, right?"

They quickly reached the top of the crater where the other Paul was waiting for them. He looked down at where they were hanging, and said, "It's about time, man."

Paul Two called Paul One, man. Noted.

Paul Man, the people being, said, "Well, it isn't every day you come across a tiny, nude woman at the bottom of a cave. Oh, and who doesn't understand or speak English."

Paul Two took a good, long look at Dia. She just stared back and wished they would get her out of the harness, so her bits didn't fall off.

Paul Two just said, "Interesting."

Paul Man rolled his eyes. "Help me with this."

Paul Two pulled on the rope, and they were brought over the lip of the cave onto solid ground. She unbuckled the harness immediately, stepped out a few paces, and looked around.

The place was like a war zone. The sky looked dreary—not because it was cloudy, but because of the ash and dust still in the air falling to the ground.

All of the trees and fields were destroyed. There were beings like the Pauls everywhere. Some were giving aid to the wounded. Some were helping those who needed food and shelter.

She did this. Her landing created this mess.

Dia quickly put her head down and turned back to the Pauls. They were staring at her, wondering what she'd do next, but all she did was drop to her knees and start weeping.

CHAPTER 7
SHE'S KINDA WEIRD, ISN'T SHE?

P aul Man came over, pulled Dia to her feet, and put an arm around her. At first, she wanted to shove it off, but it had been nice to her so far, so she let it. "Let's go find you some proper clothes and a meal, shall we?"

The tears were still rolling down her cheeks as Paul Man walked her to one of the big things lining the makeshift path through the debris. They were full of the people beings handing out what looked like food and supplies to the victims of her destruction. She didn't realize how exposed she felt until she walked past these survivors. They glanced her way and didn't seem to give her much thought since she looked like a victim just as they were. If they only knew.

She stumbled around the rocks and realized she missed the boots and clothes she had been wearing. Her feet hurt, but Paul seemed to be watching her as they went. What was it thinking?

They both approached the back of one of the big things. It had clothes in it, and a nice being that looked a lot like her came out from the back. If it resembled her, was it she? Yes, she was going to be she.

The she said, "Paul! How are ya, sweetie?" She looked at Dia. "Well, what do we have here? Hello, darlin'."

Again, Dia didn't understand, but Paul helped. Paul had to be he, maybe? He was now he. He said, "Hiya, Maeve. She was found wanderin' naked as a jay bird at the bottom of the crater. Please don't ask how or why because I have no clue. All I did was rescue the poor dear. Oh, and she can't speak or understand English."

Maeve didn't take her eyes off Dia. "Well, did ya try Spanish or French or sumfin?"

Paul's mouth opened and closed. "Well, no," he admitted. "I don't know Spanish or French!"

"Or sumfin?"

Paul released an exasperated breath and said, "No, Maeve. Right now, my priority is to get her properly dressed and fed so we can figure out what to do with her."

Maeve, not breaking eye contact with Dia, smiled and said, "I think I can help out with that." Maeve pointed to a small set of steps that led into the back of the thing. "Come on, darlin'. Let's get you cleaned up and dressed."

Dia glanced at Paul for a moment in fear. He saw her apprehension and smiled. "It's okay. Maeve'll take care of you and get you set up in something much more comfortable than my old coat. I'll be back around in a little while to collect you."

She just stared at him with those huge brown eyes and slowly went up the stairs. Maeve took her hand at the top and said, "It's okay, honey; he's good on his word."

Maeve was short like her but much larger around. She looked like she was older than her, too, with short brown hair and friendly blue eyes. She followed Maeve into the back of the large thing and found it to be much warmer. When they made it to the very back, Maeve stopped and picked up what looked like a pair of underclothes. Maeve turned to her. "I know this is awkward, but I can't determine what size clothes to give you under that huge jacket." Maeve handed her a thin, white robe. "Can you put this on?"

Dia took the robe and gazed at Maeve for a moment. She went ahead and took off the jacket, not bothering with the robe. She began going through the piles of underclothes, completely nude again, searching for something that would fit.

Maeve was taken aback for a moment before letting out a laugh. "Okay, we can pick out something now, then get you cleaned up before ya get dressed."

Maeve made sure there was nobody else in the truck with them. The weird lady made her uncomfortable only because she seemed too trusting of those around her. That made Maeve concerned for the woman's safety. She was a beautiful, tiny little thing. Skinny, but very toned and definitely well-fed and healthy. As a matter of fact, there didn't seem to be a blemish on the girl's body.

They settled on a pair of skinny jeans, a tan blouse, a pink hoodie, and a pair of hiking shoes. The shoes were a size too big, but they only had so much to work with. Maeve took the strange girl to a small room with a sink and toilet. She gave the girl some soap, a comb, a washcloth, and a towel. "This is all I have, honey," she said. "When you get cleaned up, we'll get you dressed and fed."

Dia looked at Maeve and blinked. She understood nothing any of the beings said, but they seemed so kind. She wondered if everyone out there was like that. She went into the washroom and studied herself in the small mirror. Her whole body was covered in mud and dirt, and her hair was a filthy mess of knots.

She turned on the warm water and did everything she could to get clean. As the water ran through her hair, she was able to comb most of the tangles out. She washed her face and body with the soap and washcloth as best she could. Once finished, she dried off and stood in front of the mirror again.

Dia didn't recognize herself. She had no idea who she was, and it terrified her. The Florian took a deep breath and swallowed the tears welling up in her eyes before peeking out the door.

Maeve saw her. "Ready for your clothes?"

Knowing all she would get was a large-eyed stare, Maeve handed the girl her things, and she went back into the small washroom to put on the clothes. None of it fit very well, but it was much better than running around naked in an unknown place.

The girl walked out of the washroom and stood there. Maeve scanned her up and down and was taken aback again. It was easy to see she was beautiful when she'd been covered in mud and bundled in a fireman's coat, but washed up and dressed properly, she was *too* pretty. There was something very odd about her, and Maeve was starting to get uneasy. For the first time, Maeve noticed the rings on her left hand. She had one on her index and one on her middle finger. They were both black and looked to be made of stone and had what looked like gold and silver bands woven throughout.

She pointed at the rings and said, "I know you can't understand me, but those are beautiful rings."

The girl glanced down at her hand and spun the one on her middle finger for a moment. She looked back at Maeve with a sad, longing expression.

Maeve offered her a weary smile. "Let's go, deary. We need to get you some food and find Paul."

As they were walking out, Dia saw Paul's coat on the floor and quickly snatched it up and put it back on. She was dressed, but the coat made her feel safer for some reason.

***

As they were climbing out of the thing, Paul walked up to them and said, "Oh, wow! Look at you!"

Like Maeve, Paul was a little unsettled by how much prettier she'd become just by washing her face and brushing her hair. He couldn't help but stare at her, and she looked back at him with those haunting eyes. If his fiancée saw him right now, he'd be castrated for sure!

The girl peered past Paul and saw the world had become a little bit brighter. A natural breeze had kicked up and blown some of the dust and ash away. She looked at the suffering people and widespread destruction. Unfortunately, that couldn't be so easily blown away.

Paul gestured down the line of things and said, "They made a mean chili down at the mess tent! Have you ever had chili, ma'am?"

"It's just habit to talk to her even though you get no answers in return, huh?" Maeve asked.

Paul nodded. He was a little sad she couldn't talk. She walked between him and Maeve down the lane that had been cleared for foot traffic. Many of the other refugees watched the strange, pale woman with huge, upturned eyes. Dia was starting to feel underlying anger in this place. Did they know she was the meteor? She kept her head low to keep from showing her frustration and fear. She needed to get away.

***

They made it to the mess tent where a long line of beleaguered and displaced people waited for a hot meal. Dia wanted to leave, but Maeve took her by the arm and quietly said, "Stay close, deary."

Just then, Paul's radio crackled to life, right next to her ear. The sound didn't affect her, but she felt an uncontrollable urge to reach out to the energy in the device. She shut her eyes tight and turned away.

"Are you okay?" Paul asked. She refused to look back at him.

A voice came across the radio. "Four-two-one-one, please return to staging. Four-two-one-one, return to staging."

Paul clicked a button on the side of the radio and replied, "On my way." Then he was gone.

Dia's heart pounded, and she felt like an animal trapped in a cage. Her body instinctively sent out invisible feelers to seek out the closest and strongest energy source. She closed her eyes and took several deep breaths. When she opened her eyes again, Maeve was looking at her with a quizzical grin.

"Can you really not talk?" she asked.

Dia's inability to understand was starting to wear on her. The Florian felt ashamed for not knowing what to do. She didn't know what they expected from her.

Maeve patted her hand. "Well, even if you truly don't understand us, we still need to give you a name. Whatever happens, people will need to call you something." Maeve looked up as if thinking hard and said, "Hm, how about... Heather!"

Dia's unearthly stare focused on her. Maeve put her hand over her own heart and said, "I'm Maeve." She then placed her hand over the girl's heart. "You're Heather."

The girl started to understand. Maeve did the back and forth of the names again, then said, "Say Maeve. Maaaeeve."

The girl tentatively opened her mouth and squeaked, "Maavvv."

Maeve laughed. "No, silly. Maaeevve."

"Maeve," the girl repeated quietly. "Maeve."

What neither of them realized was the people around them in line were listening. When the girl said Maeve's name, they all cheered. She was startled, but their celebration made her smile.

Now Maeve put her hand on the girl's heart again and said, "Heather."

"H-Heather. Heather."

More cheers. Maeve hugged the girl, which was a little nerve-racking, but it did feel like a breakthrough.

Dia was now Heather.

CHAPTER 8
IS SHE A WHISKEY GIRL?

A fter their meal, which Heather devoured due to being completely famished, Maeve and her went to seek out Paul. Even though Heather felt safe in his coat, she felt the need to return it. They walked down to where the fire brigades were staged and saw a group of firefighters sorting through their gear. Paul was among them and noticed the women approaching.

Heather was hoping he would be happy to see them, but instead, he jogged over and said, "Uh, now's not a good time, ladies. I'll come find you soon."

Heather took off his coat and held it out to him. "Paul."

It was the first time he'd heard her voice. It was quiet and sweet. He tried and failed to hide his smile. "It's okay; go ahead and keep it for now. I'll be back for it later." He turned to Maeve and asked, "Can you keep an eye on her for a while? I asked my superiors what we should do with her, but she's the last of their worries right now."

Maeve nodded. "I'm sure I can find a job for her in the truck."

As the women turned to walk away, Maeve called back to Paul, "By the way, I named her Heather. She seems to like it."

Paul nodded and hid his smile behind his hand. What a weird day.

***

The ladies made it back to the truck to find the line of people in need of clothes had grown. Maeve turned to Heather. "I need your help. You need to do what I show you."

Without waiting for a response, Maeve jumped up onto the bumper and opened the door. She went to help Heather up, but the girl was already beside her, waiting for instructions. Maeve let four people into the truck at a time to pick through the selection, and Heather fell into a rhythm of helping people find what they needed. Maeve told everyone as they came up that Heather couldn't speak or understand English, but she could help find sizes. They both worked for hours without stopping for even a minute. Despite the language barrier, Maeve heard her laughing with children or giving a reassuring hug to a mother who had lost her only son. To Maeve, the mystery only deepened.

Once the last person was done, and their truck was almost empty, the ladies sat down for a moment. Maeve reached under her worktable and pulled out a box. She opened it and took out two small glasses and a bottle of brown liquid. Heather watched her curiously as she poured a small amount of the liquid into each glass. She capped the bottle and passed one of the glasses to Heather.

Maeve smiled and said, "A toast to a job well done, deary. You're a natural at this kind of work." She reached over and touched her glass to Heather's with a small clink.

Heather smiled and did the same back to Maeve's glass. She watched as Maeve took a sip, then raised the glass to her lips and let the liquid touch them. It was strong and had a medicinal taste to it. She wrinkled her nose and glanced at Maeve, who laughed at her.

"Not a whiskey girl, huh?" Maeve said.

Heather put the glass back to her lips and took another sip. It was a little bit smoother that time, and she smiled. Maybe she was a whiskey girl.

The women sat in the truck, quietly gazing out over the destruction. Moments like that made Heather sad and anxious. What were Paul's superiors going to do with her? Especially if they found out the damage was her fault.

Speaking of Paul, she watched him come around the corner and walk toward the truck—as she'd heard Maeve call it earlier. Only, he wasn't alone. There was a pretty girl with red hair and green eyes walking hand in hand with him.

***

Heather had taken Paul's coat off and put it aside earlier while she was working. She ran to the back to grab it, and when she got back, Paul and his friend were talking to Maeve.

Heather noticed Paul's friend give her the most disdainful of looks. She was full of resentment; Heather could actually feel the energy her anger emitted. That couldn't be good. Heather sheepishly handed the coat back to Paul, hoping he would take it this time, and said, "Paul." Thankfully, he did.

"I thought you said she couldn't talk," his friend said.

Paul looked uncomfortable. "Sweetie, I think all she can say is Paul, Maeve, and Heather. Names she just learned today."

The girl rolled her eyes. "Of course, she learned *your* name."

Maeve seemed to be getting irritated. "Well, deary, he did rescue her from a giant crater. Learning his name is a nice start," she said.

Heather could feel the girl's anger increasing. It made her uneasy. Being able to detect energy from a living being was fine, but she was never supposed to attract or absorb it. She didn't even have to try and consider why that would be a bad thing.

Finally, Paul said, "Thank you both." He glanced at Heather. "We're going to be working hard to get all the displaced people and support workers out of here tomorrow, due to the cave's instability. But the Red Cross should be here in the morning to talk to you. Hopefully, they'll have some answers."

Heather just nodded, not knowing what he said.

She kept her gaze away from the girl, but she said, "Goodnight, Heather. My name is Robin. Will you remember that in the morning?"

Heather said nothing.

***

Paul and Robin walked off, arguing. Maeve and Heather watched them until they rounded the corner back onto the walkway. Maeve sighed. "She doesn't deserve that man. She has no idea how good she has it."

Heather studied Maeve's face and could tell by her expression that what she said was true. She looked down and saw her whiskey glass on the floor. There was still a little left in the bottom, so she picked it up and drank it all at once. She sputtered and coughed for a moment, making Maeve laugh hard at her. Heather caught her breath and laughed as well.

Maeve clapped her hand on Heather's back. "You know, girl, I might just tell the Red Cross to piss off and offer you a job myself."

Heather started to feel the whiskey's effects. Her head was spinning a little, and she blurted out a laugh.

Maeve stood and said, "Okay! Here's how the sleeping arrangements are going to be." She turned to lead Heather to the back of the truck, but the girl had already lain down on a pile of clothes and fallen fast asleep. She was even snoring quietly. Maeve smiled at her new, curious friend.

Who *was* she?

Maeve couldn't have known the strange girl happened to be Commanding General Dia Harlow, leader of the Florian Army, protector of the peoples of the planet Rygone. Nor that she was 1,248,152 Earth years old.

And she was sorely missed.

CHAPTER 9
SHIPS, TRAITORS, AND NALONS

T roy was a passive, calm, and calculating person. However, at that particular moment, he was full of more rage than he'd ever been in his long life.

"You're a fucking traitor! What the hell are you doin—" Troy was cut off by Veronica slapping him as hard as she could. He stumbled back, catching himself on a chair. The triumphant look on Veronica's face quickly turned to fear when she saw him turn and lunge at her. Troy was no longer in bindings; they were in an enclosed room, and he was just struck by a traitor to his world. He wished he could kill her.

Just as he got to her, she screamed as loud as she could, and the door immediately burst open. The room flooded with male Coronian beasts, but they didn't get to him before he was able to wrap his hands around her throat. His dark eyes locked on hers, and he growled, "Someday, you'll regr—"

Before he could finish, Troy was ripped off her and thrown face down on the desk by a colossal beast. It shoved its knee against Troy's back and pressed all its weight against the doctor. Troy gasped as his indestructible body flexed in response to being crushed. However, that didn't mean he wasn't struggling to breathe or that the pain wasn't excruciating.

Veronica was helped up by one of the Coronians. She leaned over the desk and whispered in Troy's ear, "What was that my dear doctor?"

Those words made Troy use his last bit of strength to try and get at her, but there was no moving from under that thing. Veronica ordered, "Bind his hands and feet and gag him. Take him to the private prison cells. I'll deal with him shortly."

The beast on his back moved off and pulled Troy to his feet. As he tried to catch his breath, he caught a quick glimpse of Veronica as she breezed out of the room, barking orders at one of the female Coronians. The beasts put on his restraints and gagged him. Troy didn't resist. What was the point? There was nowhere to go, and the leader of this operation was a former *Florian* assistant of his. They took him out of the room and practically dragged him down a dark hall. They came to a door marked "Public Cells" in Coronian.

One of the beasts growled, "It's time to parade the pretty boy in front of the hungry mob."

Troy was a medical doctor before anything else. For over a million years, he'd traveled to many of the systems within their galaxy, helping civilizations recover from plague, disasters, and many other things. The point was, he'd smelled some horrible things in his time, and he had a pretty strong stomach. When they shoved him into that room, there was no way to describe what he experienced. He almost instantly became horribly nauseous. He choked it back because of the gag, and he refused to give the beasts any other reason to torture him.

The room was lined with cells on both sides. There were two to three prisoners of all different species in each cell. As expected, the moment they saw him, there was a loud uproar of voices, all shouting at him. A few of the more interesting tidbits he was able to make out were:

"Ooo, a Florian! I like to gnaw on them."

"Purty clothes! I bets they would be purdier on the floor of my cell."

"I heard if you smash a Florian's head against the floor three times, a genie appears, and you get three wishes!"

"How's big do y'all thinks his head is?"

"Dumbass, you can *see* his head right there!"

"Dat's not the one I'm talkin' 'bout."

With that, there was a deafening roar of laughter.

Troy thought, *Bigger than you would expect, gentlemen.*

His captors stopped in the middle of the room, much to Troy's chagrin. He was fairly sure there was about to be a show—and he was the star.

Troy watched as the beasts who brought him in walked around the room slowly, studying the prisoners in each cell. The prisoners began screaming.

"Pick me! Pick me!"

"I want to taste him!"

"I'm going to be the first to kill a Florian!"

As one of the beasts removed his binding and gag, Troy sighed and thought back to that morning. It seemed so far away. Dia and him rushing to her new DREX, the one Oscar had built just for her. The two of them speeding through the caves, unaware they were flying right into a trap. He could still hear her panicked screams as he ejected her into oblivion. *I really hope you make it somewhere safe, my love,* he thought.

Troy's daydreaming caught him off guard as his first rival took advantage of his distraction. It was a Nalon warrior. It hit Troy in the jaw so hard he would've bitten through his tongue if it were possible. Troy came right back up and swung at the Nalon, barely missing. His exhaustion was definitely going to show in this fight. He hadn't eaten or drank any water in over a day, and he still needed to piss.

The Nalon ran right at Troy, but he was lighter on his feet and quickly moved out of the way. Turning the Nalon's momentum against him, Troy kicked it as hard as he could in the back. The Nalon lost its footing and crashed into the bars of a closed cell, knocking it out cold.

Troy wanted to feel elation, but he knew better. His next opponent was a female Bartle trader from Jaokle. She gave him a disgusting grin, showing off her teeth, which were crawling with some sort of creature.

He wrinkled his nose. "I bet there's something that can cure your affliction there."

She growled at him. "Yup, breaking your face, pretty boy!"

Troy just shook his head and let her come at him, but she was faster than he expected. She dove between his long legs and punched the back of his left knee, buckling him right down on top of her. Then, much to his displeasure, she bit his right ass cheek. Troy yelled in anger. He turned and viciously punched her in the head, knocking her out. By the sounds of it, the audience really loved that show.

Troy stumbled to his feet and was blindsided from behind and thrown to the ground. Unlike before, he couldn't get back up right away from how much his head was spinning. Part of him was screaming to stand and keep fighting, but the part that just wanted to fall unconscious was winning. He felt himself being lifted off the ground. *Well*, he thought, *this can't be good.*

***

When Troy woke up, he was in darkness. His head still hurt, and he felt like he was paralyzed. After a moment, he realized he was tied, naked, to a metal table. He wiggled the fingers of his left hand to see if his rings were still there. They weren't, which meant the Coronians had Dia's memories. *Fuck*! he thought.

As if on cue, a door opened to his left. He tried to turn and look, but even his head was tied to the table. He heard footsteps; they were slow and deliberate, not the steps of a Coronian. Veronica.

A light above him turned on, and he squinted against the brightness. It was indeed Veronica. She leaned up against the table with her rear, eating a piece of fruit. She deliberately let some of the juice drip on his arm.

"Oh no," she said. "Should I get that?"

"Don't. You. Dare."

She giggled. "You know, Troy, you need to lighten up. You were always so serious."

He knew where she was going with that, so he interrupted her and said, "What're you getting out of this?"

She took another bite of fruit, letting the juice run down her arm just so she could lick it off. Her answer was an inquisitive, innocent hum.

"For fuck's sake. What the hell are you doing with the Coronians? What's this all about?"

She traced a sticky finger along the edge of his jaw. "Well, honestly, I wanted your wife. But I guess I'll have to do with the man who created what she now is."

Troy glared at her with disdain. "Why? What do you think she is?"

"Oh, Dr. Harlow, don't play with me. I *know* Dia is a weapon. The Coronians want that weapon, and I want to deliver it." She leaned in and whispered, "Or if I can't have her, maybe you can make me into one."

***

Troy lay on the piece of garbage the Coronians considered a mattress, staring at the ceiling of his cell. He thought about the exchange he'd had with Veronica, or Maria, after the fights in the prison cells. There was no way he could ever replicate the results he got with Dia because it'd been an accident. And even if he could, he never wanted to do it again. He absolutely did make his wife into a weapon. A weapon, although not initially intended for her, that he thought would be useful to protect their people. Troy had tried for many years to find the perfect candidate who could tolerate the energy immersion but to no avail. Until one day, Dia came into his lab and waited at his desk for him to finish a test so they could go to lunch. His test went horribly wrong, and the EIP discharged, bonding to Dia instantly.

Every other attempt at bonding a Florian to the system resulted in them collapsing from the pain until the energy dissipated from their body, or the energy simply bounced off harmlessly. No one seemed to have the perfect genetic makeup to bond with the EIP.

Nobody until Dia.

The Energy Immersion Power immediately spread itself throughout her body, and she inadvertently absorbed the energy from his desk lamp before falling to the ground. He ran over, scared that he may have actually hurt her, but she sat up, laughing, and said, "Hey, honey. What the hell did you just do to me?"

Panicked, he asked her, "Are you okay? Do you feel any pain?"

Dia giggled. "On the contrary, it's kind of tingly."

Only his wife would think being hit with a gigantic bolt of particle energy was "tingly."

He helped her up, and she turned to get her bag, putting her hand down hard on the desk for support.

And it promptly blew up.

CHAPTER 10
A MOTHER'S LOVE: PART 1

J eannie Harlow aimlessly pushed her food around her plate, staring into oblivion. She heard a distant voice say, "Come on, honey, you must eat something."

Jeannie slowly looked at her husband, Dr. John Harlow, across the table. "Why?"

It had been six weeks since Troy and Dia disappeared. They knew Troy was being held captive by the Coronians, but there had been no word where he was being imprisoned. Troy Harlow was their only child. He meant more to Jeannie than anyone on Rygone.

John sighed and said quietly, "Because that's what Troy would want you to do."

She rolled her eyes. "Is that so, John? Then go rescue him and bring him home so he can tell me himself," she said.

Jeannie had always possessed a serious flare for the dramatic, but she had a good excuse that time. All of Rygone was in an uproar with the kidnapping of their general and doctor. Dia and Troy were the faces of their planet. Children were raised to want to be just like them. The immense burden Rygone put on them both was sometimes almost too much for the couple to bear.

Mrs. Harlow took a large bite of whatever it was their cook had made and chewed it loudly for John. She swallowed that bite down, picked up the flagon of wine on the table between them, and drank half of it. Standing up, some of her dinner fell off her lap, and she said, "I'm going for a walk."

Jeannie strode proudly past her husband. John just stared at the wall, helpless. Jeannie tended to get depressed, but she lived vicariously through their son enough to keep her grounded. Now? He didn't know what to do.

John watched his wife walk out of the apartment. He called Eno on his communicator.

Eno answered and said in his monotone Tradeon voice, "Dr. Harlow, how can I help you?"

"Eno, Mrs. Harlow has just left our apartment for a walk. Can you please keep an eye on her for me? Discreetly."

"Of course, Doctor. I will call you when she's approaching your door. Or if she tries to flee the city again."

"Thank you, Eno. You're truly invaluable."

The line went dead. John knew that Eno was the only one in Baltica who could keep track of Jeannie without being detected. As a Tradeon, he was naturally able to camouflage himself and move silently without others noticing him. Tragically, he was the last of his kind.

***

Eno left his small quarters and did a neuro scan of the building for Jeannie Harlow's signature. He was able to detect her location on the main floor of Baltica City. She was sitting in the mezzanine, just like she'd been for many days over the past few weeks.

Eno traveled down the Flash Lift and walked against the wall until he could see her sitting in the middle of the courtyard, staring at the far wall.

The chancellor and Lady Strom, at the request of the people, commissioned several artists to paint detailed murals of Dia and Troy in the city center. The people of Rygone were mourning the loss of not just one, but two of their most beloved citizens. The murals were nearly twenty feet tall and took up almost the entire main courtyard wall. The chancellor wanted them to be seen from all forty levels of Baltica City.

Jeannie sat on her bench and stared at the incredible paintings. Dia was portrayed in her dress uniform. The jacket was black, trimmed with gold, and fitted to her body. Her high collar bore the gold insignia of the Florian Army, which was the head of a roaring wildcat with crossed silver and black swords underneath. On her shoulders were three gold stars representing the commanding general. She wore slim black slacks and knee-high black leather boots. Dia always wore her long, light-brown hair in a signature braid woven with her silver Kalow Warrior Ribbon. They painted her large brown eyes with black liner; her lips were the color of crimson, and there was a touch of blush on her peach-porcelain cheeks. If Jeannie didn't know better, she would've thought Dia herself was going to step off the wall.

Next, she turned to her son's mural. She looked at his handsome face and felt tears welling up in her eyes. Troy was also portrayed in his dress uniform, but it was much different than that of the army. His form-fitting jacket was a light gray with a single blue stripe that traveled from his right shoulder, across his body at an angle, and stopped at the bottom left. His high collar was the same blue as the stripe and bore the Florian Science Corp. insignia—a dark blue globe representing Rygone with a set of open, black hands beneath it. On his shoulder were three of the same globes from his collar, representing his role as head of Health and Science. Like Dia, Troy wore slim black slacks and knee-high black boots. His dark-brown hair was close cropped on the sides and in the back, so his Harlow birthmark was always visible, but it was longer on top and always swept perfectly to the side. The painters captured his appearance flawlessly, but there was something about him that wasn't quite right.

Troy had uniquely colored eyes that many people found unsettling. They were a rich, dark brown, but they often looked completely black, especially when he was angry. It could be disturbing to people when they first met him, so she'd convinced him to wear color-changing lenses to lighten the brown when he was young. Since most of the residents of Rygone didn't know about his actual eye color, the artists painted his eyes lighter. Jeannie wanted her son represented as he truly was. She would find out who to contact to have his eyes corrected.

Jeannie knew she'd been there too long, and John was probably worried. She didn't always intend to be so hard on him about how she was feeling, but her heart hurt so badly.

Eno watched as Jeannie stood and slowly walked to a small dessert shop across the courtyard. That part of the city contained all the shops and markets the residents needed on a daily basis. Jeannie's favorite treat was an Obalie. It was a dessert with shaved glacier ice mixed with sweet cream and blended fruit. She and Troy's favorite flavor was malson fruit.

As she made her purchase, the young Bayron girl working the register quietly said, "We're all wishing hard for the safe return of your son."

Jeannie stared at the girl for a moment. She'd heard the same exact sentiment from hundreds—no, thousands—of people in the past several weeks. But the girl didn't know that, and she was just being kind. Jeannie faked a smile and quietly replied, "Thank you. I appreciate your wishes."

The girl smiled with pride as Jeannie left the shop. She made her way back to the Flash Lift to go home.

Eno had stayed in his place against the wall, unnoticed, the entire time. He watched as Mrs. Harlow entered the Lift. He took note of what floor was lit up on the wall—thirty-eight—and got into the Lift on his side of the courtyard. As he stepped off on the opposite side of the thirty-eighth floor, he saw she was strolling down the hall toward her apartment, savoring her dessert. Eno activated his communicator and called Dr. Harlow. "Doctor, your wife is coming down the hall toward your home. I will wait here until she is inside."

"Thank you, Eno," Dr. Harlow said.

Just as John cut off with Eno, Jeannie came through the door. Walking up to her husband, she held out her dessert and asked, "Do you want some?"

John chuckled. "No, dear, that's your treat."

Jeannie took another bite and looked down into the cup. John saw a tear running down her lovely dark-brown cheek. With the bite of sweet cream still in her mouth, she mumbled, "His eyes are wrong, John. They're too light; they need to be his real eyes."

He took the cup from her hands and placed it on the table. He pulled her close and held her tight. Jeannie buried her face in her husband's shoulder and began to weep.

CHAPTER 11
MAYBE IT ISN'T SO NICE HERE AFTER ALL

Heather woke up to the sound of the truck door being slid open. There was also a blissful aroma in the air that she'd never smelled before, and she was curious about where it was coming from.

Maeve was standing by the open door and noticed Heather stirring. "Good morning, sleepy head!" she said. "Would you like some coffee?" As usual, Heather only gawked at her, this time with an air of sleepiness. Maeve shrugged and mumbled, "I need to teach you to speak, girl." She moved to her little desk, where there were two cups and a small device hissing with steam.

Heather could feel the warm energy coming off the machine and realized that was where the aroma was coming from. She got up and shuffled over to the desk to watch the device with wonder. There was a glass container with a small spout and a little stream of hot, brown liquid spilling out. Heather went to reach for the container, but Maeve placed her hand on her arm and said, "Oh no, sweetie, that's hot! I'll pour when it's done."

Maeve watched the girl closely, amazed that she didn't even know what a coffee maker was, yet she'd caught on almost immediately with helping people find clothes. Finally, the coffee sputtered and finished brewing. Maeve poured some into each cup. She figured Heather had never had coffee, so she put cream and sugar in hers. The girl watched Maeve in amazement.

Maeve handed her the cup. "Be careful now; it's hot."

Heather took the cup by the handle, put it up to her nose, and drew in a long breath. The smell was wonderful, and she hoped the taste was as good. Heather drank the entire cup in one gulp with no regard for how hot it was, as that wasn't a problem for her. As a matter of fact, Heather was pleased to realize that she absorbed the energy from the hot liquid as she drank.

Once the cup was empty, she lowered it and smiled up at Maeve. But Maeve wasn't smiling back. She was staring at Heather with fearful curiosity. "What are you, girly?" she whispered.

Heather didn't know what Maeve meant, until she looked down at her hands. Her fingertips had begun to glow slightly, and she watched a cool-green flame, barely visible, travel up her arms. Even without looking, Heather knew her eyes were turning emerald-green, and a yellow mist was flowing across her face.

She glanced back up at Maeve, wondering what she'd do. To Heather's surprise, Maeve seemed concerned but not scared. She didn't alert anyone else of Heather's strange appearance after drinking a cup of coffee. Heather wondered if it'd happened yesterday at lunch when she ate the chili. Maybe not, though, as it was much cooler than the hot coffee.

Maeve grabbed Heather by the arm and pushed her back into the truck, then closed the door. She looked around, trying to think of what to do. "I wish you understood me."

Heather just blinked at her. Maeve could tell she at least seemed to comprehend that whatever made her glow like that wasn't something other people around here needed to see.

Maeve nodded and said, mostly to herself, "Well, the Red Cross will probably be here soon to determine what they're going to do with you. I'll try to convince them I have a job for you in Brownsville at the thrift store so you can stay with me."

At first, Maeve struggled to rationalize with herself why she should help Heather. She could see firsthand there was something different, perhaps even potentially dangerous, about her. But Maeve couldn't help thinking that she wasn't dangerous at all. Just a lost, confused girl—who was maybe an alien? Perhaps she escaped a secret government program? It didn't matter to her; she was committed to helping Heather, and that was that.

Then Maeve watched Heather do something even more amazing. The girl gently placed her glowing fingers on the coffee decanter. The light— or whatever it was—surrounding her seemed to flow into the pot. As it hit the liquid, Maeve could see the coffee boil slightly, and the power around the girl diminished until she was back to normal. Maeve went to pick up the pot to see if anything was different, but Heather grabbed her hand. "Hot."

Maeve laughed. "Yes! Four words now!"

A knock came from the roller door of the truck, startling both women. Maeve glanced back at Heather to make sure the girl wasn't glowing anymore before going to open it. There were two men from the Red Cross standing outside. The one holding a clipboard was tall with shaggy, sandy-blonde hair and a big nose. The other had yellow hair that almost looked fake, and he was shorter and very thin. He also had a pock-marked face.

The tall one nodded at them. "Hello, we're from the Red Cross. I understand you have a victim who needs help finding shelter. Can we please come up?"

Maeve reluctantly lowered the steps and said, "Sure! But I think we have it figured out. I'm going to take her with me back to Brownsville. She seems to be getting on quite well here."

Both of the men looked over at Heather. They seemed to be very curious about her almost immediately, just like most of the people who'd seen her since she came out of the cave. Heather stared back uncomfortably.

"Hello, ma'am," the shorter man said. "How are you this morning?"

Heather looked at Maeve, knowing she would help with the language barrier, who said, "She doesn't know much, but she's learned a few names in the one day she's been here. Oh, and the word 'hot.'"

The Red Cross volunteer asked Heather as if he didn't believe Maeve, "Can you talk, ma'am?"

"Maeve, Paul, Robin," Heather replied.

"Are those people you know here?"

Like always, Heather just stared at him with her strange brown eyes.

Maeve said, "Like I said, she doesn't speak much, but I would like to take her back to Brownsville and help her find her way."

The first volunteer glanced at the other. "What do you think? She seems okay here, and we have so many others who need shelter space right now."

The other volunteer shrugged. "Fine by me," he said. He turned to Maeve. "We'll need you to sign a waiver for her. That way, we know exactly where she went, and if something happens, the Red Cross won't be held responsible."

"Fine by me," Maeve echoed.

The taller volunteer took a packet of paperwork off his clipboard. "Please fill these out." He looked back to Heather. "We'll wait."

Maeve rolled her eyes and sat down at her desk. "Bureaucracy," she mumbled.

As Maeve worked, the volunteers walked around the truck, periodically stopping to stare at Heather. She felt uncomfortable, mostly because she didn't understand what was going on. Finally, the shorter volunteer asked, "Your name is Heather? What's your last name? Do you know that, at least?"

Heather glanced at Maeve nervously. Without looking up, she said, "Her last name is Stone. Heather Stone."

Heather committed the word "Stone" to her memory. It was significant; she could feel it.

The volunteer nodded and continued to scan the truck. The other said, "You did well with the clothing donations. Your truck is almost empty."

Maeve kept writing as she answered, "Yeah, but I hear there'll be more to stock back up with at the next location. I just wish they'd tell us where that's supposed to be, since we're leaving tomorrow."

He nodded again. "I hear ya."

Maeve finished with the packet and handed it back. "There you go, gentlemen. Miss Stone will be safe with me."

They both smiled at the ladies, and the tall one said, "Thank you both."

As they climbed down the stairs, the yellow-haired man turned and looked at Heather directly. "I hope you find your way, ma'am," he said. "This world can be an unforgiving place, as you can see by this disaster."

His tone made Heather uneasy, but she managed a small smile anyway.

The volunteers waved as they walked off. Maeve and Heather watched as they rounded the corner. Maeve said, "Well, girl, it's official; you're now my responsibility. I never had kids, but I bet this will be sort of like that."

Heather smiled. "Maeve."

Maeve patted Heather on the shoulder. "Let's go find some breakfast; I'm starving." She pointed at the coffee pot and said, "No."

Heather stared at the pot and back at Maeve. "No."

"Good girl. Now let's go."

The two women made their way toward the mess tent. Much of the makeshift command post was already being torn down, getting ready to be moved. However, there were now two mess tents, unlike the single one yesterday, so there was no line to contend with, which made Heather feel better. They walked up to the servers and Maeve said, "Just give the girl here some cold stuff. She has a canker sore, and the eggs and oatmeal might hurt."

The server gave Maeve a weird look but said, "Okay." She placed a small box of Cheerios, a carton of milk, and a banana on Heather's tray. Heather looked at the food, not knowing what it was, and smiled at the girl.

To make it easier for Heather, Maeve got the same thing. They sat at a table on the far end of the tent. She showed Heather what to do with the cereal and milk and demonstrated how to open the banana. Heather thought the cereal was bland, but the cold milk was good. She really liked the banana and wished she could have another.

As if Maeve could read her mind, she offered Heather half of hers. "Go on, girl. You're so damn skinny. We need to shove as much food into you as we can!"

Heather accepted the banana. "Maeve."

Maeve laughed. "Today will be spent teaching you some more words."

Heather took a bite of her banana and, with a full mouth, said, "Words."

Just then, Heather saw a small screen on the far side of the tent light up. There were people talking and words scrolling across the bottom.

Maeve turned and followed her gaze. "Ah, the news. I wonder how much they're covering this disaster. I haven't seen many reporters," she said.

Heather couldn't understand the people, but she knew the images. They showed different angles of a fireball streaking across the sky toward the Earth. In each video, Heather could hear panicked voices as they watched the fiery object race closer. Each time it impacted the ground, the people screamed and tried to run. Most of the time, they were swallowed by the dust and ash cloud that rushed after them.

Heather was absolutely horrified, and Maeve saw it. "It's terrible, isn't it?" she asked. "I would think all those videos made it out with survivors, but I suspect there are many out there we'll never see."

Tears began to fill Heather's eyes, and all she wanted to do was run, but nobody knew she was the cause of the devastation. It was probably for the best that Heather couldn't understand what the reporters were saying. At present, there were 3,408 deaths and another eight thousand injured. Preliminary estimates were saying there was around two billion dollars' worth of damages.

Heather turned away from the screen and saw Paul and Robin walk into the tent. She tried to look away so as not to attract attention from Robin, but it was too late. Robin feigned excitement and waved her hand like she wanted to come and sit by them. Heather could see it made Paul uncomfortable, but he didn't say or do anything to stop her.

Once they got their food, they came over, and Robin said giddily, "Can we sit with you guys?"

Maeve eyed them warily. "Sure, but we were just getting ready to go."

"Aw, that's okay," Robin said. "It will only be for a few minutes, anyway. Right, honey?"

"Yeah, only a few minutes," he quietly agreed.

Heather didn't glance up from her breakfast tray. Between the news report and Robin and Paul's appearance, she was beginning to feel like a trapped animal again. Her body was instinctively searching for energy sources around her. There were many—she could absorb a lot of power between the lights, the screen, and the cooking stations. She took a few deep breaths and closed her eyes, trying to suppress the danger that resided within her.

Robin decided to feed on Heather's discomfort. "Good morning, Heather!" she said, sickly-sweet. "Do you remember me?"

Without looking up, Heather said, "Robin."

Clapping, she said, "Outstanding! Have you learned any other new words today? Because, you know, invalids don't make it very far in the world these days."

Maeve angrily stood up and snapped, "Is that really necessary? Can you be kind to anybody, girl?" Maeve pulled Heather up by her arm. "Let's go, deary; we have work to do."

Paul took a deep breath and said, "Have a good morning, ladies."

As Heather stood up, she secretly reached out two fingers of her left hand and pulled a small amount of energy from a light nearby. Nobody noticed the bulb dim slightly. She turned to Robin, glared at her dead in the eye, energy illuminating the curve of her irises with an emerald-green flash, and said, "Words."

Robin just gaped at her in shock. Paul noticed Heather as well, but by the time he saw her face, she had already pushed the energy back to the light, and her eyes were brown again.

"Come on, now," Maeve said, pulling on the girl's arm.

Heather gave Robin a sly smile as she walked away with Maeve.

Robin watched as they strode off and asked Paul, exasperated, "Did you see that?"

Paul took a bite of his eggs. "See what?"

"That bitch's eyes. They turned a weird, shiny green for a few seconds. It was evil-looking!"

Paul swallowed and watched Maeve and Heather exit the tent. He shook his head. "No, I didn't see anything."

"Why didn't you just leave her in that hole?" Robin hissed accusingly at him.

Paul looked long and hard at Robin. When they first met, she'd been such a nice person who cared about others. Now, all she cared about was making him miserable for doing his job, or hell, just for being in public. He stood up with his breakfast tray. "Because it's my job. Remember? I help people for a living. All people, even weird women stuck in craters with glowing green eyes." He walked away and put his tray by the trash, leaving Robin sitting there with her mouth hanging open in shock.

Paul knew he would regret it later, but it felt good right then.

***

For the rest of the day, Maeve and Heather packed up what was left in the truck and helped out other crews get their stuff ready to go. The Red Cross and donation vehicles would leave first thing in the morning. That included Maeve.

Most of the camp heard the story of the small, pretty girl pulled out of the bottom of the crater. Workers and survivors alike would stop by just to get a glimpse of Heather. She thought it was strange and didn't like the attention, but she smiled at the visitors anyway.

Maeve also used the time to try to teach her more words. By dinner time, Heather knew yes, no, stop, help, food, water, clothes, tent, truck, and coffee.

Heather had really started to enjoy Maeve's company. She was kind and seemed to genuinely care about her. She felt Paul would've been the same way, but Robin kept him from doing so.

That evening, when the truck was completely packed and ready to go, Heather cleaned up again and changed into a fresh pair of clothes that she scrounged from what was left. She found an old leather jacket that she liked, and Maeve was happy to let her have it. Heather also found a red blouse with white flowers and a pair of skinny black slacks. She kept the hiking shoes, as they were comfortable despite being the wrong size. She thought about the boots she'd been wearing in space and suddenly remembered how much more comfortable they were. *I wonder where they came from*, she thought.

The two women walked back to the mess tents and saw they were mostly taken down as well. A few volunteers were handing out packages containing cold meals and bottles of water. Heather hoped they'd have more bananas, but they didn't.

Maeve read off the different options from the pouches. "Chicken and noodles, beef stew, or ham and potatoes." She said to Heather, "I'd ask you what you want, but I'm sure you don't know."

Maeve took two of the packages and handed them to Heather. "Chicken and noodles, and beef stew. We can share and get some variety," she said as she grabbed two bottles of water.

"Share," Heather repeated.

***

They made it back to the truck and sat at Maeve's desk to eat. They had a pleasant time, considering their situation. Maeve worked with Heather on starting to put questions and sentences together. She was amazed at how fast the girl learned.

After dinner, Heather went to the bathroom, but when she returned, Maeve was gone. Heather didn't think she'd leave without telling her, so maybe she'd be back soon.

She waited for a long time, but there was no sign of Maeve. Heather was getting worried and decided to search for her. She considered absorbing a small amount of energy from a light in the truck but was afraid it would be visible in the dark camp. Heather knew Maeve couldn't be far, so she went down the steps into the cool night air. Most of the dust and ash had settled, and there was no breeze.

Heather looked both ways. "Maeve?" She walked a few steps toward the path and repeated her name. Nothing.

She started to get nervous and thought maybe she should go back to the truck and wait. But Maeve had been so friendly, and she didn't want to leave her to be hurt if she could help it.

Walking around the truck next to theirs, Heather called Maeve's name again. Suddenly, two men stepped into the light at the far end of the trailer. Heather felt panic fill her heart, wishing that she had absorbed the energy from the lamp. She turned to go back the other way, only to find two more men behind her. She was trapped.

As the first two started to approach her, one laughed. "I told you, boys. Fresh and hot."

Heather recognized his voice. It was the yellow-haired Red Cross volunteer from earlier that morning. She flicked her eyes between the pairs of men approaching her and tried to calm her mind in order to figure out how to flee. From the other direction, one of the men said, "Oh, honey, don't try to look for an escape. It ain't gonna happen."

Heather backed herself up against the truck and tried to feel for energy, but there was nothing. Her best hope was to find a way to get closer to Maeve's, where the lamp was still on.

Out of desperation, she tried to crawl under the truck opposite Maeve's, but one of the men caught her by the ankle and dragged her back into the open. He pulled her to her feet and pinned her arms behind her back. She tried to scream, but another slapped tape over her mouth. He got right in her face and said in a raspy, teasing voice, "No, no, no."

Heather struggled against the man holding her as much as she could, and he was having a hard time keeping her still. "Fuck man," he grunted. "She's stronger than she looks; hurry the fuck up!"

The man with the yellow hair reached down and grabbed her pants and tried to pull them down. She heard another one of them say, "Oh, I can't wait to see what's under there!"

He had her pants nearly down, then pulled her away from the other man and smashed her against Maeve's truck, where she felt the faintest bit of power from the lamp. As he pressed his bare skin against hers, she reached out and pulled all the power she could from it. With a blast of green flame, she pushed off from the truck, using all the energy to propel her and her attacker into the other trailer.

Knowing she had to act while they were still shocked, Heather pulled her pants up to run, but unfortunately, one of the men was still paying enough attention and ran after her. He caught her before she could clear the truck and slammed her to the ground. He spun her around, and she saw it was the other Red Cross volunteer. He leaned close to her and snarled, "The only place you're going after we get a piece of you is back into that fucking hole."

Something in her—an instinct of sorts—came alive. She smiled beneath the tape.

Before he knew what hit him, Heather brought her hand up and jammed her fingertips into his throat as hard as she could. As he reached for his damaged larynx, he released the weight pressing down on her, and she shoved him off. She kicked him in the crotch, punched him in the head, and then ripped the tape off her mouth. As he lay in agony, his friends came running at her, but Heather was ready.

All three came at her at once, but she was already running away lightning fast.

She heard the one who had held her arms back say, "See, I told you she was strong—and that green flame shit? Let's get the fuck out of here!"

"We gotta catch her and get the cops or something!" another cried.

Although it was hard while running, Heather sent out feelers for energy. She discovered a large source nearby—a running generator. By that point, some of the camp seemed to have been alerted to the struggle and were coming out of their tents and trucks to see what was happening. The three men were starting to gain on her. She made a beeline for the generator, and as she got close, she showed the whole area what she was capable of.

And all hell broke loose.

CHAPTER 12
SOMETIMES IT'S HARD TO BE STRONG

"You know, Chancellor, you can always confide in me. Even more than Mom sometimes."

Chancellor Strom looked up at his son Dominic, his head of security and the one responsible for his protection. "I know," he said quietly. "I just don't know what to say."

It'd been six weeks since Dia and Troy's disappearance, and like Jeannie Harlow, the chancellor was having a harder time handling it than expected. At least they knew who had Troy; Dia had been ejected into space, and she couldn't be located. Several DREX had been searching all around the planet and the surrounding quadrant. There was no sign of his daughter anywhere. Plus, the documents from the wreckage were a particular source of distress. *Why did they leave? Were they ever going to come back?* he wondered.

He asked, "Do you think they left because of the Energy Immersion Project?"

Dominic answered, "Absolutely. According to Oscar, Troy was making Dia into the ultimate Rygonian weapon, and they must've discovered something that wasn't supposed to happen. The Coronians probably found out, and they wanted to get away before the planet was attacked—and before she could fall into their hands."

"How do you think they found out about the EIP? I wonder if there was something more to the project that we don't know."

Dominic shrugged. "That's something you'll need to take up with Oscar. Troy never told me much."

Troy and Dominic were never close, but they were cordial. Dominic knew for many years that Troy was working on something big, but he never talked much about it, and with all of the other innovations he produced, Dominic never questioned the EIP. At least, not until Dia became involved by no fault of her own. Troy didn't take enough precautions, which wasn't like him, and Dia became the unwitting recipient of the power. That made Dominic's relationship with his brother-in-law go south fast.

The chancellor sighed. "I have, several times. He's just as secretive as Troy. Plus, Troy, Dia, and Oscar's work and personal information has been searched repeatedly. There's nothing out of the ordinary. Whatever reason prompted them to leave, they covered their tracks well."

Dominic suspected his brother knew something more about the situation than he was saying. Whatever it was that Troy and Dia were running from, it was bad.

Warren stood up and walked to his office window, one that looked down over the mezzanine. Even from the thirty-ninth floor, he could see the giant murals of Dia and Troy painted in the courtyard. The people of Rygone all knew the Coronians were involved in their leaders' disappearance. They knew how terrible their enemies were, especially to Florians, so most of the population believed Troy and Dia were gone forever. Therefore, it hadn't taken his people long to want a memorial of their beloved general and doctor. *Do they not have faith that I will do whatever I can to bring them home?* he thought.

There were two painters touching up Troy's eyes, making them darker. He was sure that was by Mrs. Harlow's request, which seemed strange, as Troy never went into public without his color-changing lenses because of people's reactions in the past. Most of Rygone had no idea his eyes were so different. Though, he figured if something about Dia's image weren't right, he'd want it changed as well. Her mural was perfect.

He turned around to find Dominic still sitting down, watching his father intently. His son asked, "What do you want me to do, Chancellor?"

"Put together a team of the best secret corps people in Dia's inner circle. Find out where the Coronians have Troy."

"And rescue him?"

The chancellor shook his head. "Not yet; we need to figure out what the final piece of this puzzle is—and I think we'll only find out after the Coronians get Troy to either talk or recreate the EIP for them."

"So, we're leaving your son-in-law in the hands of our greatest enemy to be forced to create another weapon that can be used against us?" Dominic asked.

"You make it sound like I want to," the chancellor said. "They need him; they want to know what the EIP can do just as much as we do, and that weapon is probably drifting through space as a frozen piece of living debris." He immediately regretted saying that. "I didn't mean it that way. Dia has to be somewhere close enough to find. We just have to keep trying."

Dominic stood up. "Do you want my honest opinion, Dad?" he asked.

Chancellor Strom said, "No, but I'm sure you're going to tell me anyway."

"We should go get Troy now; hopefully, he hasn't been forced to build them anything yet."

"And Dia?"

Dominic swallowed and said, "We should stop the search for Dia. It's been six weeks, and there's no telling where she drifted. I think further searching for her is a moot point."

A flash of anger crossed Warren's face. "No matter the cost, we will always search for your sister, Dominic."

Dominic sighed, exasperated. "Okay. But for now, I'm on my way to find Troy and bring him home. Whether you want me to or not."

CHAPTER 13
KENTUCKY, WE HAVE A PROBLEM

D ia wasn't a frozen piece of space debris. She had crash-landed on a planet halfway across the quadrant. She had no memory, no idea where she was, or even *what* she was. All she had was her new name—Heather Stone—and her incredible, terrifying powers.

***

Heather was still running away from her attackers when she noticed the power from the generator. Instinctively, as she ran by the machine, she reached out her hand and pulled the energy from the running engine. The lights around her dimmed as she took it, and once she had it all, the engine stopped.

At that point, all of the people left in the camp had come out to see the commotion, only to be confronted with a woman pulling what appeared to be a green flame from a generator and absorbing it into her body. Her hair went from light brown to a yellow-white. Her eyes shone like iridescent, green emeralds, and she was emitting yellow mist across the sides of her face. Her fingertips glowed as bright as a star, ready to dispense whatever power she desired.

They couldn't believe what they were seeing. People started screaming and running as Heather stopped and turned, confronting her pursuers head-on. As they saw what she'd become, they cried out and tried to turn the other way, but Heather's rage was inescapable. She raised her hands out in front of her and shot several small balls of green flame toward them. They hit each man in the back, sending them flying at least twenty feet and catching their clothes on fire. They screamed as they struggled out of their burning jackets and ran into the night.

Utter chaos reigned throughout the camp. Heather returned to the generator, intending to release the energy back into the machinery, but she was confronted by two sheriff's deputies who were scared out of their minds. She stopped and stared at them, not realizing how terrifying she appeared to everyone.

One of the deputies pointed his gun at her and shouted with a shaky voice, "S-Stop right there! Don't take another step!"

Heather had no idea what he was saying, but she could tell he was an authority figure, so she stayed where she was. Since the generator was only about five feet behind the deputies, she thought it would be a good idea to send the energy back. *Stupid, Heather, just stupid.*

As she raised her hand and started to push the energy back toward the engine, the deputies, rightfully so, thought she was attacking them. One fired his weapon and shot Heather three times. She jolted from the impact of the bullets but was otherwise unharmed. She dropped her hand and touched where one of the bullets had made a hole in her leather jacket.

What was even more interesting, she realized, was that her power increased with the impact of the bullets. Her body had absorbed the kinetic energy from the rounds when they hit her.

Both of the deputies were frightened and didn't know what to do. Heather started to walk toward them, not with any ill intentions, since she still only wanted to put the energy back into the generator. The deputies opened fire on her. Heather jolted from each impact but kept coming.

One of the deputies started screaming, "Stop! Stop now!"

They were almost out of bullets, and Heather was nearly to them when from her side, Paul came running toward her. She smiled. "Paul."

He looked at her, horrified. "Heather? What the hell is happening!?"

One of the panicked deputies cried, "What is it?!"

"She won't hurt you! I promise," Paul told them.

From behind Paul, more people were running toward them. Still calm but powered, Heather stepped around him to see how many there were when a single shot rang out from the group. It was intended for her but missed its mark and went straight through Paul's heart.

Paul lurched forward and sputtered for a moment, and Heather watched, dismayed, as he coughed up blood. He collapsed against her, and she grabbed him, sinking to the ground. Heather felt his life energy drain away, and within moments, he was dead.

Rage welled up inside her as the group of people surrounding her waited to see what the strange creature would do. Heather gently laid Paul's body on the ground before screaming, her eyes and fingertips becoming brighter. Panicked, the armed people in the crowd all started firing at once.

Heather expected this reaction. Knowing she could absorb the bullets' kinetic energy, she took in as much as she could before they realized their mistake. The gunfire stopped almost simultaneously as the onlookers saw she was glowing with so much green energy, they almost couldn't recognize her as a person. She took a deep breath and shrieked again, bursting out enough power to blow most of the crowd back at least ten feet. Heather scanned the area around the camp for an escape route, but the landscape was all the same from the impact damage.

With nothing else to do, she ran away as fast as she could. She didn't know where she was going or what she would do, but she needed to flee. The Florian obviously didn't belong there, or anywhere, for that matter. *Who and what am I?* she thought, terrified.

She fled into the darkness of the night, emitting her own light. She remembered the strange voice, in the language she thought in. *Release all of the power inside you. Who is he? Where is he?* she wondered desperately.

Heather slowed down as her power began to dwindle. She looked around and realized she must've gone very far because there were no lights, sounds, or absorbable energy around her—only darkness. For the first time, the events of the evening began to flood back into her head. Maeve leaving the truck, and the four men trying to attack her. She could still feel the bare skin of the yellow-haired volunteer on her back side. Her escape from them, but the mistake with the generator. She should've known better than to absorb that much energy around people.

Heather thought about that for a moment. Instinctively, she spun the ring on her middle finger as she considered what to do next. How did she know so much about the rules of her power but nothing else? Who or what erased who she was?

She shook off that thought and remembered Paul. He was the first person she'd met on this world and had been so kind to her. He only cared for others, even when Robin tried to put him down. Heather touched her jacket where Paul fell against her; she could feel his dried blood. Tears filled her eyes. She felt all alone. She would rather be speeding through space than be stuck here on a world full of people she couldn't understand.

Heather still had a small amount of energy stored, so she was glowing ever so slightly. That made it easy for the police helicopter to spot her from above. It flew over her head, scaring her into running again. The helicopter stayed low, close enough for her to feel the power from its engine. She debated on absorbing it, but she didn't want to crash the vehicle. Her intent wasn't to kill or hurt anybody. Heather just wanted to escape.

Over a loudspeaker, a voice called, "Stop! Stop running, or we *will* shoot!"

Maeve had taught her the word "stop," so she froze in an open field, her energy entirely spent, and craned her neck toward the helicopter hovering above her. The lights and wind from the rotor made it hard to concentrate, but she tried to stay calm.

"Put your hands behind your head and get on your knees!" the voice said.

Heather began to panic because she didn't understand and was afraid of how the people in the helicopter would respond. She just continued to stare at them, hoping they'd realize she didn't know what they were saying. Unfortunately, that wasn't the case.

"Get on your knees, or we'll shoot!"

Heather stood there, unmoving. Tears were beginning to well in her eyes again as the fear started to get the best of her. Suddenly, the helicopter lurched closer. She didn't know if it was intentional or not, but it scared her enough that she pulled power from the engine and took off again.

As she ran away, she could hear the motor whine up and down as the helicopter tried to compensate for the lack of power. She glanced over her shoulder just as the chopper hit the ground hard. The tears finally came.

You're only making things worse! she berated herself.

It wasn't long before more helicopters were flying close to her. She was running for, what—her life? Could she die? She didn't know, but she just wanted to get away. A voice from one of the helicopters yelled, "Stop! Or we'll use deadly force!"

That time, Heather kept running. She didn't have much stored energy left, but she would use all she had to escape. Suddenly, Heather heard a loud boom and saw a bright light that blinded her. She was blown off her feet and landed in a ditch. She sat up and shook her head. After a moment, she realized she'd absorbed a large amount of power and immediately stood up and ran. Whatever weapon they used against her had the opposite effect. Not only did it not stop her, it helped her!

Heather was running incredibly fast, but she knew it wouldn't last long. She could see the land around her and noticed there were vehicles on the ground starting to form a circle around her. As she searched for the best escape route, she realized she was being funneled. The ground vehicles were closing in on both sides and behind her, and three helicopters flew above. Just as Heather planned to pull as much energy from them all so she could stand her ground, a familiar voice distracted her.

Maeve came from over a loudspeaker. "Heather!" she cried. "Honey, please stop! Don't hurt anyone, and they won't hurt you!"

Heather didn't understand, but it was Maeve, so she stopped. One of the vehicles came racing toward her, and Heather tensed, ready to defend herself. The truck stopped about fifteen feet away, and Maeve jumped out.

Heather started to run to her, crying, "Maeve! Maeve!" But she didn't get far.

From behind, Heather was hit with what felt like a ton of bricks. Disorientated, she fell forward. Several men descended on her and began putting chains on her arms and legs. Another one gagged her and put a cloth bag over her head.

The last thing she heard was Maeve plead, "You promised you wouldn't hurt her!"

A man's voice replied, "I haven't. Not yet at least."

CHAPTER 14
MORE COFFEE PLEASE

W hen Heather finally woke up, she was lying on a concrete block with a thin mat for a mattress. There was a small amount of light coming from a window in the ceiling, but she could barely see. Heather squinted and saw that the only items in the small room were the concrete block she was lying on, a concrete table with concrete stools on two sides, and what looked like a metal toilet in the corner. One wall had a large mirror. She figured that was how her captors would watch her. The room she was in must've been well-insulated, as she couldn't detect any absorbable energy from in or outside of the space.

She sat up and saw she was wearing a comfortable light top with matching pants, along with soft white socks and thin shoes. She also realized she'd been bathed, and her hair had been washed and braided.

While she was unconscious, some unknown person undressed and washed her body without her knowing. Heather didn't like that. She went to spin the ring on her middle finger for comfort but found it wasn't there. Both rings were gone. The only part of her existence before the strange man's voice, gone.

She gazed at her surroundings for a long time, not moving or even thinking much. Finally, a voice came over an unseen speaker and said, "Good morning, Heather."

Heather still didn't move. After a few minutes, the voice said, "Maeve said you liked bananas. Would you like a banana?"

She could barely understand the language, yet she felt the voice was being condescending. Heather lay back down and turned her back to the mirror. She only wanted her freedom, and she was sure that wouldn't happen anytime soon, so she might as well sleep.

Heather drifted off for what seemed like a few hours but was really only a few minutes. When she heard the door open, she whirled around to see who was coming in. It was a tall woman with ash-blonde hair and green eyes. Her face seemed friendly, but Heather wasn't buying it. The woman had a tray with food on it.

She placed it on the table. "I know you can't understand what I'm saying, but food is universal." She pointed at the tray and said, "Come and eat something, Heather."

Using her absorbed power took a lot of her own body's energy, so she *was* starving. However, she just warily stared at the woman.

"My name is Helen," the woman said. "I'm here for you, Heather. If you need anything, just knock on that mirror."

Heather glanced at the mirror, then back at the woman. Helen clapped her hands together and said, "Well, I doubt you'll even think about eating while I'm in the room, so I'll step out." She smiled warmly at Heather. "I hope we'll make a real connection soon."

Helen got up and left the room. Heather could hear the door lock.

The Florian hungrily stared at the food. To her pleasant surprise, there was a cup of coffee on the tray. She got up and slowly moved to the table, all the while staring into the mirror, wondering how many people other than Helen were watching her.

Heather sat down and inspected the food. Besides the coffee, there was a plate with two round, flat cakes with a small square of creamy yellow stuff on top and a sweet brown liquid on the side. There was also what she could only describe as some kind of meat pressed into a circle. Another cup contained an orange liquid that also smelled sweet. That was the first thing Heather tasted. It was lovely. She drank the orange juice in almost one gulp, savoring the sweetness.

Next, she tried the meat circle. She picked it up with her fork and nibbled on the edge. She thought about it for a minute, then she decided it was good and devoured the piece in just a few bites. The yellow, creamy stuff on the cake circle had melted, so she spread it around with her finger and licked it off, giving the mirror a side glance. She dumped all of the brown, sweet liquid on top of the cakes. Using her fork to cut the cakes up, she basically shoved them down her throat. At least the food was good.

Once she was finished eating, she turned her attention to the cup of coffee. It was still hot. She picked it up, holding it in her hands, feeling the warmth. Heather quickly drank the coffee, savoring the energy she absorbed from it. Once she was finished, she set the cup on the tray and offered the mirror a sweet smile.

Before the crew in the observation room could react, Heather jumped up and used the energy from the heat in the coffee to rip the door off its hinges. Unlike her room, there were lights on the ceiling in the hallway, and as Heather ran down the corridor, she raised her hands, absorbing the power they emitted. By the time she reached the end of the hall, she was glowing with green fire, and her eyes were as bright as flaming emeralds. She heard several people at the other end of the hallway yelling for her to stop. She turned to them, gave a sinister grin, and kicked in the door.

Heather found herself in another corridor just like the first one. She continued to pull the energy from the lights as she ran. She came to the end of the hall, but before she could blast through the door, Helen threw it open and yelled, "Please! Stop, we can help you!"

Heather gave Helen a shrug of her shoulders, literally picked up the woman, spun, and put her down. "No."

She ran down another corridor and spotted a door with a window revealing the the courtyard beyond. She sprinted toward her freedom, but before she could make it, ten guards in riot gear came flooding into the hallway in front of her. She turned on her heel to go back the other way, but there were more, all converging on her. Heather, no matter the situation, didn't want to hurt anyone.

They were surrounding her with riot shields and batons. Many looked anxious, not yet knowing what she was capable of. She gave them a little taste. Heather took in a deep breath, dropping the air pressure. All the guards were confused at the sudden, strange feeling. Next, she did a huge backflip and she landed, there was a loud crack, almost like thunder, and the floor beneath everyone began to buckle, knocking people down. Confusion and chaos tore through the guards, and Heather was able to easily run over their sprawling bodies to the end of the hall. She ripped open the door, only for a rope to come out of nowhere and encircle her neck.

Unfortunately, Heather had released most of her energy with the floor stunt and couldn't get the rope off her neck before several more were thrown around various parts of her body, dragging her to the ground. She wasted the rest of her absorbed energy trying to escape, to no avail.

Next time, she'd have a better plan.

CHAPTER 15
MUSIC SOOTHES THE SAVAGE FLORIAN

M ajor Jason Mallory watched the woman, or thing, lying on the concrete bed. She was now in a full-body papoose and just staring at the ceiling. He could only imagine what was going through her head. He whispered to the glass, "What the fuck are you, lady?"

Dr. Helen Grace came up next to him and said, "Today was incredible, huh, Major?"

He looked at her with disdain. "Did you know she could do that? With the coffee? She fucking destroyed an entire hallway and took out twenty guards with a cup of coffee and a backflip!"

"For the record, the worst injury sustained by any of those twenty guards was a sprained ankle," she retorted, opening a folder she was holding. "Even at the recovery camp, the worst wounds were second-degree burns three men sustained from a targeted attack. Some witnesses think they were trying to rape her."

"But wasn't there a death?" Mallory asked. "The firefighter? She knew him."

Helen nodded. "Yes, Paul Dixon. He was the one who pulled her from the cave. But she didn't kill him. He was caught in the crossfire and basically died in her arms, sparking more anger."

"What do you mean?"

"Well, she obviously doesn't know who or where she is. She can't communicate with anyone very well, and a nice man helps her out. Then a bunch of assholes try to rape her, and a few minutes later, her friend is shot by a bullet meant for her and dies in her arms. Hell yes, the girl had the right to be upset, yet the reason she was hunted wasn't that she hurt anyone; it was because nobody understood what she was doing."

"Understandably so," Mallory said. He looked back into the mirror. Heather hadn't moved a muscle. "What do we do with her? The chain of command is already drooling over getting her out of this unsecured facility so they can start weaponizing her power."

Helen said, "And that's what they'll do. My job is to help her learn our language and how we do things as much as possible before they get here." She placed a hand on his shoulder and added, "And you need to figure out what the hell she can do before we let a dangerous alien loose on the United States. I'm going to go in there and try to connect with her."

"Good luck," Mallory said, "and don't take coffee."

Helen shook her head and laughed. "This girl will only get cold food from now on."

Mallory watched through the mirror as Helen entered the room. The woman didn't move or acknowledge her presence. Helen sat down at the table and took out her phone. She didn't say a word, just turned on the phone and played some classical music. Mallory watched as both women sat still, not talking or even blinking for what seemed like forever. When the third piece came on, Mallory saw the woman shift a little bit in the papoose. She closed her eyes and seemed to be listening intently to that particular piece. When it ended, she looked at Helen for a moment, and without saying anything, the doctor repeated the song. They said music soothed the savage beast; well, it just calmed a woman who could destroy a building with a cup of coffee.

***

Helen watched Heather intently as she listened to the music. It seemed either that particular piece was familiar to her or reminded her of a lost memory. After playing the song for the fourth time, Helen said, "Soon, in the work you and I will be doing together, I want to know what it is that made you react so much to that particular song. We'll listen to it at the beginning and end of each day."

Heather just stared at the ceiling for a while. Suddenly, she opened her mouth as if to say something, then closed it. Helen asked, "Did you want to say something?"

A tear rolled down Heather's cheek. She said quietly, "Paul."

Helen wanted to comfort Heather, but she didn't want to get too close after what had happened earlier that day. "I was told you and Paul Dixon knew each other. I'm sorry for your loss, my dear."

Heather examined her and said, "The song. Paul."

Taken by surprise, Helen asked, "The song reminds you of Paul? You understood what I said a few minutes ago?"

"Some," Heather said.

Helen nodded excitedly. "Well, this may go smoother than I thought. We start fresh tomorrow."

As Helen got up to leave, Heather said, "Banana, please."

She nodded. "I'll make sure you get a banana with dinner and that they take you out of that infernal thing. However, you'll never get coffee again."

"Damn," Heather whispered.

CHAPTER 16
MEET THE TEAM; PLEASE DON'T HURT THEM

T he next morning, three more people were in the room behind the mirror, staring at Heather. She was sitting on the concrete bed, glaring at the glass.

One of the newbies said, "Damn, she's pretty, but those eyes are creepy as hell!"

Another, a woman, added, "I think her eyes are pretty. They're so different and mysterious. I can't wait to get in there and talk to her!"

Dr. Carl Johnson, the leader of the three and a physicist, shook his head. "Wait until you see the footage of what happened at the recovery camp in Kentucky and the hall yesterday. I heard things got hairy. That woman is incredibly dangerous. I'm not sure how eager you'll be after that."

With that, the three turned around and joined Dr. Grace and Major Mallory at a conference table.

Dr. Grace cleared her throat. "As you already know, Heather Stone—who was named by one of the camp volunteers—was rescued from the impact crater. She had absolutely nothing on, except these rings." Dr. Grace pointed to Heather's rings in a small ceramic dish on the table. "She didn't speak or understand English but seemed harmless at the time. The camp volunteer, Maeve Marco, said that local fire and rescue asked her to watch the girl, and she seemed scared but friendly. By the end of the first day after being rescued, she was able to help Marco hand out clothes and supplies to the survivors. Marco said she felt nervous around Heather at first but was put at ease quickly."

Grace dimmed the lights and turned on a television on the far wall. She continued, "These first pictures are some of what the camp survivors took of Heather before anything happened. As you can see, she was nervous but calm and seemed to cling to Marco. On the evening of the attack, Marco said she was called away from the truck suddenly and left the girl there by herself. She wasn't sure what happened after that because it was less than an hour later that the attack occurred at the generator."

Helen scanned through a few of the pictures so the rest of the team could get an idea of how their new friend behaved before the attack. "From what we put together, eyewitnesses said Heather left the truck to find Maeve and was attacked by four men, probably with the intention of sexual assault. She escaped from them, and witnesses said she ran by a generator and literally *pulled* the energy from the engine with a sort of green, glowing flame."

She clicked a button on the remote and said, "Here is the first cell phone video we have. Be prepared, though it's grainy and quite graphic."

The three watched as Heather stopped running and turned around. The video showed three men running toward her, and that she was glowing green with bright white fingertips and emerald-green eyes. Heather raised her hands out in front of her and shot several green fireballs from her palms that sped away and hit the men. They were thrown back at least twenty feet, and their clothes were on fire, but they seemed to get away relatively unharmed.

Penny Singleton, the team's physician's assistant, said, "Geez. That's crazy!"

"That's just the beginning," Major Mallory told her.

Dr. Grace clicked to the next cell phone video and said, "From what it looks like, we think she was trying to put the energy back into the generator, but the deputies didn't understand that which makes sense as she didn't obey their orders."

The three watched the amateur video show Heather walking toward the police officers with her hands out in front of her, not unlike how they were when she shot her attackers. They were yelling at her to stop, but she kept walking. Finally, one of the cops shot her three times. Amazingly, not only did the bullets not harm her, but they seemed to make her stronger.

"This next part is where things really went off the rails," Grace warned them.

The trio watched as a man came running up to Heather's side. She smiled and seemed happy to see him. From behind, they could see a mob of people rushing toward them. A shot was heard, and the man buckled forward into Heather. She screamed what must've been his name and fell to her knees, holding him as he died. She shrieked again, and several people in the crowd opened fire, shooting countless rounds directly at her. To their bewilderment, they were only making her more powerful. She stood up and the three gasped. Heather was almost engulfed in the green flame; her eyes were the brightest of green gems with a yellow fire flowing down the side of her face. Her hair went from light brown to a bright yellow-white. She crouched down, balling her fists against her chest, and burst out a wave of the green flame all around her. The rush of power hit all the people, including the cell phone holder. The screen went dark.

They were quiet for a moment, trying to process what they just saw, until Dr. Johnson asked, "How's that possible?" He glanced back at the tiny woman through the mirror, sitting on the bed and staring intently at the glass. He got a shiver up his spine. It felt like she was staring angrily into his soul.

"We have no fucking idea, Doctor," Major Mallory said. "That's why you're here."

Brody Patterson, the technology expert for the team, asked, "Did she have any devices that could be used to attract that kind of energy? That power should've killed her instantly."

Mallory scoffed. "Again, that's why you're here."

"Was there any footage after that? How was she caught?" Penny asked.

Dr. Grace answered, "The footage taken after that was by the military and police presence and hasn't been released to us. But we do know she ran twenty-seven miles from the camp. Twenty-seven miles in four minutes. If she wouldn't have run low on the power she seemed to have absorbed, she would've gotten farther, and I doubt we would have found her. Someone in one of the helicopters got the bright idea to shoot her with a launchable grenade and gave her a boost but not enough to get too far. By the time we caught her again, she was hit from behind with a battering ram, rendering her unconscious for several hours. That's how we got her here."

"But there was an incident yesterday as well," Dr. Johnson said. "What happened?"

Major Mallory and Dr. Grace looked at each other. She reluctantly turned on the television again, and the events of the day before played out for the new team. They were amazed Heather could do all of that damage with just the heat energy from the coffee and a few overhead lights. Johnson said, "She may not be able to talk, but she's damn smart. Dangerously so and cooped up like a rabid wolf. We must figure out what to do fast, or she could become a serious liability for not just us but the entire world."

Penny said, "I don't mean to play the devil's advocate, but I don't really see her as all that dangerous. Yes, she's attacked and demonstrated this incredible power but think about all the circumstances behind why she did it. First, those men tried to assault her, so she defended herself. The police, although right, shot her because they didn't understand what she was doing, and now we think she could've been trying to put that energy back into the generator. In both cases, we can't prove she was trying to hurt anyone. She ran because she was scared and wanted to escape. Dr. Johnson, I think you're right; she's backed into a corner like a rabid wolf and is dangerous, but only because she's confused and misunderstood. We need to help her, not demonize her."

Carl considered her words for a moment. "Sure, makes sense. However, she's still dangerous and unpredictable. What if she's just waiting for the right moment to use her abilities to hurt us? We don't know enough and need to take precautions."

At that moment, everyone in the room noticed movement on the other side of the glass. They turned to watch Heather get off the bed and walk up to the mirror. Everyone became tense, unsure of what she could do, even without any energy. She placed her hand on the glass and gave a sly smile. "Hear you," she said.

Shocked, Major Mallory asked, "She can hear us?"

Heather echoed him, broken but mockingly. "She hear us?" She smiled again.

"Yup, she's dangerous," Penny said, shuddering.

Heather just laughed, walked back to her bed, and sat down, staring at them again with her eerie eyes.

The brief exchange rattled the entire team. Heather had heard everything they said about her, and she seemed to be able to understand certain phrases, and even more unsettlingly, she was responding to them in her own way.

***

Dr. Grace glared at the others with frustration. "I went in there yesterday, and she didn't show any aggression toward me. She even likes music. That's the avenue I think we need to start with. Pick something she likes and build on it. She's obviously highly intelligent; I don't think it will be long before we have her under control."

The rest of the team just stared at the psychologist.

"Or lose control, Dr. Grace. You have too much optimism this early in the game." Mallory barked at her, "Just play some of that music you were listening to yesterday through the speakers and see what she does."

Helen took out her phone and connected it to the sound system that fed into Heather's room. She started the classical playlist from the day before. They all watched Heather intently, but she didn't shift her eyes from the mirror. As the third track was about to start, Dr. Grace said, "This was the piece she responded to. She told me it reminded her of the man who rescued her from the crater. The one who was killed."

Heather didn't respond how they were expecting her to this time. She yawned and lay down, turning her back to the glass. Brody said, "I'm thinking that was intentional."

Dr. Johnson exhaled hard. "What kind of timeline do we have? When are the brass going to be here to pick this chick up?"

"Two weeks," Major Mallory answered.

Johnson continued, "We need to get her medically vetted, speaking and understanding the language, and figure out what she's capable of in two weeks?"

Mallory nodded. "Yeah, sounds about right."

"And if we can't?" Penny asked.

"Then they'll find someone else who will. We already know this thing is a liability, but the powers-that-be want to start with the soft route first. In other words, you people."

"You people," Dr. Grace repeated with disdain.

The room fell silent except for the classical music. Finally, Johnson clapped his hands together and said, "Well fuck, let's get started then." He turned to the group, ignoring Mallory, and said, "Let's go introduce ourselves to the little lady, shall we?"

Penny and Brody tried to resist, but Dr. Johnson wasn't having it. "Suck it up. If you want to help this woman, or thing, we have to do this." He actually couldn't care less about Heather. Carl had his own reasons for ensuring she didn't get sent to a different location or to another team.

The four of them walked into the hall together. Penny and Brody seemed to huddle behind Dr. Johnson and Grace.

Grace frowned at them. "She isn't that bad. Really." Nobody believed her.

Dr. Johnson took a deep breath and unlocked the door. "Everyone get in behind me fast; I want to get the door closed and locked quickly."

They all nodded, and Carl opened the door. The others pushed him into the room, almost knocking him over. They stumbled over themselves as he turned and struggled with the door. Once locked, Carl saw that his companions were gaping at Heather like she was an atomic bomb about to detonate, even Dr. Grace, who'd assured them all she was safe.

Carl looked past them at Heather, and to his surprise, she was giggling. Focusing on him, she said, "Hi."

He hadn't been expecting her to speak. "Uh, hi. Um, my name is Dr. Carl Johnson." He waved, gesturing at his colleagues. "Say hello, everyone."

"Hi," Penny said in a squeaky voice.

"Yo." Brody lifted his hand in acknowledgment.

Dr. Grace said, "We've met."

Heather scrutinized them for a long moment and giggled again. She looked at Carl and placed her hand over her heart, just like Maeve did when she first named her. "Heather. Heather... Stone."

"Heather is such a pretty name," Penny told her.

Carl cleared his throat. "Hello, Heather, this is my team. I'd appreciate it if you refrained from hurting them because we're the only four people who can keep you from being sent somewhere much less pleasant."

Helen added, "With no bananas."

"No bananas," Heather repeated quietly.

Carl shook off the weird exchange and pointed to Penny. "This is Penny Singleton. She's going to perform a few medical tests to make sure you're healthy and not carrying any toxic alien disease that'll kill us all."

Penny waved happily, but Heather didn't say or do anything.

He continued, "Once we get all of that done, Brody and I will try to find out what kinda shit you can do because it's clear you aren't human."

Heather said, "Shit I can do."

Dr. Grace looked at Carl and said, "Nice." She turned back to Heather. "And I'm here to teach you to talk and tell you about our world, okay?"

"Our world," Heather echoed.

For some reason, hearing Heather say "our world" like that was unsettling to the team. Was it really her world now, too?

CHAPTER 17
FRUITLESS SCIENCE

Troy stood in his new lab, wearing his new clothes, dreading his new life.

In her desperation to please her Coronian benefactors, Veronica had built a state-of-the-art lab on the Coronian home plant of Darsayn for Troy to work on the EIP. It didn't matter how many times he told her there was no way he could replicate the results he got with Dia; she wouldn't listen. His disagreement was considered insurrection, and he would be punished. Sometimes, he'd be submerged into a tank of rancid water. It would fill his lungs, stomach, and digestive system for a few days, then he'd be taken out to lay in his cell while his body slowly and painfully expelled the water and toxins. During the entire process, Troy was awake and aware of the pain. It was the perfect torture for someone who couldn't die.

On that particularly trying day, Troy struggled with a piece of equipment he'd never seen before. Veronica would watch him work from an open gallery above the lab. He never had an issue being watched like that in the past. He actually used to teach certain surgery courses, and entire classes of students would watch him perform a complete procedure while he explained everything he was doing. Having Veronica watch him struggle with something that would never work was absolutely nerve-racking. Finally, he peered up at her and asked, just loud enough for her to hear, "Can you please come down here?"

Veronica feigned that she hadn't heard him and cupped her hand to her ear and said, "Say what, my dear Doctor?"

Pissed off, Troy yelled, "Can you please come down here, oh Queen of the Coronians!"

Troy was still trying to control his mouth. He'd never been one to take too much shit from anyone, but there were consequences for his outbursts here.

Two guards came from the door, and Troy just stood there, waiting to be grabbed and dragged away, when Veronica yelled down in Coronian, "Stop! I'll deal with him!"

They relented, gave a slight bow to her, and backed away. Troy watched as she descended a flight of stairs. She was wearing a white jumpsuit with a gold-colored belt. Over the jumpsuit was a sheer white cape that went down to her calves. She also wore brown knee-high boots made of soft leather. Her long blonde hair was pulled into an ornate ponytail, and her face was made up perfectly. She truly looked like a queen. A beautiful, manipulative, traitorous bitch of a queen.

She stopped on the other side of the table from him, flashed her winning smile, and asked, "What is it, Doctor?"

Troy stared at her for a moment, debating whether he wanted to spew the horrible tirade in his brain or just be cordial and ask for what he needed. He erred on the side of caution and said, "I need a lab assistant. Someone who's familiar with all of this equipment. I've never seen a lot of these machines, and I need to know what I'm dealing with."

"Well, we gave you the manuals for everything, didn't we? Figure it out, genius."

Troy shook his head. "With equipment this sensitive, you need more than just a manual. In order for me to make sure I know what I'm working with and to reduce the risk of accidentally blowing us all to hell, I need someone here to help me. Preferably another of the scientists you're holding as a prisoner here. The Cralion."

Shocked, Veronica studied his face and asked, "How did you know about him?"

Troy gave her a sarcastic grin and said, "You know that rancid cesspool you like to marinate me in? It's close to whatever it is you're having him work on. I can hear everything he says and just how frustrated he is with *his* work. Maybe he and I could help each other and get you and your new friends closer to taking over the galaxy."

She knew he had to have ulterior motives, but the two of them could indeed help each other. Nodding to the guards, she said, "Take him back to his cell."

Troy hoped she was debating the possibility. As he was unnecessarily shoved down the hall to his cell, the wheels in his brilliant mind began to turn with the possibility of working with another prisoner who could help them both escape.

About half an hour later, Troy realized he was mistaken.

***

When Troy and Dia were young, they didn't interact much. She'd gone off to the Academy and Troy worked with his father, traveling the galaxy, and becoming a doctor. One day, when he was actually at home, he received an invitation to a wedding. Dia's wedding.

She'd met a prince from Kalow 9 and had fallen head over heels in love, which Troy never thought possible. Still, since Kalow 9 was a beautiful planet filled with pristine beaches, majestic mountains, and gorgeous women, he was game for a vacation.

One of the traditions for a royal bride-to-be was having to perform the planet's anthem before the wedding ceremony. The ceremony was on a beach at sundown. There was a small stage set up, ringed with torches. Drummers and flute players were scattered all around. Children dressed in grass skirts and silk tank tops wore crowns of reeds woven with gold ribbon and kata orchids.

A woman in a long white gown adorned with white crystals came onto the stage. Her light-brown hair was pulled up in an elaborate updo woven with more crystals and gold ribbon. She wore a sheer veil inlaid with gold thread and kata orchids. Her large, brown eyes sparkled with the dancing firelight. Surprisingly, she had the symbol of the Florian Army painted on her cheek in gold.

The crowd was in awe of her. Most of the Kalowians had never seen a Florian before. Her family and friends didn't know what to think either, as Dia usually wore a dirty uniform or sweaty exercise clothes. Now, she was Princess Dia Kekoa of Kalow.

Her appearance made her stunning; her voice made her absolutely dazzling.

She began to chant low in the Kalowian language, and the drums and flutes joined her. The children danced around in a magical performance. Her singing was mesmerizing, and Troy was completely entranced while watching her. She moved deliberately with the young performers around her. On top of the music, he could hear the tinkling of the crystals as she danced, which only made the performance more beautiful. He felt a pang of jealously toward Prince Ben Kekoa.

That was the memory Troy held on to as his body struggled not to breathe in the hot sand he had just been buried in. In his desperation to make his situation better, he'd once again miscalculated his enemy; both of his enemies. Troy was certain Veronica was willing to have the Cralion work with him, but maybe the Coronians didn't want that. Perhaps she didn't have as much power as he initially thought.

He was smart, but this was new to him. He wasn't used to fighting for his existence; that was Dia's department.

What would she do? She would think before she opened her fucking mouth, Troy, that's what Dia would do, he thought.

CHAPTER 18
THIS IS THE START OF SOMETHING STRANGE

Heather slowly opened her eyes and realized she was in a different room.

She was lying on a soft bed with silky sheets. She ran her hand over them, taking in the cool, smooth fabric. She was also wearing a white satin nightgown that felt lovely against her skin.

The light in the room was dim and blue, like just before dawn. She glanced over her shoulder at the large window covered in sheer drapes and could make out what looked like mountains in the distance. The room was decorated simply but nicely. Wherever they had her now, she was going to be much more comfortable.

Heather rolled toward the center of the bed and realized a man was lying next to her. At first, she wanted to panic, but something inside her felt she would be okay.

He was on his side, facing away from her. She could tell he was still asleep by his even, constant breathing. He had thick, dark-brown hair and as far as she could tell, he was tall and slim. Her curiosity got the best of her, and she reached out and gently traced a finger down his spine. He shivered and gave a quiet sigh. Heather was a little concerned about her bold move and sat motionless, wondering what he would do.

For a moment, he was still again. Then, he stretched. He said something quietly that she didn't understand and started to turn over toward her. Heather was genuinely curious to see who the dark-haired man in her bed was, but as he turned, his hair changed to a bright yellow. His face turned splotchy and pock-marked. It was the Red Cross volunteer.

Heather panicked and tried to scream. He lunged forward and grabbed her by the shoulders, pinning her to the bed. "The only place you're going after I get a piece of you is back into that fucking hole!" he growled in her face.

***

Heather sat straight up, screaming. She was gasping for air and realized she was in the concrete room with the large mirror. *It was a nightmare. Just a nightmare*, she thought.

However, how much better was her reality? She wanted to escape so badly, but where could she go?

She pulled her knees to her chest and buried her face against them. She was starting to get the trapped-animal feeling again, only this time, there was a very slim chance of escape.

***

Dr. Johnson had come in early that morning to try and get their work started as soon as possible. When he arrived, he was the only one in the observation room, watching Heather sleep.

He was trying to decide if she was the answer he'd been searching for all these years and felt she might be. She was unpredictable, dangerous, and needed to learn a lot, but after having seen her power up close, he was confident she could do what he needed, maybe even more. Carl was anxious to get going.

Suddenly, she sat straight up and screamed. He guessed she must've had a nightmare, which surprised him. He debated the risk of going into her room and seeing if she was okay. After all, she couldn't absorb any energy, and maybe he should try to connect with her. Or not.

She crouched with her head between her knees. Even though she wasn't human, he could tell she was scared. He sighed and muttered, "Fuck it."

***

Heather heard the lock on her door being turned, and the door began to open slowly. She tried to cram herself as far into the corner as possible, in case it was the yellow-haired man from her dream. Instead, it was the leader of the team. Carl, wasn't it?

He was tall and relatively young. He had scruffy black hair, a matching beard, and bright green eyes. His clothes were clean but disheveled, like he'd slept in them. His appearance confused her, as he didn't seem like much of a leader, but she also didn't really know him yet.

He stiffly sat down on one of the concrete stools. Hesitantly, he asked, "Are you okay? I heard you scream." Before he'd even finished talking, he realized she probably didn't understand a word he said.

He was surprised when she nodded and seemed to relax a little bit. But now, he had no idea what to do; he couldn't really hold a conversation with her, and her unpredictability made him nervous, but he tried anyway. "How much do you understand when we talk to you?"

She looked at him for a moment, then down at her hands. He was afraid she didn't comprehend at first, but she said quietly, "Want to understand."

Carl contemplated how fantastic or dangerous her quick level of awareness could be. "You want to understand us?" he asked.

She nodded.

At that moment, Carl got an idea. It was a bold, risky move, but he thought it could be a huge step in getting her to learn about them and their language.

He put up his finger and stood. "Just a minute." Carl left the room.

Heather shrugged her shoulders and leaned her face against her knees again, but he was back after only a few moments.

In his hands, he held a small tablet. As if on cue, just as Heather sensed the power in the device, he said, "Don't you fucking dare take the energy from this thing. I don't want to have to beat you with it."

Heather glared at him. Figuring he was trying to help her, at least for the time being, she didn't mess with the tablet.

He sat down next to her on the concrete bed and showed her the tablet. It had pictures moving across the screen like the television in the mess tent. But this time, the pictures weren't showing the devastation from the "meteor." The images were of young people—children, she guessed— and a large purple thing dancing around, singing songs. Heather couldn't take her eyes off it. She sat back against the wall and put the tablet against her knees, quickly becoming entranced by the images on the screen.

Carl watched her until he was pretty certain she wouldn't pull some shit like she had yesterday with the coffee. "There you go, love. Enjoy some *Barney*."

She smiled at him as Carl was getting up to leave.

"Carl!" she called to him before he could reach the door.

He was surprised she remembered his name. Looking back, he said, "Yes?"

"Breakfast? A banana?" she asked.

He nodded with a smile. "I'll see about that right now."

Don't start liking her, man, she may not work out, and you know what happens then, he thought as he locked the door behind him.

CHAPTER 19
DREAMS AREN'T REAL, BUT NIGHTMARES CAN BE

Troy slowly opened his eyes. It took him a moment, but he realized he was sleeping in his own bed, in his own bedroom. He was lying on his side, looking toward the window. He could see through the sheer drapes that the mountains in the distance had their first snow on the peaks. The light outside was dim and blue, like just before dawn. Everything must've been just a horrible dream.

Troy rolled over and saw Dia lying next to him. She was facing away, toward the center of their bedroom. Her long hair was in a mass of tangled curls, and she was quietly snoring. He smiled at the mundane familiarity.

He reached out and ran his long fingers down her spine, over the smooth fabric of her white nightgown. She sighed and shivered, making him smile again. Troy moved closer, slipping his arm around her waist, and nuzzled his face against the back of her neck. Dia sighed again and pressed her body back against his.

Troy was beginning to get excited as she started to roll over. Her light-brown hair brushed against his face, but as she moved, he watched her hair change to blonde. Instead of her lovely brown eyes looking over at him, they were blue. Veronica.

Troy pulled away in horror, but she grabbed the arm he had put around her and said seductively, "You know, Troy, you need to lighten up. You were always so serious."

***

Troy's eyes shot open. He was met with the cold blackness of his cell on Darsayn. He sucked in a few deep breaths and tried to calm himself down. Shaking his head, he couldn't believe he was actually relieved to be in this prison rather than his own bed, with that snake of a woman beside him.

But the brief thought of Dia lying next to him made his heart long for her. His guilt for the entire predicament they were in was starting to wear on him heavily. If it weren't for the EIP bonding with Dia, they'd both be home, safe and sound—or as safe as she could ever be as the leader of the Florian Army. Had she made it somewhere safe? Had she been able to start a new life, or would she float in the vacuum of space for eternity?

In the darkness, Troy's eyes began to fill with tears. It wasn't just the EIP that brought them to their current plight. Several mistakes along the way had snowballed into their need to flee. Some of which Dia knew nothing about.

Troy heard the door of his cell begin to open. His throat tightened as he waited to see who it was. Was it Veronica there to take him to the lab to perform useless work? Was it the guard who loved to torture Troy when he wasn't supposed to? Or would it be the small, deformed Coronian woman who brought him his food and emptied his chamber bucket? Luckily, it was her.

Her name was Corky, and she was rather pleasant. She even knew a few Rygonian words and would communicate with Troy as best she could. If he were ever able to escape this hellhole, maybe he would take her with him.

From the dim light that came in through the open door, he saw her give him a crooked smile. In broken Rygonian, she said, "Good morn, Doc. Breakfast."

She put down a small tray with stale brown bread and a bowl of some kind of grain-based paste, resembling porridge. However, it didn't taste anything like porridge. There was also murky water to drink. It was all gross, but he was punished when he *didn't* eat because they knew he could survive without it. Coronians were fucking experts at the art of torture.

"Thank you," Troy said in Coronian.

She smiled and nodded, then went to the corner and picked up the bucket. Troy always felt so uncomfortable about that thing, but it was the only place he could go.

She left and closed the door. Troy heard the guard lock it and a small light came on in the corner. He knew it wasn't only a light but a camera to spy on him. Usually, all he ever did was sit motionless on his bed, sleep, or eat the garbage they called food.

Troy put the tray on his lap and choked down his meal. The paste was particularly dry that morning and he nearly vomited it back up, but he didn't want to give the assholes watching him the satisfaction.

Once finished, he placed the tray on the small table and lay back down, putting his back to the camera. Even though it had turned into a nightmare, Troy tried to imagine Dia lying next to him in their bed. He could even smell the kata orchid shampoo she loved that she could only get from Kalow 9. He could feel the warmth of her body, higher ever since the EIP, and the smooth fabric of her nightgown. Dia was a natural fighter, a true female warrior who was never afraid to get injured or dirty for her people, but she also loved the finer things. Pretty dresses, beautiful jewelry, but mostly she loved fine, soft nightgowns. At first, Troy thought it was out of her character, but just because she was a fighter didn't mean she wanted to be less of a woman. It was one of the many things he loved about his wife.

The door opened again; this time, it was the guard. He grunted with a smile. "Shower."

Troy had always been a clean person. His job caused him to get dirty quite often, but he always cleaned up as fast as possible. But getting— yes, *getting*—a shower there was a whole different story.

Troy reluctantly stood up and let the guard grab him by the arm and pull him into the hall. Luckily, the guard understood little Rygonian, so Troy enjoyed uttering horrible insults at him. Today, he said, "If I ever get away from all of you assholes, I'll take great pleasure in shoving a grenade up your ass and enjoying the show when it goes off."

The guard just grunted.

When they made it to the shower room, the typical scene played out. Troy was never given a shower with the other prisoners. So, he had the room all to himself, except for two female Coronians who always took pride in scrubbing him down themselves.

The guard grunted again and left Troy there. He kept his chin up as he walked toward his shower molesters, ready to get the embarrassing situation over with. Once he reached them, both staring at him with contempt and anticipation, he quickly removed his clothes and said, "Okay, do your worst."

Out in the hall, he heard a familiar voice and cringed. Veronica came into the shower room and barked, "Leave us," at the two women.

The Coronian women bowed and threw Troy a disappointed look as they left. Once they were gone, Veronica turned to Troy. "Good morning, Doctor." She glanced down at his nakedness and added, "It's cold in here, huh?"

"Fuck you," Troy quietly replied.

She slowly took a few steps closer to him and said disappointedly, "You've been here for some time now. Why haven't you begun to let go of your animosity toward me?"

Troy huffed and snapped, "I could be here for thousands of years, and that still wouldn't happen."

She took another couple of steps toward him. "I've already told you what you can do to make your life here much better."

"I'm okay with being miserable, thanks," he said as he stepped away.

"Don't worry, Dr. Harlow," she said with a sly smile. "It won't be long before you come to me. I guarantee it." She cleared her throat. "I wonder what happened to your wife. Such a waste."

Troy merely shrugged and said, "Her demise was not a waste." He nearly choked on those words.

Veronica laughed. "You don't fucking believe that, and you know it." Then she turned around and yelled for the two Coronian women to come back for his shower. As the bitingly cold water was turned on, he heard Veronica say, "If you just say yes, this will stop."

Troy saw one of the women holding a rough scrub brush and said in Coronian, "My back is particularly dirty."

He watched Veronica as she walked away, shaking her head.

CHAPTER 20
A MOTHER'S LOVE: PART 2

P amela Strom stared out of the large window in their living room overlooking the plains. In the distance, the Raltain Mountains were capped with the first snow of the season. She sighed, thinking about Dia and how much she loved going to the mountains during this time.

The news of the attack, Troy's capture, and Dia's disappearance had spread quickly around the globe. The citizens of Rygone were on edge, waiting to be attacked by their biggest enemy again. Especially because one of their beloved leaders had been taken and the other had completely disappeared. Fear and unrest were beginning to grip the population.

Pamela heard a door close behind her. She turned around and saw Dominic walking into the room. He came up and hugged her. "Dad is sending me to find Troy."

She shook her head and pulled away. "What about Dia?" she asked.

"He still has several DREX units searching for her, but it's almost impossible to know where she went." He swallowed and bowed his head. "I don't think there's much hope, Mom. For either of them."

Just like her husband, Pamela said, "We will *not* give up on them." She walked up to the window that looked into the center of the city and added, "Even if we wanted to, I don't think *they* would allow it."

Dominic went and stood behind his mother, peering down into the inner mezzanine. There were hundreds of citizens of all different races camped out in front of the murals in the courtyard. They had mourning lights and were singing songs about their missing leaders.

"We're fully capable of taking care of our people, but we made Dia and Troy into such a big presence, they don't realize it," Pamela said.

"They think we're lost without them. We need to prove to them that we aren't."

Pamela nodded and asked, "Has there been any contact from the Coronians?"

"No, nothing," Dominic told her. "They aren't trying to ransom Troy, and all of our patrols and outposts are on the hunt for any indication they'll attack Rygone or our allies. Silence. They're much more intelligent than we give them credit for. Even Dia spoke about how much they humbled her after Breger Dunes." *Of all of us, she was the one who lost the most back then,* he thought.

Pamela nodded. She remembered the late-night conversations she'd have with her daughter after that war. At times, Pam wondered how Dia wasn't in one of the many Florian mental facilities on Rygone due to that time in her life. Despite all of Dia's struggles throughout her long life, She was stronger than anyone.

"It has to have something to do with Troy's secret project. They didn't get Dia, but they have him. Maybe they think he can recreate it," Dominic said with concern.

Pamela said, "For all of our sakes, I hope he can't."

"Except Troy. Who knows what they're doing to him."

Pamela was surprised to hear Dominic say that. Troy was never his favorite person, though this was an extraordinary situation.

Dominic turned toward his room. "Well, I'm going to pack a few things so I can fly through space with my ex-wife and look for my wayward brother-in-law."

"You're going with Renee?" Pamela asked. "Shouldn't she be here, taking over some of Dia's duties?"

"Well, according to Renee, finding Troy *would* be one of Dia's responsibilities. She's Dia's best friend and is losing her mind over trying to sit back and complete her day-to-day duties. She's a pilot; she needs a hands-on job to keep her sane."

Pamela smiled and asked, "And she asked for you to go with her?"

Dominic laughed loudly. "Hell no, I told her the only way she was going would be by being my pilot. She almost decided to stay home."

As Dominic walked off to his room, Pamela reflected on her extraordinary children.

Dominic had been married to three different Florian women, all ending in relatively fast divorces. Dominic was Pamela's wild child and had no kids from any of them. His third wife was Renee Conner, one of Dia's star recruits and best friends.

Dia had been married twice. Her first marriage was a hastily put together union with Kalowian Prince Ben Kekoa. Dia had only been eighty-two years old at the time. They met in a bar on the planet Emerotl while she was a pilot for her father as he traveled the galaxy working as an ambassador to Rygone. Dia and Ben ruled Kalow happily; they had three beautiful, incredibly brilliant children. Tomas became one of the most beloved kings in Kalowian history. Princess Victoria was a staunch ambassador and activist, forming programs and building infrastructure that still stood to that day. Young Prince Edward was Dia's precious baby. He grew up wanting to be just like his mother and became an accomplished fighter pilot for the Kalowian air corp. Sadly, he was killed in action at the tender age of twenty-four. Edward's death was Dia's first taste of loss, and it devasted her. Losing her family one by one while never aging a day nearly drove Dia mad. She stayed on Kalow for almost fifteen thousand years, watching and assisting her husband, children, and descendants bring Kalow back to its former glory. Once she returned to Rygone, she made a vow to never fall in love with a mortal again. And she never did.

After nearly four hundred thousand years, Dia and Troy finally admitted their love for each other and married. Pam had waited for the day they'd finally have a child, but the pair always had an excuse as to why they wanted to wait longer.

So far, her only hope for a typical Florian family was *her* baby, Oscar. He married his first love, Samantha, another Florian, very early. They had three kids so far and would probably be Pamela's only Florian grandchildren.

Pamela sighed and cast her attention back into the mezzanine, contemplating going down into the courtyard to grieve with her citizens. Her husband and children were all working to protect and take care of them. The least she could do was let the people know they were being thought about.

When Dominic came out of his room with his away bag, she asked him, "Can you please call two of your best security guards to accompany me down to the courtyard?"

Dominic frowned. "I don't recommend that, Mom. The people are on the edge and unpredictable. The Lady of Rygone could be a target for their fear."

Pamela countered, "Which is why I want you to call me your best two guards. I can't sit back and watch us ignore our people as we struggle to figure out what step to take next. I need to let them know we're still thinking about them. Try to quell some of their fears."

"Or fan them," Dominic said.

"Dom."

"Fine, Mom. I'll call in two of my best. But promise me something."

"What's that?"

"The moment something doesn't seem right, *leave*."

Pamela nodded and said, "I promise. I'll also have Eno watch the edge of the crowd for anything suspicious and have him keep in touch with the guards. How about that?"

"That's good." He walked over and kissed his mom on the forehead. "I'm needed on the flight deck. I'll be gone before you get back, and I have no idea how long we'll be out there."

"I know. Just make sure you keep in touch with your father, so we know what's happening."

Dominic called and had two of his guards dispatched to go with Lady Pamela. Meanwhile, Pam called Eno and asked him to go down first and scope out the crowd to make sure it was safe. He could move through the people unseen and was a valuable asset in that type of situation.

Once Eno confirmed the crowd was calm, Pamela got on the Flash Lift and went down to the courtyard. She took a deep breath as the door opened, and she stepped out. Her guards stayed close, and she made eye contact with Eno on the other side of the crowd.

The throng recognized her immediately. She smiled and shook their hands and gave hugs. They praised her and her husband; they expressed their sadness and worry for Dia and hoped the Strom family was doing well. She took pictures with children and hugged soldiers, who were with their families before being deployed the next day to protect their home. Pamela expressed how proud she was of them for defending the freedom of their world.

Pamela took a quick moment to glance up at the murals of Dia and Troy. It was the first time she had seen them up close, and they were breathtaking. The details were perfect, and Pamela felt her throat tighten as tears fought their way into her eyes. It was almost as if her daughter had been taken from real life and placed on that wall. Why did the murals have to be commissioned so quickly?

The crowd brought her back to reality when the calm demeanor began to change. The questions and comments went from kind and supportive to doubts about the safety of Rygone. Who was working to protect them from another Coronian attack? How were the relief efforts from the initial attack going? Who was trying to find General and Doctor Harlow?

Pamela tried to answer as calmly as possible, but the unrest Dominic was afraid of started to show. One of her guards grabbed her arm, and the other said, "Okay, folks, that's enough for the day. Lady Strom must return to the Command Center to help find the answers to your questions."

Pamela appreciated his efforts to quell the growing problem, but it didn't work. As the frustration turned to yelling, the guards pulled Pamela toward Eno, who'd been able to clear a route to the Flash Lift. By the time they were safely inside, a crowd had gathered to get back on once it returned.

One of the guards called to have the Lifts shut down. All floors of the city were restricted to personal verification access. Only the residents and employees would be allowed on each floor. It would be verified by retina scan, fingerprint examination, and physical identity by a guard at the door of the stairs. It was an aggressive response, but they needed to get the order restored before addressing the problem.

Baltica City was more of a massive residential apartment and government building than a city itself. All but six floors were built into the flatlands of the Odogen Plain. The Florians had built their city and its outer defenses well enough that they didn't take internal assaults too seriously. Over the city's million-plus years of existence, there'd only been a handful of domestic conflicts, and they were all unrest caused by their own kind. And this was turning into one of those disputes.

Pamela's guilt was overwhelming. As they reached the thirty-eighth floor, she said, "I do want to go to the Command Center. I must see the chancellor."

The guards shared a concerned glance but realized she was safer there than anywhere else in the city. So, they sent the Lift up one more floor. As they stepped off, Eno stayed behind.

Pamela turned back to him and said, "I want you to come with me and tell the chancellor what you saw and heard from the citizens when they didn't know you were there."

Eno nodded once. "Very good, my lady. There is much to tell."

The group walked silently to the Command Center. Pamela let her tears go, wondering what new problem she'd just caused in her beloved home.

CHAPTER 21
DOES ANYBODY HAVE A FLORIAN ANATOMY BOOK I CAN BORROW?

A few days had passed since Dr. Johnson had introduced Heather to television. As he'd expected, that medium served as the best source of information she could quickly absorb. Of course, Dr. Grace didn't agree; she thought Heather should learn the traditional way with the internet and Rosetta Stone, but Carl reminded her they were very short on time and felt the web might be too dangerous.

Heather already understood basic commands and questions. *Barney* was doing a great job teaching her about cooperation and what the different fruits looked like. Oh, and how to clean her room, even though she had absolutely nothing in her room.

She'd taken a shine to movies. Each member of the team chose a certain film they thought Heather would benefit from. Carl chose *Die Hard*. Heather loved it and kept saying, "Come out to the coast, we'll get together, have a few laughs."

Grace chose *Good Will Hunting*, hoping the higher intellectual quality of the film would stimulate Heather's desire to learn. Heather watched it but gave Dr. Grace a blank expression and just shook her head.

Penny chose *Miss Congeniality* because Sandra Bullock's character seemed a lot like Heather to her. The Florian enjoyed it but didn't seem to get anything out of it.

Brody was hell-bent on having her watch all eight seasons of *Game of Thrones* but *everyone*, even Carl, said no. However, they all did agree on *Fellowship of the Ring*. Heather absolutely loved it. She seemed to learn a lot from this film as she babbled on and on rather incoherently about elves, Lord Sauron, and how wonderful Samwise Gamgee was. It was decided they'd all sit together for the next two nights and watch the other *Lord of the Rings* films.

***

Penny was going through the challenging task of attempting to perform medical tests on Heather. It wasn't that Heather was too difficult—at least, not all the time—but most of the medical equipment simply didn't work on her.

Singleton had been authorized to bring a cart with different equipment and supplies, as long as they were all mechanical and needed no power. She had Heather sit on one of the concrete stools and face away from the table. Penny sat in front of Heather on a small rolling stool.

Penny took out a glass thermometer, which she didn't want to use, but it was the only one she had that didn't require any energy. She said to Heather, "Open your mouth and lift your tongue."

Heather opened her mouth but didn't understand how to lift her tongue. Upon realizing that, Penny opened her mouth, lifted her tongue, and slurred, "Li' 'his."

Carl, waiting by the door to intervene if Heather made any threatening moves, chuckled. She gave him a dirty look, and on cue, Heather turned and gave him the same expression. She turned back to Penny, opened her mouth, and lifted her tongue.

Penny giggled and whispered, "Good job."

She placed the thermometer under Heather's tongue. "Now close, gently." She was afraid Heather would bite down too hard and break the glass, spilling the mercury, but she closed gently like she was told.

They all sat quietly for a few moments before the PA said, "Open."

Heather obeyed, and Penny took the thermometer and shook it. She glared at the reading. "This is why I wanted my temporal thermometer. This thing is way off."

"What is it?" Carl asked.

"It's reading that she's a hundred and eight degrees! I can tell she runs a little bit warmer than we do, but a hundred and eight is a death sentence."

Carl shrugged. "Maybe not for this girl."

Penny sighed. "I should check it with my temporal, just in case," she said. "We can't just assume. Her life might be at stake, Carl."

Johnson had always figured Penny to be somewhat childish for her age and station, but he could see she took her work seriously. "Okay, I got it." He knocked on the mirror and said, "Brody, get the doc's temporal thermometer off the table, will ya?"

Singleton smiled in spite of herself. "I'm not a doctor, just a PA," she reminded him.

Carl leaned against the wall and said, "Yeah? Well, here, you're a doctor."

She blushed for a moment but remembered the team wasn't allowed to get too personal with each other.

Brody knocked on the door and Carl opened it, grabbing the thermometer from his hand. He passed it to Penny, and she turned it on. Both Carl and Penny watched Heather intently to see if she'd respond to the energy, but she remained sitting still. Penny told her, "I'm going to pull this along your forehead. It won't hurt."

Heather just stared at her with wonderment as Penny took her temperature. She growled at the display, then tried again, pulling it across Heather's forehead—then stared at the device in disbelief.

"What is it?" Heather asked.

Heather's voice startled Penny. They knew Heather was learning quickly, but she was usually quiet unless actively spoke to. "It's still one-oh-eight," she explained. "Do you know if that's normal for you?"

"Normal for me?" Heather repeated.

Penny shook her head and said, "Sorry, I guess I assumed you'd know."

Heather shook her head slightly. Penny could see she wanted to help her with this problem but didn't know how.

Johnson asked quietly, "So now what? We have an alien woman who runs hot. She hasn't acted sick, and nobody who's come in contact with her has either."

"I know, but—"

Carl moved a little closer to Penny and said, "We've got to think a little outside the box on this one, Doc. We'll monitor her a few times a day and see if something changes."

Singleton nodded. Carl was a hard nut to crack. Sometimes his demeanor wasn't that of a world-class physicist, but that of a high school gym teacher. When it counted, though, Carl was a great leader.

She returned the thermometer to him. "Have Brody come take this back, just in case."

Carl smiled at her and said, "Good idea."

Penny turned back to Heather. "Okay, now for your blood pressure."

She took her manual cuff and placed it on Heather's arm. She didn't resist or anything, just watched Penny work. Placing her stethoscope in her ears, Penny pressed the chest piece below the cuff. Heather was fascinated by the bulb as Penny pumped air into the cuff. She couldn't help but laugh as it became tighter and tighter.

"Shh," Penny said.

Heather sat quietly for the rest of the test. When Penny released the air in the cuff, she wore the same confused look as she'd had with the temperature.

"Now what?" Carl asked.

Penny furrowed her eyebrows and answered, "Her blood pressure is two ten over one-eighty. That's an even bigger death sentence."

Carl said, "Again, we'll just have to keep an eye on it." He turned to Heather. "Right, love?"

Heather shrugged. "We can monitor it."

Penny shook her head. "Okay, hopefully not your funeral."

"What's a funeral?" Heather asked curiously.

Carl laughed. "I'll let you take this one, Doc."

Penny only said, "Never mind, Heather. Let's try for a blood sample."

That was the part Penny was most nervous about. From what they'd seen of Heather's actions, she seemed pretty damn indestructible. Therefore, she doubted they'd even be able to puncture her skin for blood or other samples. And even if they could, how would Heather react?

She took the needed items out of her kit and laid them on the table. Heather was watching Penny intently as she picked up the rubber band. "Please hold your arm out. Like this." She demonstrated, and Heather followed her lead.

Penny tentatively put the rubber band around Heather's arm above her elbow and pulled it tight. Heather winced, more in anticipation than pain. Penny glanced from Heather's face to her arm. She pressed on the elbow and was surprised to see a few strong veins. She picked up the alcohol pad and cleaned the area she was going to poke, all the while keeping a close eye on Heather's facial expressions. Mostly, it was curiosity, but Penny could feel that she was also confused, which might not be good. Singleton picked up the needle and took a deep breath.

"Okay," Penny said, "here we go. If this works, you'll feel a bit of a poke. It'll be like a bee sting."

"She doesn't know what the hell a bee is," Johnson reminded her.

Penny shot a mean glance at him. "Shut up, Carl."

"Shut up, Carl," Heather whispered.

Turning her attention back to Heather, Penny pressed the needle into her arm. Heather tensed for a brief moment, but relaxed. Penny tried as hard as she could to get the needle to penetrate Heather's skin, but it wouldn't go through. Finally, after almost a minute of struggling, she lifted the needle and sat back. She looked at Heather, who, thankfully, didn't seem phased one bit. "I'm pretty sure no matter what I do, I'll never get a blood sample from you."

Heather said, "I'm sorry."

Penny laughed and reassured her, "There's no need for you to be sorry. You just aren't like us, so I need to think of something else!"

"Okay," Heather said.

Carl asked, "Now what?" He was beginning to sound like a parrot.

Penny rolled backward on her stool to the wall and stared at her patient. She thought back to the notes from the night the tiny woman in front of her was brought in. They explained how Heather must've been shot over one hundred times, yet she only had a few minor abrasions. What's more, those abrasions miraculously healed within an hour of her being cleaned up. Her body defied the laws of physics and nature, yet there she was.

Heather was truly beautiful. Not just beautiful, but perfect. Her fit body was unchanging, perfectly proportioned for her size. Her large, upturned eyes were strangely entrancing. At times, Penny thought her pupils would actually elongate like that of a cat! Her smile, her high cheekbones, her incredible hair that didn't even seem to need washing. Penny was deeply curious about their new friend, but as Heather looked back at her inquisitively, she thought, *Where are you from, beautiful?*

Singleton rolled back to Heather. "Hold on, let's see if this works," she said, reaching out. She grabbed an errant hair on top of Heather's head and pulled it. Much to Penny's delight and Heather's confusion, the hair came out. She continued, "I'll take this and a swab from her cheek and go from there. Other than that, I don't think there's anything else we can do."

Carl nodded. "Gotcha; let's get that all done so we can get lunch."

Penny narrowed her eyes at him suspiciously. "You're in quite a rush, Carl. Do you have a date?"

"Nope, just hungry."

Heather asked, "What's a date?"

Johnson and Penny shared an amused glance. She said, "Uh, that's for a later time."

As Penny was getting ready to leave, she arranged for Heather's lunch. Heather was also given her tablet to watch television for the rest of the afternoon.

Unbeknownst to the team, Heather had figured out her new world by way of that tablet. They were so worried she'd absorb the energy, but she used it to absorb knowledge instead. When they thought she was watching *Barney* or *Hannah Montana*, she researched the world on the internet. Helen would be proud.

Heather knew the entire English language. She knew exactly what they were saying all the time. She knew all about humans and Earth. As for what Carl said, well, she knew what the hell a bee was.

She was going to figure out a way to escape soon. Then she was going to find who was behind that voice. *Release all of the power inside you.*

Not before watching the last two *Lord of the Rings* movies, though. They were too good to pass up.

CHAPTER 22
OKAY, LOVE, SHOW US WHAT YOU CAN DO

On the morning of the first day of testing, the team was on edge. It was going to be the first time, other than to shower, that Heather was being let out of her cell since her escape. The guards and facility's managers had mapped out the fastest route with the least amount of energy sources to get them to the warehouse.

The four members of Heather's team were outside of her door early. They were all given uniforms that were unique from the rest of the facility. Carl wasn't too thrilled about it, but Major Mallory wanted to make sure their team stood out. You know, like targets.

Mallory met them in the hall and said, "Well, are you ready? You don't have too much more time before we send her away." He got close to Carl's face. "I already know you don't want that, Dr. Johnson, do you? Gotta save face with the Feds, I guess."

None of the rest of his team knew why they were chosen for their current assignment, but Mallory just gave them a big reason to start asking questions. Carl narrowed his eyes at the major and said, "Feds, brass, who gives a fuck, right? Just as long at the woman, or whatever the hell she is, gets her learnin' done. Huh, Major?"

The tension had gone up exponentially between them all. Although they thought she was still asleep, Heather was standing behind the door, listening. She placed her hand on the door and could feel the negative energy they were all putting off. She was curious what Carl meant by the Feds and brass. Her research on the tablet usually revolved around what she heard in their conversations, from top-secret discussions about her to restaurants they were going to eat at for dinner, but she'd never heard those words. The Florian was trying to learn as much as possible. But for now, she needed to play dumb. Heather knew they'd be coming into the room to get her, so she lay down on the bed and waited until she heard the lock being turned.

Heather sat up and stretched. Penny came into her room and said, "Good morning, Heather. Today's a big day; therefore, I have a new set of clothes for you. A different gray outfit versus your gray PJ's." Penny tried to smile, but Heather could tell she was nervous.

She took the clothes, and Penny stepped back out. It didn't matter; Heather had been changing in front of the observation mirror the whole time. Dr. Grace had mentioned the mirror was changed to opaque for her privacy when Heather changed her clothes, washed up, or went to the bathroom. She didn't believe that.

She changed into the new clothes and realized she preferred these over her PJ's because she could hide the fact that she wasn't wearing a bra. They kept giving her one when they brought her clean PJ's, but she refused to put it on. Both Penny and Grace tried to convince her of the benefits, but Heather wasn't buying that either.

When she was ready, she pounded on the door, and Carl opened it for her. The lights in the hall were turned off, so she could barely make the team out. Carl waved her into the corridor, and Heather wasn't surprised to see a large group of guards lining the dark walkway. It looked like today everyone was going on a field trip. Heather smiled to herself. She'd found the schematics for the facility on her tablet and had memorized every inch of the compound. Soon enough, she'd use that information against them all.

Carl turned her toward the south exit and said quietly, "Let's get going. We've got a lot to do today, love."

Heather would need to look up why he always called her "love."

She could feel energy reaching out from everywhere. They thought they'd taken so many precautions, but she could pull in enough from one of the light sockets to get her off the grounds. The temptation was strong, but she needed to be patient.

The group of nervous people walked alongside Heather, regarding her as some sort of unpredictable god or something. She'd studied a lot of the humans' gods. Their beliefs were fascinating.

They walked into a large courtyard, and the feel of the cool breeze, smell of distant rain, and sight of the clouds made her head swoon. It'd only been a few days, but it felt as if she'd been trapped inside for years. Heather took in a deep breath and smiled.

"Smells good," she said.

Brody nodded. "Yep, the weatherman said thunderstorms are forecast all day. I love the rain."

Heather breathed, "Rain."

Carl suddenly became very uneasy. He put his hand on the small of Heather's back and gently began to push her. He murmured, "Okay, love, let's move faster."

Heather was a little confused at first, but she caught on quickly as she began to feel the buzz of electricity in the air from the approaching storm. She feigned innocence as she said, "Okay. Why?"

Carl studied her face. Heather knew he would catch onto her fast, which would be fine once she found out what his deal was. He smiled and said, "Don't want to get caught out in the rain, now do we?"

Heather just nodded. This could be interesting.

The storm didn't get close enough to Heather before they made it to the warehouse. Once inside, she felt shut off from the storm's electrical energy, her senses now muffled. She looked around the large building and saw why they were using it for her.

It was large enough to hold a Boeing 747 with some extra space to spare. The building was solid concrete except for a ring of large, high windows circling the whole warehouse, which was its only source of light during the day. On one end, there was just a small, standard door. On the other end was a large bay door that went three-quarters of the way up and all the way across the wall. That door was closed.

"No internal sources of energy. Everything we're going to use, we brought with us," Carl said.

Three of the guards brought in cases with some equipment and put them by the small door they'd just entered. As they were leaving, they glanced at Heather as if she was an alien freak. Wait, she *was* an alien freak to them.

Brody and Penny started to open the boxes and take out equipment. There were a few tables already set up for them to stage their work, and Heather watched them attentively.

Patterson came up to Heather with a small device in his hand. She could feel a small amount of energy coming off of it, but strangely, the device was reaching out to her. Brody walked around her, waving the machine up and down, reading her body. Heather stood still and waited for him to tell her what he was doing. When he was finished, he just glanced at her face and walked away. She frustratingly wanted to ask him what he did, but luckily Carl beat her to it.

"Brody, why're you just now checking her for radioactive energy? Shouldn't that have been done the first day?" Carl asked.

Brody shrugged as he put the Geiger counter away and said, "Probably. Luckily, she's not radioactive."

Even Heather was happy to hear that. In her exploration on the internet, she researched the different types of energy that humans had classified. What they called radioactive, or nuclear power, was one of the most dangerous.

Next, Brody came over to her with a harness to go on Heather's chest. There was another device on the front that would rest over her heart. Brody hadn't been too close to her until now, and he realized she made him more nervous than he expected. He asked Penny to come over. "Please demonstrate for her what I need her to do. I hate this communication barrier."

Heather smiled internally again. It was fun knowing so much more than they did.

"Lift your arms out to your side," Brody said.

Penny lifted her arms and Heather mirrored her. Patterson delicately placed one side of the harness over her right arm and slowly walked behind her to put it on the other side.

Irritated, Carl sighed. "Have you seen what she can do? You ain't gonna break her by putting on a vest quickly."

Heather wanted to laugh but held it in. Carl was funny sometimes.

Brody glanced at his boss and quickly placed the vest on Heather's left arm, then went to buckle it in the front. At that moment, he realized a design flaw: he would have to touch her breasts to buckle the vest properly.

Looking over his shoulder, Heather was once again trying not to laugh. She couldn't wait to see what he would do, but Penny realized his dilemma and came to his aid. Penny buckled the vest and nodded at Heather before walking back to her place to demonstrate movements for Heather.

Next, Brody took a remote out of his pocket and clicked on a switch. Heather felt the device on her chest power up, and she had an uncontrollable need to absorb the energy. The team watched in shock as the instrument began to shut down, and Heather began to glow with green fire.

Carl ran toward Brody, shouting, "Turn it off!"

Helpless, Brody yelled back, "I can't turn something that doesn't have power off! She took it all!"

Heather didn't want to use her abilities like this. She had to try and push it back into the device, so they didn't think she was dangerous yet. She closed her eyes tight and concentrated on the device and her energy. She breathed deeply as she pushed the power back into the box until her green fire dissipated.

Heather growled at Brody, "Warn me."

Carl nodded, glaring at him. "That's a good fucking idea, kid."

Brody took a few breaths and calmed down. He said, "I'm sorry, I didn't know that would happen."

"It's okay," Heather said. Honestly, she hadn't known it would either.

Penny and Helen were the assistants for this part of Heather's training, or whatever it was, so they just stood back and watched. Patterson asked Penny, "Did you monitor her heart rate during her medical tests?"

Singleton realized her results of the blood pressure and temperature tests were so shocking she forgot about Heather's heart rate. "No, I forgot. What is it?"

Brody looked at Penny, almost accusingly, and answered, "Two hundred and eighty."

They all gasped, even Carl. Penny walked up to Heather, who was faking obliviousness, and lifted her wrist and took her pulse. When she was done, she studied Heather's face. There was no indication her vitals were a sign of health issues. She was still waiting on the results of the

DNA tests on Heather's cheek swab and hair sample, but Penny knew she probably wouldn't get anything. If there were any doubt that Heather Stone was from Earth, in her eyes, it was crushed.

Penny stepped back from Heather. "Continue testing. I don't think her vitals are anything to worry about."

Confused, Helen asked, "Why? Those numbers will kill her."

Penny, more serious than she'd ever been, said, "Those numbers would kill a human. I'm pretty sure we're not in the presence of a human."

Heather thought, *No, dear Penny, you're not.*

Brody, who was still a little shaken, directed his attention back to his work. He moved out of Heather's way and pointed to the other side of the warehouse. There were three barrels lined up along the far wall with the big door. "Do you see those barrels?" he asked.

She nodded.

"If you can, I'd like you to reabsorb the energy from the device on your chest and destroy—"

Heather immediately absorbed the energy, lifted her right hand, and sent three green fireballs across the warehouse. They hit the barrels directly, completely destroying them. It took all of five seconds—child's play.

The team was in shock and completely speechless, but they all had different thoughts about what just happened.

Oh shit! from Penny. *Well, the government wanted a weapon; they got one!*

Dr. Grace shuddered. *This is* not *good; she could kill the entire world! Holy fuck, that was awesome*! Brody thought.

She's the answer, Carl realized. *She's definitely the answer. Now, how do I convince the rest of this lot of my plan?*

Heather turned around to see what the team thought. The reactions from Brody, Helen, and Penny were expected, but the sinister grin Carl was giving her seemed unsettling. It made her very curious about what his intentions for her were. It had nothing to do with Feds or brass; she was sure of it.

He crossed his arms and slowly walked up to Heather. She shifted on her feet, showing uncertainty for the first time since arriving in the facility. The other three were left wondering what was going on.

Carl stopped in front of the Florian General and looked down into her eyes. She stared right back, hiding her fear. He said, "I'm quite sure that what you did in the hallway and right here is the smallest tip of the iceberg. Am I right, love?"

She leaned in closer, only being tall enough to speak at him just below his chin and said quietly, so only he could hear, "You have no idea, Dr. Carl Gregory Johnson. Born on May fifth in Spokane, Washington. Your parents are Betty and Gregory John—"

Carl felt anger rising in his chest, and Heather could feel it, too, making her smile with satisfaction. He clenched his jaw. "I knew the tablet would be good for you, but it seems you're smarter than I thought. You and I have a lot to talk about, don't we, love?"

Heather leaned in and whispered, "Oh, yes we do, Carl. And stop calling me love."

Carl nodded and said, "Fair enough, bitch."

CHAPTER 23
WAREHOUSE

The rest of the team watched the interaction between Heather and Dr. Johnson in bewilderment. When Carl turned away from their test subject, he said, "Okay, pack up. We're done for today."

Brody objected, "But there's a lot more I wanted to test. Don't we need to know more about what she can do?"

"That test you just pulled was all we needed to see," Carl told him. "With only a small amount of energy, she was able to follow your order and destroy her target with precision. And all it took was that little thing you strapped to her chest. Do you really think we need to keep testing the same scenario on a larger and larger scale? That's all they want us to do."

Heather innocently watched Brody to see how the young man would answer his boss. She could tell he wanted to argue because he wanted to test out more of his equipment, but Carl was right. The rest of the team took the experiment as a sign that they needed to focus on other areas to get her ready, but Carl knew that was all he needed to prepare her for *his* plans.

Heather stood motionless as Penny took the harness off and handed it to Brody. She observed Heather curiously for a moment, then asked, "Are you okay, Heather?"

Pulling herself from her far-away thoughts, she smiled at Penny. "Yes."

Penny tentatively nodded and turned toward Carl. He was also staring off into space. "What did you say to her, Doctor?"

Carl studied Penny's face for a moment. "Nothing of importance," he answered. "Our little friend is coming along nicely."

Penny glared at him, knowing if she were to press him for the truth, she wouldn't get it. She walked away and helped the guards and Brody get the gear ready to go. Carl and Heather were standing rather close, but neither looked at the other. Carl was thinking about the best way to get her alone to talk about how she managed to learn everything about Earth, including his personal information, in five days. Heather was thinking about how she could use Carl's desire to get her to do something for him to her advantage. Either way, the two of them could be a perfect team or a perfect disaster.

In the distance, there was a rumble of thunder. Carl glanced at Heather and found she was daydreaming as if she didn't notice her surroundings. He barked an order at the others, saying, "Let's go; we need to get across to the cell block before that storm gets any closer."

Heather let the slightest of grins cross her lips as she thought about using the storm as a testing moment for her captors. She figured she'd make that decision once they were outside and could see their proximity to the storm.

Carl grabbed Heather by the arm. "We ain't waiting. Let's go."

As they approached the open door, Heather felt a surge of electrical energy and pushed Carl away, screaming, "No!"

Johnson stumbled back in shock when a huge bolt of lightning struck directly in the courtyard, which pushed him and Heather back into the warehouse. Heather had unintentionally absorbed the power, which blew Carl off his feet. Before they could move farther back from the door, another strike hit in almost the same place. Since Heather was still close to the open door and was too disoriented to move away, she absorbed that energy as well. It didn't take anyone long to realize she was actually attracting the lightning.

Brody came in from the side and pulled Carl to safety as one of the guards slammed the door closed just as another bolt hit, almost directly in front of the building.

All of the people in the warehouse were scared out of their minds, especially Carl. Heather wasn't only scared but energized, and she knew she wouldn't be able to hold her power much longer. If she released what she had stored, she could hurt or kill everyone in the warehouse.

Heather just lay on the ground, taking deep breaths, trying to figure out what to do. The only time anybody present had seen her at full power was on the videos from Kentucky. She was glowing like green wildfire, and her hands were as white as the lightning she received the power from.

Johnson came back and knelt next to her and asked, "What now?"

She said quietly, "Get everyone out."

"How long can you hold it? Can you move?"

She shrugged. "Not much longer, but I can move."

Outside, there was more lighting, and the thunder was deafening, but Carl needed to get the people out of that warehouse before she blew. He jumped up despite his head still spinning and yelled, "Grab the shit and get out; run back to the cell block *now!*"

The people started gathering gear, but Helen protested, "We can't go out there now! Not with all that rain and lightning!"

Carl pointed at Heather, who was still lying on the ground. "Do you see her?" he asked. "She just absorbed the energy of *two* bolts of lightning; she can't keep that in, and if she blows in this warehouse, we're all dead! We have to take our chances out there. It's only a quarter of a mile; we'll be fine, Helen."

Helen's fear was visible, tears welling in her eyes. Gently, Carl said, "Run with me, Helen. I'll take care of you as best as I can."

She nodded apprehensively. Johnson checked to see if everyone was ready. He yelled to Brody, "Go now! We'll be right there."

Heather saw they were about to open the door. As to not draw more lightning, she scrambled up and ran to the center of the warehouse, glancing back at Carl, nodding.

He and Helen ran to the group, and they all left. Carl was the last one out, and he turned to look at the glowing, green woman standing in the middle of that giant warehouse. He hoped for his own sake she lived through whatever happened.

Carl pulled the door closed, and they all ran toward the cell blocks. The rain and lightning were relentless, but everyone made it to the other building without incident. Once they were inside, Carl and his team went into one of the side offices with a window facing the warehouse. They were all quiet except for their panting and the sound of water dripping off their clothes onto the floor. None of them knew what Heather would do; all they could do was wait, helpless.

***

Heather stood in the middle of the building and concentrated on the sound of the thunder. She was counting the flashes of light through the windows and noticed that the storm was weakening, and the lightning was abating. However, Heather knew she couldn't hold the power in her veins long enough to wait until the storm had passed entirely. If she went outside now, all she would do was keep drawing in the lightning and making the situation worse. She'd have to release the energy inside the warehouse.

She could feel the power moving through her. It settled in her blood and flowed through her veins, moving slowly to every part of her body. The longer she held it, the harder it was to endure. It wasn't pain, but more of a torturous passage, like someone ceaselessly tickling her.

When she couldn't hold on anymore, Heather crouched down and tensed. She flexed every muscle and pushed the power from her body. It came out as an enormous pulse that burst in all directions. As the pulse hit the walls of the warehouse, she heard the concrete buckle and the glass windows shatter. Before she could even register what was happening, she was crushed under the collapsing roof.

***

The team watched from the cell block building in horror as the entire warehouse collapsed in a ball of green flame.

"Fuck," Carl quietly said.

CHAPTER 24
RUBBLE

Major Mallory entered the office and walked up behind Carl's team. He stopped next to Carl and said, "What a shame. She had promise."

Johnson shook his head. "That woman ain't dead."

Mallory rolled his eyes at Carl. "There's no way. Not even that woman could survive such a collapse." He looked back at the pile of debris, being pummeled by the rain, and said, "Don't get me wrong, I'm disappointed her story ended like this, but she's gone, Johnson."

"No, I don't think so. She has to be alive. The moment this fucking rain stops, I want teams of people out there combing the debris for her body. She's as valuable to me as she is to you."

The major gave Carl a sly smile. "Fine, we'll look for her. But if she's still alive, that changes things. I'll have to make sure she's sent away faster."

"Don't fuck with me, Colonel," Carl said. "We had a deal, and I still have time to work with her. If she's still alive, we get to continue our work for at least another *week*."

Major Mallory studied Dr. Johnson's face for a moment. He knew the doctor had alternate plans for the woman, but Mallory wasn't sure what they were yet. He needed to find out fast before he missed out on a promotion for getting the bitch to a place where she could be made into a tool to further the defense of his country. Turning back to the window, he observed, "Rain is slowing down. Let's get some workers and heavy equipment. We need to dig out a body."

Carl turned away from the major and said to Brody, "Go help get some gear together. I want all of us out there searching. She was in the center of the building when I closed the door, so I'm pretty sure that's where she was when the roof collapsed."

Johnson hadn't taken any time to consider the emotional condition of his team. Penny was quiet, staring at her hands with wet cheeks from crying. Helen was sitting on the desk with her arms crossed, mumbling to herself, trying to make sense of what happened. Brody was upset because Heather was going to be the biggest project he'd ever work on, and she was gone in an instant.

Finally, Penny asked Carl, "Do you really believe she's still alive?"

Carl nodded. "I'm pretty sure. This chick has a lot more to her than we know. But we won't find out until we get out there."

Brody left and went to the guard station to get them all access to the site with the recovery crew. The rain had stopped, and the late afternoon sun was shining. They all walked back across what was left of the courtyard toward the pile of steaming rubble.

The rain had quickly put out any fire that had remained when Heather's energy pulse took down the building. Since the blast hit the walls on all sides in the same place, it looked as if the walls had blown in half with the windows bringing down the roof on top of Heather.

Now that he was closer to the damage, Carl began to second guess his insistence that Heather was alive. The building was all concrete, steel, and glass, and had collapsed onto a one-hundred-pound woman. Alien or not, it was doubtful she was even still intact, let alone alive.

The crews began tackling the massive pile of debris and tried to make their way closer to the center of the mess. Carl was directing them to where he saw her last when he closed the door. Of course, that was where stability was the worst. They brought in a few cranes and small excavators to move the biggest items. Brody climbed onto the rubble pile and tried to get as close to where Carl said Heather was with a FLIR to see if there was a heat signature that could be human. Unfortunately, the rubble below was still so hot from her energy pulse that he couldn't get a reading.

The sun was setting, and the light was failing. Large sodium lights were brought in to keep the search going through the night. Carl was standing just off to the left side of the rubble, watching the work, when Penny came up beside him. She said, "You know, they're going to have different shifts come in overnight. Are we staying here?"

"I am," he said, not tearing his gaze away from the frenzy, "but you all need to go home. You can help in the morning if we don't find her before then."

Penny was concerned about Carl. Something happened to him today that made his view of Heather completely change. It was disconcerting. *What's he up to?* she wondered.

"Maybe we should all stay," she said.

Carl snapped his head to her. "No, you all should go home. Get some rest and be ready to go to work tomorrow."

"And if she's dead?"

"Well, we'll be looking for other jobs then, won't we?" Carl turned and walked away, leaving Penny speechless.

She found Brody and Helen watching her and Carl's exchange. She went up to them and said, "We're supposed to go home and get rest."

Brody said, "I want to stay and help. He can't make us leave."

"He can fire you, Brody," Helen reminded him.

He shrugged. "Maybe, but I doubt he would."

Penny shook her head and said, "No, he just might. Something's different about him. I've worked with him occasionally over the past few years, but I've never seen him like this."

Helen said, "He's never found the person he was looking for, let alone an alien. He doesn't want to let Heather slip through his fingers."

Brody addressed Helen. "Do you know why he's been trying to find someone with abilities like her?" he asked. "I always thought projects like this were a waste of time and resources."

"They usually are. I've done this work for nearly twenty-five years and been there to test hundreds of subjects; nothing has ever come close to this woman."

Penny said, "She's worth the most to the highest bidder. Major Mallory wants to give her to the military researchers, but he was instructed to allow Dr. Johnson to test her first. Why, I don't know, but they both want her."

Helen sighed. "I doubt it's good. Plus, Heather is catching on very fast and has her own mind. If anyone pushes her too far, she could become a real liability to the world."

Just then, Carl returned and said, "Please go home. There's no way they'll get through that rubble tonight, and I'll need you fresh tomorrow."

Suddenly, Brody demanded, "Why? What's going to happen tomorrow if they don't find her? Do we stand around and watch everyone else do the heavy lifting until they scrape what's left of her off the bottom of a rafter?" As soon as the words left his mouth, Brody realized how harsh his statement was, not only to Carl, but to their subject. He cast his eyes down and said, "Sorry."

Carl said, "Nope, you're right. I want you fresh for when they scrape her off the bottom of a rafter. So, go home, all of you."

Carl turned and stormed away from his team. He did feel bad for being that way, but he needed to get to Heather before anyone else. He needed to get her away from the facility, dead or alive.

The rest of the team slowly walked away. Helen called after Carl, "Carl! If they find her, will you at least call one of us?"

He nodded. However, he had no intention of following through. The three of them did as they were told and went home, all wondering what was happening on the debris site.

***

It'd gotten completely dark, and Carl could see lightning in the distance, making him nervous. If a storm made its way too close, everything would have to be shut down until it passed. Plus, if Heather was somehow still alive under the rubble and able to attract the lightning, they could all be in big trouble. He hadn't been under this much stress since his second divorce hearing.

As Carl closely monitored the skies, one of the guards came running up to him. "Sir!" he yelled breathlessly. "I think we may have found something! This way!"

Carl followed the guard as they climbed over a large part of the debris pile to a spot in the middle, where several people were working to dig a hole around a ceiling beam. As Carl approached, the foreman stopped him. "We need to keep the amount of weight around that hole at a minimum," he explained, "but we believe we've found where her body is."

Johnson was filled with excitement and concern. "Can I get up there and look? Can you see her?"

The foreman called for two of his people to leave the hole so he and Carl could approach without adding extra weight. The foreman said, "Approach the hole on your belly. This area isn't completely stable, and it'll only get worse as we remove more material."

Dr. Johnson nodded and lay down on top of a large, relatively intact roof slat. Leaning over the edge, he peered down into the hole. The workers had directed floodlights into it, and sure enough, at the bottom of the debris hole, Carl could see the very top of Heather's head. She wasn't moving, so Carl called her name, "Heather! Are you okay?"

The workers gave each other confused glances as the foreman said, "Sir, based on how the debris is laying that beam," he leaned down and pointed to a large, red steel beam, "is running right across her torso. Sir, Miss Stone is definitely deceased."

Carl rolled on his side to look at the foreman. "Were you here this afternoon during the thunderstorm that caused this mess?"

The foreman shook his head. "No, sir, I wasn't."

Raising up on his elbow, Carl said, "Miss Stone absorbed the power of not one, but *two* lightning strikes while standing right next to me. If she can survive that, then that beam ain't shit. We need to get down to her. *Now!*" He stood back up.

"Okay," the foreman said, "but I just have to say, sir, don't get your hopes up."

"There's another storm in the distance," Carl said quietly. "This needs to get done quickly, do you understand?"

"Yes, sir."

As the crew resumed work on the debris around the hole, Carl grabbed a pickaxe to help. He was exhausted and starving, but he couldn't let anyone else get to Heather before him. That way, he could at least get her back to her room or the infirmary under his supervision. As he worked, he thought about the way the day had gone. He'd insisted to Helen that the internet was too risky, but he knew Heather would figure it out. He was very impressed by her ability to learn what she did from the tablet. When he'd taken it back from her, he'd scoured the tablet for any history of what she looked at, but he usually only found a few sites like language pages or Earth history. He never saw anything that would indicate she knew how to research their backgrounds. All that told him was she was much more intelligent and dangerous than he'd thought. He couldn't wait to get her out on the streets.

Something else stuck with him about that afternoon. When she'd felt the initial buzz of energy from the first bolt of lightning, she'd actually tried to pull Carl to safety. She also made sure she ran far away from the door when they opened it to escape so she wouldn't absorb any more energy. As he thought about all the interactions Heather had had with humans since showing up a couple of weeks ago, he realized she was never the aggressor. She only attacked when she was threatened first, and when she tried to escape, the only damage she did was to property. So far, she didn't *seem* to want to hurt anybody.

After a few hours of working, Carl saw they were out of luck for avoiding the rain. It was almost one a.m. when a large storm approached, and they had to shut down the operation. Carl had to reluctantly leave the debris pile and his prisoner trapped beneath the rubble. He went back into the office where he and the team had observed the warehouse collapse and stared out the window. The orange facility lights left an eerie glow over the site. Carl felt helpless; he was starting to feel sorry for Heather personally and was scared she was dead. If she was alive, she was out there all alone, trapped.

Carl sighed and decided to sit down for a few minutes while he waited for the storm to pass. Once it was over, he would get back up and help the crew again.

***

It was past six a.m. when Brody nudged a sleeping Carl on the shoulder. His boss had stretched out on top of the desk and was snoring loudly. Brody figured it had to have been a long night. Carl opened his eyes and sat straight up. "What the hell—what time is it? I sent you home; why the fuck are you here, Brody?"

The young man answered, "Doc, it's past six. I came *back* early. It looks like it rained most of the night. Is that why you're in here?"

Rubbing his eyes, Carl slid off the desk. He looked out the windows and saw the crews were just getting back to work. He yawned. "We need coffee, then we must get out there. They found where she's trapped. It's just a matter of getting down to her now."

Brody perked up. "Awesome!" he said. "Was she moving?"

"I'm not sure. All I could see was the very top of her head. She didn't respond when I called to her. We need to get out there now, so we're the first people to get to her. Who knows what'll happen if we aren't, but first—coffee."

Brody knew that cue was for him, but as he turned to go buy some from the commissary, Penny walked in with a tray and four cups. "Did someone say coffee?" she asked.

Carl smiled. "Aren't you a dear. Good job."

She trained her eyes up and down Carl. "Did you sleep here last night? You look horrible."

Carl merely gave her a dirty look, grabbed his coffee, and turned to walk down the hall.

"Wait, what's the plan?" Penny called after him.

"The plan is to rescue a living or dead alien from that pile and keep her from the ever-increasing threat of being turned into a major military weapon."

Brody and Penny looked at each other and shrugged. They grabbed their coffees as well and followed Carl. The last cup belonging to Helen sat on the desk. It would go untouched.

***

Helen was sitting across from Major Mallory in his office, going over what she witnessed yesterday. He asked her, "So, what the hell happened? How did my warehouse get destroyed, Helen?"

She shrugged. "Honestly, I would like to say it was recklessness by Dr. Johnson, but that was more of an unforeseen accident. Mother Nature took her turn at our new little friend, and Heather absorbed the power of two lightning bolts like it was nothing. Interestingly, when she realized she had to release her energy, she ensured we were all outside of the building and away from her. She doesn't seem to have any inclination to harm anyone yet."

Mallory huffed. "Yet." He shifted in his seat and asked, "Do you think she's still alive under all that rubble?"

Helen nodded. "I do. I don't know how, but I do. I'm sure Carl is back out there now, trying to get at her."

"The night foreman said they were able to get a small hole down to see the top of her head," Mallory told her. "He said Carl tried to call to her, but there was no response. Our workers don't have much faith she made it. I guess the location of her body puts a massive roof support beam going right across her. That girl is done for, Helen."

Helen shrugged and stood up. She grabbed her jacket off the back of the chair, walked around to the other side of the desk, leaned down, and kissed Major Mallory deeply. As she stood back up, he smiled and said, "Thank you, Dr. Grace. Now, go get me my alien, dead or alive."

Dr. Helen Grace smiled seductively at him. "Yes, sir." She turned and walked out of his office to head to the debris site.

***

When Helen got outside, the sun was shining brightly, and the area was alive with activity. She saw her teammates standing on a small platform close to the debris. She walked up beside Carl and asked, "How much have I missed?"

Carl didn't look at her as he said, "They found her body last night, and this morning they were able to get about half of the large debris in that area moved. The morning foreman said we should be able to get to her by early afternoon."

"Great! Has anyone made contact with her? Do we know whether she's dead or alive?"

"Well, there are a hell of a lot of bets and money flying around," Brody told her. "It's almost tempting to put in a wager since I know she's alive."

Carl slowly turned to Brody. "And what the hell do you mean by that?"

Brody smiled. "Yesterday, when I put the harness on Heather, you all know there was a heart rate monitor attached to the power module. Penny, when you took off her vest, one of the wireless leads must've gotten stuck to her shirt. When I checked my gear this morning before coming back in, I saw that the power module was still monitoring her heart! Her heart rate is running between eighty and a hundred. Heather is still alive."

Again, all for different reasons, the other team members were elated to hear that news.

Thank God! Penny thought. *She deserves to be free of this prison.*

Carl thought, *Things will move on as planned, as long as this cunt doesn't fuck it up for me.*

Mallory will be so happy. I just have to keep this asshole from ruining things for me, Helen thought.

Just then, one of the workers from the top of the pile yelled down to the foreman, and many people scrambled into action. The team ran over as well, eager to find out what was happening.

The worker on top of the pile said, "We made it down to the beam faster than expected. We can get the area on both sides of the lady cleared, but honestly, sir, I don't think there's much left to recover."

Brody narrowed his eyes and called back to him, "Why do you say that? What's the condition of her body?"

The man seemed a little taken aback by the question, so the foreman answered for him. "What does it matter? She's dead. We can collect the rest of her remains when the whole area is cleaned."

Johnson stepped forward and got into the foreman's face. "Now listen to me, this isn't some regular girl with a notion of a superpower; she's the focus of a critical government study, and whether she's dead, alive, or in pieces, you will do whatever it takes to get her out of there, *now*."

The foreman glanced over Carl's shoulder and saw Major Mallory approaching. Johnson followed his gaze and said, "Good morning, Mallory."

Mallory nodded to Carl and said to the foreman, "Dr. Johnson is right. We need to get whatever is left of Miss Stone out of there today."

The foreman shrugged and started directing his men to get the equipment up there to lift the beam.

Carl said to Mallory, "So, you wanna walk up there with me and see what's left of her?"

The major sniffed and crossed his arms. He considered it but said, "No, not today. I'm sure you'll take care of her remains, Johnson."

With that, Mallory turned and walked back to the cellblock, glancing at Helen. She knew what she had to do.

Carl turned to Penny. "I want you to come with me. Whether she's alive or not, I think having a med doctor up there is a good idea."

Helen said, "But she isn't a med—"

Pausing beside Helen on his way to climb up the debris, he said, "She is to me."

Penny beamed internally and followed Carl up the rubble. When they got to the top, Penny breathed, "Holy shit. All of this fell on her. I think Brody's monitor must be reading something else. She couldn't have survived this."

Johnson said, "I dunno; I still have faith she's gonna make it."

They both stood well away from the workers on a flat piece of the slate roof and watched the debris being removed. After about half an hour of silent observing, one of the workers in the hole yelled, "We're ready for the crane! The people who want the body need to get over here now because I don't know what'll happen when this beam moves!"

With that, Penny and Carl made their way over to the edge of the hole. When Carl looked down, everything was cleared except for the beam on the cracked floor of the warehouse. Heather was lying on her stomach, and the beam had landed right across the small of her back. Carl heard Penny whimper. He rested his hand on her arm and said, "It's okay. She went fast, hun."

The ball of the crane swung over their heads and lowered down into the hole. Carl watched as the riggers put the straps around the beam. The foreman looked at Carl and said, "You can climb down that side. It's probably best that you're down there when the beam is lifted to keep the body from sticking to it, and… you know, being—"

"Stuck to the beam and taken on a ride for all the world to see?" Carl interrupted. "Yeah. I got it." To Penny, he said, "Ready, love?"

Penny nodded and took his hand as they made their way down. She was a medical professional and had been in some pretty hairy situations and seen some horrible things. She'd even responded to a plane crash where eighteen kids were killed, but for some reason, this was messing with her head.

They made it past the riggers, who were impatiently waiting to get moving, and down to the left side of the beam, next to Heather's legs. Now that they were next to her, both Penny and Carl were struggling, but he knew it had to be this way. They both knelt and held down Heather's legs. He nodded to the closest rigger, and the command was given to start the lift.

Penny heard the crane's engine rev and felt the beam start to lift. She squeezed her eyes shut, expecting to hear horrible bone-crunching or flesh-tearing sounds, but there was nothing. She kept her eyes closed for a few more moments until she was sure the beam was well into the air. She opened them and looked first at Carl, who was staring in disbelief at Heather.

Singleton followed his gaze to the body of the beautiful brown-haired, brown-eyed woman with flawless skin and perfect teeth. To Penny and everyone else's amazement and horror, Heather's body was still intact, with no visible injuries other than where the beam had been resting across her back. Her back was completely flat except for a small ridge that must have been her nearly-flat spine. There should've been blood and gore everywhere, but not a drop was visible. Penny's curiosity got the better of her, and she lifted Heather's shirt and touched the skin on her flattened back. It was completely intact and uninjured, but there was nothing other than the skin and her compressed spine. Heather's organs and other bones had been *pushed* to either side of the beam when it landed. Yet, from what she could tell, they were undamaged and fully functional. Penny and Carl watched Heather's upper body raise and lower as she was still breathing normally. Singleton picked up her wrist and took her pulse, which was eighty-two, just like Brody had said.

Penny turned her gaze to Carl's. "She really is alive," she whispered. "This is fucking insane."

Carl was speechless, and Penny could see he was completely freaked out. She peeked up and saw the entire crew of workers were all frozen, watching them. "How are we going to get her out of here?" she asked Carl.

Heather was still unconscious, and she was technically cut in half. Moving her out of that hole was going to be extremely difficult.

Suddenly, Heather's upper torso lurched, and she coughed. Her whole body began to shake, and she screamed in pain. Penny was now afraid that since the beam had been removed, she was going to die. Just as she started to yell back up to the foreman to lower the beam back down, Carl grabbed her arm and cried, "Look!"

Before all of their eyes, Heather slowly contorted and twisted herself back into one piece. Penny could only imagine how much pain she was in. Her screams were horrible. But after only three or four minutes, she was back to being whole and perfectly alive.

Heather was lying on her back with her arms over her eyes, sobbing. Penny knelt down beside her and told Carl, "Get the gawkers out of here. Let the woman recover in peace."

Carl, who was shaken to his core, stood up and mumbled to the crowd, "Please leave us be for a few minutes." He watched as the curious onlookers moved back from the hole's edge. He then dropped back down to his knees next to them.

Penny placed her hand on Heather's shoulder and said, "Hi, Heather, it's Penny."

Through her tears, Heather said, "I know. I want to go to bed, please."

Penny didn't think much of it, but she was impressed by Heather's ability to speak so clearly. To Carl, she said, "How do you want to do this? She can't walk out of here."

Johnson stared at Heather. His own heart and body hurt tremendously for her at that moment. He whistled loudly, and about ten people poked their heads over the edge. "Get us a rescue basket to lift her out of here."

"We can have it over to you in about fifteen minutes," the foreman told him.

Carl nodded and returned his attention to Heather. She'd rolled onto her side and was staring at his knee. Penny and Carl didn't know what to do or say. How did you comfort someone who just spent nearly twenty-four hours having been cut in half by a ten-ton beam of steel, then miraculously mended herself while experiencing immense pain?

Johnson just sat next to her, silent, and Penny rubbed her shoulder. They were all quiet for a few minutes until Heather began to dry heave.

She pushed herself onto her hands and knees and choked out, "Move."

Carl and Penny jumped back and watched, again in horror, as Heather vomited a large amount of blood and bile. When she couldn't wretch anymore, she collapsed onto her back again. "Well, there's your blood sample," she said to Penny. "Do you still want it?"

CHAPTER 25
MAKE IT LOOK LIKE THIS NEVER HAPPENED

T he crane lifted the rescue basket out of the hole and swung around to where Brody and Helen were standing. It'd taken Carl and Penny a little bit to get Heather into the basket, but they got her out of the hole safely.

As the basket was lowered to the ground, Brody noticed all the men and women on-site silently staring at them. Most of them had seen Heather's body when it was still under the beam, and they'd known she was dead. But there she was, whole and alive, struggling to climb out of the basket.

Patterson helped her out and onto a gurney that was standing by. Carl and Penny made their way over.

"We need to go with her straight to the infirmary," Singleton said. "I need to examine her for any additional injuries."

Carl said quietly, "Only you're going to examine her. This is a critical time. If Mallory is going to grab her, he's going to do it now."

Penny agreed. While they were in the hole, not only had Penny's suspicions that Carl had another agenda for Heather been confirmed, but she'd discovered Heather had been working to better herself. She'd stared at her in astonishment when Heather had asked about the blood sample.

Carl, apparently unsurprised, had said, "This one is too fuckin' smart for her own good."

Heather had been too sick and in pain to respond. Penny just looked at her beleaguered face and said, "Yeah, I guess. How long have you been able to understand us fully?"

"About two days," Heather choked out.

Singleton shook her head and asked, "How? How did you learn so much so quickly?"

Heather pointed at Carl and dropped her head back to the ground with a groan. Penny looked at Carl, who explained, "The tablet. I knew she'd use it for more than *Barney*. Turns out she learned a lot more than I figured she would."

It was then that the rescue basket arrived. They got Heather loaded up and sent it to Brody and Helen. As Penny and Carl had been about to climb out, he stopped Penny. "Now, I'm taking a chance in sharing this with you because I trust you more than any of these other assholes."

She blushed and asked like a schoolgirl, "You trust me?"

He shook his head. "Only to a certain extent, but don't get your panties in a bunch. There's a lot at stake, and I ain't letting anyone know the whole story."

"What's going on?"

Carl waved for her to start climbing and told her, "I don't want Heather to get too close to Mallory or Dr. Grace. I don't trust either of them. I know he wants to grab Heather and run, and I think Helen is working with him."

After a moment of thought, Penny replied, "I've never trusted Helen too much. She's too nice. She always seems to want to report to Mallory about everything. I bet they're fucking each other."

Carl let out a big laugh. "Could be, girl. They seem like each other's type. Anyway, can I trust you to at least keep our new friend away from them? Who knows what Mallory will want to do now that he knows she can survive somethin' like that."

As they reached the top of the pile of debris, Penny said, "You can trust me. I don't want any of these fuckers messing with Heather."

Johnson could tell by the defiant tone of her voice she was sincere. He thought, *One down, now for the important one.*

***

Brody was standing next to Carl as he watched Penny and Helen wheel Heather away. He didn't like seeing her so hurt, but he couldn't believe she was alive.

"Now what?" he quietly asked Carl.

Carl scanned the crowd of onlookers who were gawking at Heather. "Do these guys have cell phones? I don't see anyone tryin' to take pictures or call their significant others telling them what they were watching."

Brody said, "No, on an emergency response operation like this, they aren't allowed to have any devices. The United States government doesn't want anyone having pictures of an alien woman who should've been cut in half by a steel girder get up and shake it off." He looked around the courtyard and added, "I'm surprised Mallory doesn't have a debrief team out here."

"I'm sure he does within this lot. We just don't know who they are. One thing we have to agree with Mallory on is that this needs to be made like it never happened. We don't need TMZ showing up at the gates wanting pictures of the green fire lady."

Brody nodded and said, "I wish you were joking, but I guess the paparazzi were all over the site in Kentucky, and people who were there have been posting cell phone videos online like crazy. If they find out she's here, there could be a run on this place. It isn't necessarily ultra-secure."

Carl asked, "How do you know?"

Brody leaned in and whispered, "When we first got here, it took me all of five minutes to hack all of the servers and access all of the top-secret data on-site. I also accessed the electronic door locks and was able to map an escape route that could be run in under three minutes."

Carl was impressed but kept it to himself for the moment. "From where?"

Patterson smiled. "Dr. Johnson, you're not the only one who wants to get Heather out of here before Mallory sends her off to some group of military scientists to be poked and prodded until she does what they want. I think there are applications in the real world for her."

"So, you want to poke and prod her on your own?" Carl realized that sounded bad, but he needed to know.

Brody flushed with anger and said, "No, not really. I want to see what she can do but let her decide on her own what she wants to do with her abilities."

Carl didn't necessarily believe Brody, but he needed the kid to get her out of the facility. "Well, we're better off working together. We should form a plan, right?"

Patterson really didn't want to work with Johnson, but he had to admit the input from a physicist would come in handy. He put out his hand for a shake, and Carl took it and said, "No funny business. We're in this together."

Brody nodded. "Agreed."

Carl started to walk away, calling over his shoulder, "Penny's coming too."

Patterson groaned. *Great*, he thought.

***

Mallory watched the conversation between Dr. Johnson and the tech kid from his office window. *What are you fuckers talking about?* he wondered.

He turned from the window to the officers standing in front of his desk. Sitting down, he said, "We need to get the names of each and every worker out there. They saw the alien being taken out of the hole, and many of them know how she brought that damn warehouse down on herself. All of you need to make sure no information makes it out of the facility."

Captain Brian Pickering asked, "What would you suggest we do, Major? Most of these people are civilian contractors. They go home at night."

"Who the hell brought in civilians to work on this?"

"It was Dr. Grace," Pickering said. "I think she wanted to get the woman out as soon as possible, and we didn't have enough of our own engineers and equipment, so she called in civilian contractors."

Mallory cringed internally. Helen just wanted to impress him by getting Heather out of that hole the fastest, unknowingly possibly compromising the situation.

He cleared his throat. "Well, what's done is done. I want all of these people set up in barracks here on the grounds until the entire site is cleaned. There will be no communication in or out. Once the work is done, they'll have to sign confidentiality agreements to never talk about what they saw, or they'll go to prison for a very long time."

Captain Pickering nodded and directed the rest of his people out of the room. As he was about to follow them, he turned and asked Mallory, "Do we even know what it is?"

"Not yet," the major said, "but I plan to find out before that prick Johnson."

CHAPTER 26
A WHOLE NEW ALIEN

P enny was in the X-ray room, setting up to take some pictures of Heather. She'd have preferred a CT scan, but the facility didn't have one. Her infirmary was only set up for minor emergencies and routine tests. Not aliens being cut in half and—regenerating? Resealing? Who knew what her body did.

Heather was lying on the table, staring at the ceiling. She wasn't quite back to herself and had no idea how long it would take to heal from her ordeal. She thought back to the moment she'd released her energy.

The first thing Heather noticed when the warehouse came down on her wasn't the immense pressure of the beam across her body but the immediate darkness. She struggled to breathe through the smoke and dust but finally realized she was pinned under the beam. That was when she felt the pain—such unimaginable pain. The Florian tried to cry out, but between the shaft and dust, her voice was reduced to a small cough. Her head was spinning, and she couldn't control the panic. Tears began pouring from her eyes, and she thought, *Why am I not dead? What kind of torturous hell would keep me alive for this?!*

Finally, her body's underlying instincts kicked in, and Heather slipped into an unnatural unconscious state. Her breathing and heart rate slowed, but they were still enough to maintain her life. Since her legs were separated from her heart, the veins within them converted into their own, independent circulatory system. The blood would only flow enough to keep her legs from degenerating. Once her body was whole again, her heart would pump extra blood to her legs to restore them, but that would take time. One of the problems with being in a situation like that was the blood and waste that would usually collect below where the beam hit would gather in her stomach until she shut down to a full maintenance mode. It was why she threw up so much once she woke up. She would only reanimate if her surroundings went back to being livable.

The first thing Heather remembered from when she woke up was the light. When she slipped into the unconscious state, or survival stasis, it was dark and chokingly dusty. Then, it was bright from artificial lights. She could feel the pressure and weight from the beam was gone, and she could distantly hear Penny's voice.

The pain returned.

The pain was blinding; she could actually feel her organs and bones moving back into place. Luckily, her body repaired itself quickly, and she was whole in only a few minutes, but she wasn't fully healed yet. She felt the rush of blood return to her legs, which had been starved for a day. That made her upper body feel weaker at first, leaving her with absolutely no energy. Everything was shaking; it hurt. Then, the nausea hit, and wave after wave of blood and bile poured from her stomach.

By the time she stopped, all she could do was cry. She barely noticed Penny and Carl were there, horrified at what they'd witnessed.

She remembered bits and pieces of being lifted out of the hole and brought into this strange room. Penny came and stood by the gurney. Quietly, she said, "Okay, Heather, I need you to try and get up and walk over to the little table over here." She motioned to a big machine with arms and dim lights. "This is an X-ray machine. I need to use it to take pictures of your body to make sure you're healing properly."

Heather just said, "Okay," and tried to sit up, but she fell back, grimacing.

Penny slid her arm behind Heather and gently helped her up. As she moved her, Penny noticed the red mark on the back of Heather's neck. It looked like it could be a birthmark, but the design was more like a tattoo. Not really thinking, Penny ran her finger over the mark and asked, "Heather, what's this?"

"What?"

"This mark on your neck, what is it?"

Confused, Heather shook her head. "I don't know what you're talking about," she said.

Penny had to remember that even though Heather was learning about their world, she still didn't seem to remember her own. She said, "I'll get a mirror and show you once we're done with the X-rays."

With that, Singleton helped Heather off the gurney and into a hospital gown. She didn't even seem to care. Penny could feel her shaking, and the extra warmth she was used to feeling radiating from Heather wasn't there. *I wonder if she has her powers right now*, Penny thought.

She got Heather through the X-rays, which didn't seem to affect her powers at all, and back to her room. Carl had arranged for a much more comfortable bed to be brought in. There was a warm meal and even coffee waiting for Heather. The incident had made them realize how important it was to take care of her, rather than treat her like a prisoner.

The beleaguered woman sat down in front of the food and began to eat right away. She savored each bite; the more she ate, the more she seemed to recover. There was a pitcher of water that she drank all at once. Carl, Penny, and Brody were all in the room and watched her intently. Heather knew there were probably many more behind the mirror, but she didn't care. She needed to concentrate on getting back to full strength before striking up a conversation with Carl.

When she was finished with everything but the coffee, she lifted the cup and took a small sip. She smiled and said to Penny, "My neck."

Penny had almost forgotten about the mark. "Here," she said, "let me take a picture with my phone so I can show you."

Curious, Carl asked, "What are you talking about?"

"Come here. I'll lift her hair; you take a picture of her neck."

Carl and Brody watched as Penny lifted the mass of brown, curly hair off Heather's neck, revealing the small symbol. It was a deep but bright red, about the size of a silver dollar. It was circular and had eight flares, like a sun, but the center of the circle had a grid pattern. Penny smiled. "It's beautiful."

Heather said, irritated, "Is it now?"

"Sorry, Heather. Carl, take a picture."

Carl did as he was told and sat down across from Heather. Penny went to put Heather's hair down as Brody went to touch her neck. Singleton stopped him. "You should ask permission before touching someone. It's good manners."

Patterson gave her a dirty look. "Okay, Miss Manners. Heather, can I touch your neck?"

Heather, who just wanted to go to sleep, said, "Sure."

Brody ran his fingers over the symbol and was surprised to find it was textured. Heather had super smooth skin, but the symbol was almost as rough as sandpaper. "So odd," he said.

Carl raised an eyebrow at Brody and said sarcastically, "Are you quite finished?"

Brody nodded. "Yeah. The skin is rough."

Johnson didn't care. He watched Heather as he turned the phone so she could see the picture. "Does this mean anything to you?"

Heather took the phone and studied the imagine intently. She reached behind her neck and felt the textured skin of the symbol. After a minute, she said, "No. It means nothing."

Unsurprised, he said, "I'm going to print this picture. You need to study it as much as possible. Maybe after a while, it'll trigger some kind of memory. It had to have gotten there somehow."

She nodded. Heather drank her coffee and noted that everyone watched to see what she would do with the energy, but Heather didn't absorb anything. She knew she could, but it was too exhausting, and she had no desire to try any type of escape right now anyway. Once finished, she set the cup gently on the tray. "I need to sleep."

Penny nodded in agreement. "She really does. In the morning, we can monitor what progress you've made in your healing." She glanced at Carl. "Please come with me to the infirmary to look at her X-rays."

Carl knew she wanted to talk to him away from the mirror, but there were probably bugs and cameras in the infirmary as well. It would be hard to escape prying eyes and ears.

Penny helped Heather into the new bed, which was the most comfort she'd felt since her crash landing. Heather placed her head on the pillow and was asleep before the team had collected her tray and left, leaving her to some peace.

Heather began to dream almost immediately. She was walking on a beach with pure-white sand and crystal-clear water. There was nothing around her for as far as she could see. Finally, a bench appeared from the shimmering sand. As she got closer, she realized the bench was facing away from her, and there was a man dressed in loose white clothes sitting in the middle. The closer she got, the more she could see of him. He was tall and slender. He had dark-brown hair that shone with a touch of red in the bright sun.

As she approached, she said, "Hello."

The man neither answered nor moved. She stopped directly behind him, within touching distance. She noted his hair was cut cleanly around his neck and ears while the rest faded up to thick, wind-blown locks. To her astonishment, he had a red mark on the back of his neck, but it wasn't the same as hers. His was a hollow square with what looked like interwoven branches on the inside. Heather reached out and gently touched the side of his neck, dragging her fingers from right to left, over the mark, feeling the difference in textures. The entire time, he didn't say or do anything.

"Who are you?" Heather asked. "Do we know each other?"

That time, he raised his head a little and took a deep breath. Heather started to walk around to the other side of the bench, but, in the language she remembered from when she first landed, he said, "Stop."

Heather did, and in that same language, she asked, "Why?"

He stood up. "It's too early."

Heather tried to place his voice; she wanted it to be the voice she remembered from when she first arrived, but it was too hard to compare them.

"Too early for what?" Heather asked desperately.

He turned, but just as she was about to see his face, the cell door opened, waking her from her dream. Heather glared at Carl, angry that he'd woken her from something so lovely, not that he knew.

Johnson set a cup of coffee on the table. "Good morning, dear. How are you feelin'?"

After stretching, Heather stood up. She surprisingly felt quite good, almost back to normal except for a few aches and pains. She was sure she'd be back to 100 percent by the end of the day. "I feel much better." She pointed at the coffee and asked, "Aren't you afraid to give that to me?"

"Should I be?"

Heather walked over to sit across from him at the table and picked up the coffee cup. She took a sip and smiled. "Maybe."

Carl chuckled. "Yup. You're definitely feeling better." He cleared his throat and asked, "What were you dreamin' about?"

Heather furrowed her brow. "How did you know I was dreaming?"

Carl gave her a sidelong glance and replied, "You were twitchin' a bit and said something in a different language."

Heather looked down at her hands and figured her dream was innocent enough to say to him. Maybe he could tell her if he knew a man with the description of the one in her dream. Taking care to include every detail she could remember, Heather recounted her dream, losing herself in the memory of it.

Carl hung on to her every word, and so was the rest of the team. She hadn't even noticed they came in while she was talking. Penny blurted out, "So you didn't see his face?"

Heather shook her head.

Helen said, "Wow, you sure are talking very well now! It sounds like you're trying to bring up hidden memories from your past. This must be a man from your former life."

Shrugging, Heather said, "I don't know. I haven't been able to see his face. I had a dream—I mean, a nightmare—a few nights ago, and he was in part of that dream as well."

"Was it this man who made your first dream a nightmare?" Helen asked.

"No. But he turned into the man who did. I'm not sure what it means."

Penny said, "Helen's right. It sounds like he may be a connection to your past. Hopefully, you dream about him again, in a good way. And that you get to see his face. And you recognize him. And maybe even—"

Carl cut her off and said, "Thanks, Penny, we get it." He looked back at Heather and asked, "Are you up to working today?"

"What kind of work? I'm not sure I want to drop a building on myself again."

"Yeah, I don't want that either. But Brody has a few other pieces of equipment he wants to try on you."

Brody stepped in front of Heather. "Don't worry," he said. "I only need you to absorb energy, not release it. You should be fine."

"Should be?" Heather repeated.

Brody laughed. "Yeah, should be. If I guaranteed that everything would be fine while working with you, I'd be lying to the human race."

Heather was starting to like Brody.

CHAPTER 27
AHHH, THE GOOD OLE DAYS

Dominic waited in the strategy planning room for his pilot, Colonel Renee Conner—or, as he personally knew her, his third ex-wife.

Renee walked in precisely on time, just like her mentor, Dia, had taught her. Though she was several hundred thousand years younger than Dia, they were both cut from the same cloth. Die-hard soldiers at work and goofy jerks when they were off duty.

She walked up to the illuminated table and addressed Dominic quietly, "Good morning, Colonel."

He nodded. Renee's hair was black as night, falling to the small of her back. It was pulled into a simple braid, but he always liked to remember when she'd wear it down, wild. Her brown eyes sparkled, and her alabaster skin was smooth and flawless. Her black flight suit was perfectly form-fitted to her body. She looked more like she should be in a recruitment poster than actually flying a DREX, but she was second in talent only to his sister. And he was still in love with her.

"What are we doing today?" she asked.

Dominic pushed his personal feelings aside and said, "My father has tasked us with finding Dr. Harlow. We know the Coronians are holding him, but not what planet they have him on. My experience with them is that they're waiting for us to send a large search party to find him, maybe set up negotiations, or lure us into a trap. I'm sure they're waiting for us to send out emissaries to all the places we know they frequent."

She crossed her arms, nodding. "They may have him on a ship. Troy is a high-value target. Moving him around is their best bet to keep him from being found. They may not be waiting for us to send an emissary. Trying to find Dr. Harlow within their planetary system almost isn't worth the effort."

Although Dominic felt the same way, to a certain extent, he couldn't let her know that. He glared at her. "Don't even begin to think that way. We're going to utilize all of our resources to find him and Dia. Not just because they're valuable people to our society, but we think they both have the key to a weapon that will make our lives immensely better."

"Or worse," Renee countered. "Rumor has it something went terribly wrong, which is why they fled. I love Dia and Troy; you know that Dom. But do you really think what they have can make our lives better?"

"I don't think they wanted anyone to know exactly what they were working on. I'm still trying to get information out of Oscar because I know he had something to do with it."

Renee studied the table's screen and scanned what Dominic had mapped out. It was the Keplen system, which was where they knew at least part of the Coronian empire was. Dominic had marked certain life-sustaining planets that would be their first places to search.

"I believe they want to recreate his work," Dominic explained. "From what his lab looks like here, he has a large amount of technical equipment that he and, I think, my brother created themselves. The Coronians will have a helluva time replicating that gear. It'll make it very difficult to move him and his work around like they typically would. We need to try and find their most remote and hidden location to search first."

Renee agreed. "Very true. But what I don't understand is if Troy and Oscar created the equipment themselves, how would the Coronians duplicate it? Unless we have a suspected spy giving them information."

"That's *exactly* what I think is happening."

Renee was quiet for a moment. Reluctantly, she said, "You don't think it's—"

"As his brother," he interrupted her, "I don't want to believe it's him, but as the head of security, I have to reluctantly admit that it *is* possible, especially with how close he and Troy worked together. Hell, they're best friends." Dominic became quiet for a moment.

Renee could see the sadness cross his face. His family was falling apart. He loved his sister more than anything and always tried to protect her, even from herself. His brother was his confidant and always took Dominic seriously no matter what. Both of his parents were watching their people slip into fear and chaos. They didn't believe their leaders could both find Troy and Dia and also stave off any attacks by the Coronians. And Troy? He wasn't Dominic's favorite person, but he took care of and protected his sister. At least, up until now.

Dominic shook off his sorrow and turned his attention back to the map. He circled a series of planets with a pointer. "We need to start with these five planets. This is Pletor. We know the Coronians used to have a large outpost there a few thousand years ago. I'm not certain if they've abandoned it, but it's a good place to keep in mind." He gestured at a smaller planet. "This is Domdoele. It's probably the least likely to have a facility capable of sustaining Troy's work, but it's remote and has a lot of jungles and mountains to hide in."

Renee said, "I would try Domdoele last. James Ramsay and I flew there not too long ago, and the place is full of life, but none was intelligent. And it was fucking dangerous."

"Good to know." He moved on to his next planet. "This is Bodeolr, probably our best bet. The environment is conducive to everything they would need for Troy. Scans don't show much life, and we can't tell if what *is* there is intelligent, but knowing them, they could've disguised themselves." He shifted his pointer again. "This is Rol. It's another dangerous station, but we're sure there's a Coronian outpost there. They were observed on the planet by an ally of ours less than a year ago. We'll try this place first."

Dominic put the pointer away. Before he could turn off the table, Renee stopped him and pointed to the last of the five planets. "What about his one? You didn't say anything about it."

"Darsayn. That one is the biggest longshot of them all. We can't pinpoint its location because it actually *moves*. It would be a great place for them to work from, and it's suspected to be the seat of the Coronian empire, but that planet seems so remote, dangerous, and hard to find."

"Which is exactly why it's important. If we don't find anything on the other four, we're trying this place."

"I'm telling you, Renee, there's little chance of finding it, and it'd be dangerous. I don't think we should."

"Then why did you mark it?"

"Because I figured maybe it was a possibility at first, but I'm not so sure anymore."

Renee continued, stubbornly, "You say it's a longshot, but there's a possibility, although slim, that we could find something there."

Dominic just stared at her.

"Dominic, I learned many moons ago that the long odds can be your best and most effective bet."

"Who did you learn that from?"

She gave him a sly smile. "Your sister."

***

The next day, Dominic and Renee finished putting together their team for the journey to the Keplen system. In order to stay as inconspicuous as possible, they were only taking three DREX fighters, as they were the smallest of the ships in the Florian Army fleet. Even though they were small, they were also the most capable. DREX ranged from fighters, destroyers, and transports. Despite size differences, any ship could be used as an up-close fighter or as a deep-space freighter. Oscar Strom invented the craft a very long time ago to be versatile and easy to produce. There'd been little structural change in the hundreds of thousands of years since they were put into service. When a new model needed to be developed, he tried to keep the operations and weapon systems as close to the original as possible. This helped keep the need for retraining to a minimum. The ships were so well-built there were several still operational that were over a thousand years old. Many of the Rygonian allies, like the Kalowians, purchased DREX for their own fleets. It was the most popular extraterrestrial ship in their quadrant.

Renee decided to staff two of the DREX for operational purposes fully. The third would be manned with a pilot and copilot and carry all of their gear and equipment. In addition to herself on DREX-14 was High Colonel Strom; High Lieutenant Frank Rock, a navigations officer who knew the Keplen system very well; and Sergeant Janice Teller, weapons expert. On the other operational DREX, in addition to the pilot, copilot, and quartermaster sergeant, there was Lieutenant Joe Fox, who was the medical officer.

Dawn was barely breaking when Renee walked onto the upper flight deck. It was the highest vantage point in all of Baltica City. It was set up as four runways, arranged in a square around the top of the city. In case of emergencies, there was a collapsible deck that could be moved into place over the open center to help shield the city during an attack. Most commercial and everyday flight activity took place on the north and east runways, whereas the south and west were saved for the military and government to use.

Her three DREX were standing by, waiting to embark on their journey. Renee had always felt a kinship with her aircraft. To her, they were living beings that performed the tasks she and her fellow pilots demanded of them without question. Around the crafts, Renee could see the crews completing last-minute preparations. As she approached, Lieutenant Fox came up and saluted her.

"Good morning, Lieutenant," Renee said. "How are we looking?"

He cleared his throat. "Things are going as planned, Colonel. We should be leaving right on schedule."

"Thank you, Lieutenant Fox."

Renee couldn't help but think how much Joe Fox looked like his brother, Byron. Memories of times not too far in the past crept into her mind and she had to push them aside. *You can't fix the past, Renee, but you can save the future*, she thought.

That was when High Colonel Strom came up beside her. "You ready to go find the beloved Dr. Troy Harlow?"

She chuckled. "You know, if we find them both and everything turns out peachy, Dia is going to adore you for saving Troy."

He laughed. "I bet you'll get more of the credit."

Renee gestured to the crews working to get the ships ready. "Actually, knowing her, she would give them the credit."

Dominic just smiled.

CHAPTER 28
THE PRICE OF POWER

O scar Strom was getting worried about the knowledge others had in his involvement in Troy's affairs. Throughout the years, he'd helped Troy try to tame and control the EIP, but they were never able to until Dia. He'd never forget the day the pulse hit her.

***

Oscar heard a very loud bang, almost like that of an explosion, from down the hall. Knowing it was Troy's lab, he ran down there as fast as he could. The scene he entered into was like nothing he could've ever imagined.

Dia was lying on the floor about ten feet from where Troy's desk had been. She was conscious but confused. Troy was blown against the floor-to-ceiling windows, completely bewildered. The desk had been blown to pieces, smoldering with a green flame.

In horror, Oscar asked, "What the hell happened?"

Troy slowly shook his head, trying to clear the perplexity. He said quietly, "I think we figured it out, Oscar."

"Figured *what* out?"

Troy's eyes slowly panned over to Dia, who was still lying on the floor. She said, "Was that the project you're working on? What happened to me?" There was an air of fear in her voice.

Oscar hurried over and helped his sister up and into a chair. He tried to help Troy next, but the doctor waved him away. "It's fine. I think I'll stay here for a while."

Dia asked her husband again, with more agitation, "What just happened, Troy? Why do I feel like I have electricity flowing through my veins?"

The fire suppression systems belatedly triggered, and a large amount of sand dropped out of compartments in the ceiling. For the most part, the sand stayed within the area of the desk, but Dia was close enough to get a direct hit and was knocked out of her chair.

Both Oscar and Troy stifled laughter and went to her aid. When she stood up, her already mussed-up hair was full of sand, with more stuck to the sweat on her face and neck. Her perfectly pressed uniform was singed and sandy. She looked like she'd fought a fire-breathing sand monster and lost.

Troy hugged his wife and said, "I'm sorry, my love, you're having a shitty day, aren't you?"

Instead of hugging him back, she mumbled into his chest, "Are you going to tell me what the fuck just happened, or do I need to ask four times?"

Troy let her go and explained, "This was an experiment that was part of the project Oscar and I have been working on for some time. But something went wrong, and the power surge released too soon, hitting you."

What were you doing that made this happen, Troy? Oscar thought.

Dia started to pull out her braid and brush the sand from her hair. She contemplated what Troy had said and asked, "I thought you said nobody has been able to handle the power surge. Am I, so far? I don't know what I should be feeling."

Troy and Oscar were both having mixed feelings about the possibility that Dia had just become a carrier for the EIP, since she was *not* the person they wanted to have this happen to.

Suddenly, there was pounding on the door and three men from the fire brigade came running into Troy's lab. The captain seemed shocked as the three high-ranking officials were standing around as if nothing had happened. Well, at least Troy and Oscar were; Dia was a mess.

Troy stepped toward them with his hands raised and said, "Gentlemen, this was just a small lab incident. As you can see, the sand took out any flames and it just needs to be cleaned up. We can handle that."

The captain nervously replied, "Doctor, we need to make sure the area is safe for everyone. That no harmful materials are released into the city. It's protocol for any incident that takes place in a lab environment." The funny thing about that was Troy wrote the protocol.

Dia stepped toward her husband and whispered, "Let them do their jobs. The more you resist, the more you look like you're hiding the fact that something horrible just happened. Which I'm hoping, for my sake, didn't."

Troy got a good look at Dia's face for the first time. He leaned in close and stared at her eyes. She backed up and asked, "What is it?"

Troy turned back to the firefighters. "You're right; please take care of what you need to do. I believe the fire is out, but my desk and its contents were damaged." He glanced back at Dia and Oscar. "Let's go somewhere else, and… clean up."

"My lab," Oscar offered.

In silence, they all walked down the hall together. Dia was still trying to get the sand out of her hair when they entered Oscar's office. Troy quickly locked the door and said to Oscar, "Turn off all the lights and close the blinds."

Confused, Oscar asked, "Are you okay, Troy?"

Troy cast a hard look at his wife's face. "I'm fine, but I think we may have an explanation for why she's having that electricity feeling."

Dia didn't say anything as Oscar darkened the room. Troy pointed to a mirror on the wall and said, "When it gets all the way dark, my love, see for yourself."

As Oscar turned the last blind down, the room began to glow with a pale green light. They all stared in astonishment at Dia. She was dimly surrounded by the same green flame that destroyed the desk. She took a few steps closer to the mirror and was amazed by the faint differences in her appearance. Her hair had a light glow that painted it almost blonde. A strange yellow mist trailed from the corner of her eyes and down the sides of her face, and her fingertips were glowing white as well. But the most curious part of all were her eyes. They were usually a medium-brown color. But now, there was a bright-green, jewel-like line that circled the outer rim of her irises.

She took a few deep breaths and asked, "Is this going to hurt me, Troy?"

Oscar was still by the bank of windows and could barely make out Troy in the dark. His best friend was quiet for a moment before he finally said, "I don't know, Dia. I really have no idea."

***

Hindsight being what it was, Oscar wished he'd talked Troy out of moving forward with testing instead of trying to find a way to get the EIP out of his sister. But all three of them were seduced by the power. Dia was a powerful leader and skilled fighter before, but as she learned what she could do, she became more and more formidable. That was what made Troy and Oscar work with her as much as they could.

Troy's goal was always to create the ultimate weapon, to protect the people of Rygone. Unfortunately, they hadn't realized what that would mean once he achieved that objective.

And now they were gone.

CHAPTER 29
BITE THE BULLET

Veronica smiled widely. "I'm glad you finally gave in, Dr. Harlow."

Troy looked at her from across the desk. "Well, you said my life would get better around here if I did, so here I am."

Veronica studied his face. She knew he was up to something, but she wouldn't pass up on the chance to get him into her bed. She stood up and slowly walked around the desk, stopping in front of his chair. He watched her intently and didn't change his expression one bit. She leaned down and whispered, "Prove it."

Troy didn't move or say anything for a long moment. Finally, Veronica asked, "Well?"

He leaned forward and placed his hand on the inside of her left ankle, under her dress. Without breaking eye contact with her, he slid his hand slowly up her leg. She watched him closely, wondering how much of a lie it really was. As he reached her thigh, he moved slower, still staring up at her. He had already moved past where Veronica thought he would bluff, so to stop him, she grabbed him by the shirt and pulled him up. She kissed his lips hard.

That was the first time Troy flinched, but it wasn't enough for her to notice. "Was I moving too fast for you?" he asked quietly when they separated.

"No, not at all, but this is not the place to do such things. The Coronians have eyes everywhere."

Troy scoffed. "I'm sure they're in your room as well. Where do you know of that there are no cameras? And besides, why would they care if we have sex?" Troy only said it that way to make sure she admitted out loud that was what she wanted to do.

"They wouldn't care," Veronica said, "I just don't want them to watch."

"Whatever. I guess I'm ready to go back to my cell. I thought this would be easier." *I love being an asshole to her*, he thought.

In a panic, Veronica cried, "No! We can do this here! I just—I mean, I just…"

Troy was surprised to see her flustered. She must've really thought he'd never give in. Not that he was. He just needed to get into her office, and what better way was there than that? He sat on the edge of the desk and started spinning a pen around in circles. "I guess I'll wait, then. I can't believe it's me waiting on you."

Veronica stepped in front of him. Her face had gone soft, and she appeared legitimately sad. She took his hand and placed it against her cheek. "Did you have any feelings for me, Troy? At all?"

Troy didn't play into her need for sympathy and withdrew his hand. "No. I've told you before, you were a means to an end. And if I remember correctly, you were the one who pursued me. I was just weak."

Anger flashed across her face, just as it had back then, and she slapped him hard. Troy was expecting it and had braced himself. He shook his head and wiped a hand across his mouth. "My wife, in all of the hundreds of thousands of years we've been married, has never raised a hand to me," he said. "And I haven't to her. You don't have any class, Veronica."

Troy knew one of several things would happen then, but no matter what, they would lead him to either the lab or his cell. She screamed in frustration, "You asshole! You never intended to make love to me! What the fuck did you really want, Troy Harlow?"

With a shrug, Troy answered, "A break from the monotony, I guess."

That time she punched him, knocking him to the floor. He wanted to get up and fight back, but it wasn't a part of his plan. If he continued to vex her, he may wind up in the cesspool or sandpit. He stayed on the ground and waited for her next move. She stared down at him, her eyes full of both anger and sadness.

"I wanted to believe you would want me again. But you're still the same arrogant narcissist from the Breger Dunes." She turned to get a guard but paused to say, "You were right, though. You were weak back then. Thanks to *her*."

Veronica screamed for the guards to take Troy back to his cell, to his elation. He got to his feet before they could drag him away. Troy glanced over his shoulder as they walked out the door and saw Veronica staring at them from the corner of the room. He wondered what brought such a beautiful, smart Florian to that level. He shook his head. Who cared? She was a traitor.

The guards shoved him back into his cell. One of them barked, "No dinner."

They slammed the door and left. Wow, Troy had hit the jackpot today. He vexed Veronica, avoided dinner, and successfully procured the last item he needed to finish his work. Troy lay down on his "bed," facing the wall, like he always did.

Earlier that morning, when Veronica had come into the lab to watch him toil, he'd noticed she was wearing a dress with Hoiltle metal sewn into the fabric. Hoiltle metal was very difficult to find because it was an actual living thing, like a plant. Having it in a dress was a huge luxury, but it had much better applications in the lab. Perfect for what Troy needed.

He knew she wouldn't refuse him if he made even a slight effort to indulge her appetite for him, so he'd told the guard he needed to see her in private. Within minutes, he was led into her office. He was able to pull a piece of the wire from her dress when he was tracing his hand up her leg. When she slapped him, he put it in his mouth for safekeeping as he wiped his face. Then, he insulted her enough to be kicked out.

It went well. Which meant something would probably happen tomorrow to fuck everything up.

INTERLUDE
BATTLE OF THE BREGER DUNES

FIFTY YEARS EARLIER

War raged on Rygone. A war that threatened to bring the entire civilization to its knees. General Dia Harlow was the commanding general in charge of the defense of the planet's people against a little-known race of mortal refugees called the Waleetrs.

What the Waleetrs lacked in technology and numbers, they made up for in tenacity.

For decades before the full-blown conflict started, the Waleetrs had been trying to occupy many of the villages on the more rural, distant side of Rygone. A place called the Breger Dunes. The area was actually not made up of dunes, but mostly farmland and the massive Plato Swamp, which provided a living for many residents, as the waters were abundant with fish and other wildlife.

After several unsuccessful attempts to create a stronghold, the Waleetrs received assistance from an unknown source and didn't think twice about where it came from. With their new backing, they were able to take the Rygonians by surprise, and the minor skirmishes turned into an all-out war.

For the first half of a year, the Florian Army struggled to keep their enemy from taking over land and villages, creating a humanitarian crisis. A rearguard was established with a Field Command Center and a well-equipped field hospital. There were also refugee camps set up around the hospital to try and accommodate the citizens who were being displaced. The Waleetrs' way of fighting used innocent people as bait and collateral shields to keep the advanced weapons and airships from firing upon them. On many occasions, General Harlow argued with Chancellor Pottle to release more ground operations to get closer to their enemy, but he always refused. He didn't want to put too many of the regular Army soldiers into harm's way. Unfortunately, their enemy was evolving their ground-to-air offensive, and Dia was losing valuable craft and air crews on a regular basis.

General Harlow dealt with the hand she was given. On occasion, when the fighting in a particular area was too much for the DREX crews, she sent in secret corps soldiers against the chancellor's orders. Almost all of those missions were successful in routing an enemy stronghold out of a particular area. However, once the chancellor heard of her insubordination, General Harlow was reprimanded, but he never removed her from her command. She was certain he was adding up her insurrections to deal with after the conflict was finished. Time in the Ice Lake was going to be in her future.

During a particularly bad battle, four DREX fighters were shot down by crude rockets. All of the crews were either killed or captured. Three of the pilots, who were Hanner-Florians, were filmed being tortured and killed. The Waleetrs tracked down the pilots' families and sent the videos to them before they even knew their loved ones were missing. None of the bodies were ever recovered.

Dia returned to the capital, Baltica City, and held a special ceremony for those lives lost. She also insisted on a private meeting with the chancellor. She informed him she was going to temporarily turn over full control to General Toni Smith while she took command of flight operations. Although the chancellor was far from thrilled, he accepted her request, and Dia spent over a year fighting on the front lines, only returning to the rear when absolutely necessary.

The lack of her presence resulted in an unspoken rift between General Harlow and her husband.

Dr. Troy Harlow was the chief doctor in the field hospital. In addition to controlling the day-to-day operations, he was responsible for much of the patient care. His attention was pulled from one issue to the next constantly. Dr. Harlow enjoyed the challenge at first, but as the conflict progressed with no signs of stopping, even his spirit was breaking.

The field hospital was a refuge for people far and wide. Even citizens outside the war zone flocked there because they knew the treatment was much better than the clinics in their villages. Dr. Harlow was also the head of Health and Science for the Rygonian government. So, he tried as hard as he could to get proper doctors, nurses, and supplies to the people in outlying areas, but with the war demanding his constant attention, he was neglecting those clinics.

Dr. Harlow's eclectic nature and occasionally abrasive attitude caused him to have a revolving door of assistants. When he was fixated on something, he'd block out everything around him and get lost in his work. So far, all of the nurses assigned to him had requested to be transferred out of his service.

Until Maria Granby.

Toward the abrupt end of the war, Troy Harlow was assigned a Community Florian nurse named Maria Granby. She had long, shiny blonde hair, crystal-clear blue eyes, and a dazzling smile that could melt the hardest of hearts. Troy typically didn't look at other women, as he considered himself very loyal to his wife of almost eight hundred thousand years. However, Dia was rarely with him since taking over flight operations on the front lines. At times, Dia had to set him aside for her work due to the great responsibility she had to the people they served as he did for her on occasion. Unfortunately, this time, he was uncommonly lonely and despondent due to the struggle of war.

With Maria there, he couldn't help but notice how overpowering her presence was. She was always right by his side, ready to please at a moment's notice. She was never intimidated by him, and the combination of Troy struggling with his personal feelings toward Dia plus Maria's relentless pursuit to satisfy him brought Troy problems he'd never had before. He thought about her all the time, even though he knew it was wrong. He even felt as if she was there on purpose, to tempt and distract him.

One fateful morning, Dr. Harlow and his faithful assistant were treating new patients when a mother and son came in from a village not far from the border of Plato Swamp. They both presented with what appeared to be chemical burns, and their mucus membranes were very irritated. The mother, who was a mortal Gorman, had worse injuries than her Hanner-Florian son.

Troy walked into the small treatment room, where they were sharing a gurney. They were both wearing paper gowns, and their clothes were in a pile in the corner. He approached the side of the bed and said, "Hello, I'm Dr. Troy Harlow. What brings you here today?"

The mother was apprehensive but spoke quietly. "This morning, my son was playing on the fishing pier in our village and fell off. He didn't seem hurt at first, but he started screaming in pain after being in the water for only a few moments. I ran in after him, and by the time we were both out, our skin was on fire and these lesions started to appear."

Troy asked her to confirm, "This pier is over Plato Swamp, correct? The north portion?"

She nodded.

After putting on a glove, Troy touched the boy's arm, over the top of a burn. The boy immediately flinched. The sores on their skin were oozing puss already. He asked the mother, "How long ago did this happen? How long was he in the water, and how long were you?"

"Uh, it happened this morning, maybe three hours ago. He was in the water for less than five minutes, and I was only in there to pull him out, so maybe one or two."

Troy looked over at the clothes, perplexed. He went and picked up her jacket, then the boy's shirt. He was getting nervous about the potential cause of their injuries. The clothes were degraded and had been eaten away considerably. Without looking away, he asked, "Do you know if anyone else was in the swamp in the past few days? Did you see any dead animals or fish?"

Troy wasn't thinking about how his line of questions was affecting a mother who was comforting her child with injuries nobody could explain. When she didn't answer right away, Maria stepped in and said with a sweet voice, "It's okay. Dr. Harlow just needs as much information as possible to rule out causes of your injuries."

The woman nodded and smiled, even though her eyes were filling with tears. "I'm not sure about either."

Dr. Harlow sat down beside the bed. "I think you could possibly have a bacterial infection caused by a bloom of Drake's algae. This would explain the clothes and why nobody else has been affected. I'll take some blood and tissue samples from you both, and we'll find you a more comfortable room. I don't want you to leave until we know for sure."

Dr. Harlow allowed his bedside manner to soften. Smiling at the boy, he asked, "What's your name?"

"Josh."

"What's your favorite candy, Josh?"

The boy smiled. "Red flavor of anything."

Troy genuinely laughed. "Red flavor!" he said. "I'm stealing that." He reached into the pocket of his lab coat and pulled out two suckers. He handed them to Josh. "Only one is red; the other is purple. That's all I've got."

Josh took the candy. "Thank you, Dr. Harlow," he said.

Troy and Maria collected the samples themselves. Usually, Troy would have Maria send them to the main lab, but his concern was so great he took the samples straight to his private lab.

Maria dutifully followed him and asked, "Doctor, what do you think it is?"

"When you were in nursing school, did you take the class on crypto substances?" he asked.

"No," she answered. "I wanted to, but I didn't have the time."

"I think those two have come into contact with a crypto substance called Pexallun."

Surprised, she asked, "You know that after examining them for less than ten minutes?"

Troy didn't reply as they walked into the lab. She watched as he started working immediately. He was tenacious about everything, but a problem like that really sent him into his mind. She helped him when he let her, and when they got to the point that they were waiting on the results of the tests, they took a moment to relax.

It was at moments like this that their time together became more than a working relationship. While sitting next to each other at the lab table, Maria reached over and placed her hand on top of his. Troy looked over at her, mystified. She was smiling warmly at him. His heart raced, and he wanted to pull away, but her touch felt so good. Becoming even bolder, she tried to kiss him.

Troy backed away, surprised, and blurted out, "What are you doing?"

Undaunted, Maria said, "Trying to please you, Dr. Harlow. I know you hurt."

He stared at her for a moment. His brain was telling him to yell at her and make her leave. Unfortunately, his body and heart were failing him, and he stumbled over his words. "But—I'm married. My wife could come in at any moment."

She gave him a sly smile. "I've been here for a few weeks, and there hasn't been one mention of General Harlow coming back from the front. I can feel how sad you are, and I hurt for you. You need someone to be there for you no matter what, Troy. Unfortunately, no matter how much I'm sure your wife wants to be, she's not. But I am."

Troy's will finally broke, and he kissed her longingly. It didn't take long before they were frantically undressing and making their way to the small bed in the back of the lab that he would share with his wife when she was visiting. But Dia wasn't there, Maria was. And like she'd said, she wanted to please him no matter what.

Sadly, their timing worked against the tests he was running for the boy and his mother. The blood samples were somehow ruined before a result had been reached, and the tissue samples were inconclusive. Dr. Harlow tried to get new samples, but the two had been released. Troy researched the records from the hospital and surrounding clinics. No other cases had presented themselves, convincing him it actually was the algae bloom.

Unfortunately, the boy and his mother had been unknowing test subjects for poison in the swamp water. They hadn't been released. Their medical records were doctored, and when they died in the night, their bodies were immediately taken to the incinerator.

Troy and Maria's behavior continued. Dr. Harlow had hoped the affection he was receiving from Maria would ease his lonely, stressed heart, but it was making things worse. While they were in the act of making love, Troy was euphoric. Maria was new, exciting, and willing. It'd been so long since he'd known another woman, and it angered him to think he enjoyed her so much. Maria felt what they were doing was exciting and dangerous. If someone from the hospital found out, it'd definitely be the end of her time with him. If Dia found them, neither wanted to know how she would handle it, especially Troy.

One day, while performing rounds, Dr. Harlow was summoned to the FCC by General Smith. He went without Maria, much to her disappointment. When he arrived in Smith's office, he saw three Waleetr soldiers on their knees with their hands bound behind their backs. Two of them were beaten heavily but seemed okay. The third had a large head wound and was swaying back and forth, barely able to stay conscious.

"What's this about?" Troy asked.

Smith said, "About an hour ago, these three and about six of their comrades attempted a covert attack on this facility."

Troy was pretty sure the other six were in his morgue. "What do you need from me?"

Smith pointed at the wounded soldier. "He was their leader. I need him healthy enough to give me information."

Troy knew once he treated the man, he'd probably be tortured and perhaps killed. But Troy wasn't a fighter; he was a healer. He began examining the injured man, only for the two reasonably healthy Waleetr soldiers to start yelling at him not to touch their leader. Smith had some of his guards move them into a cell on the first level of the facility. That was the last Troy ever saw of them.

The injured man didn't respond to stimuli, and his pupils were completely dilated. Troy stood up and said to General Smith, "This man's head injury isn't going to get better, even if we sent him to Baltica City, which I wouldn't allow you to do. You're better off getting information from the other two."

General Smith swore. "You're absolutely sure?" he asked. "He can't get better?"

Troy shook his head. "He'll just be a waste of resources in the hospital until he expires."

Toni caught Troy off guard and shot the Waleetr in the head with his thermal pistol, killing him. "There, now he won't be a waste of your resources, Doctor."

Troy was frozen in shock for a moment before he yelled, "What the hell, General?"

Getting into Dr. Harlow's face, he growled, "This piece of shit coward killed two of my best guards. He deserved a much more painful death."

Troy examined the general's stoic face, then asked boldly, "Has General Harlow been informed of this attack?"

"The fighting at the front has been so intense I barely get to talk to the commander," he replied evenly, "General Harlow will be back here for a command briefing in six days. We'll talk to her about it then."

Troy felt that maybe she should be told immediately, but that wasn't his decision. "Okay, I agree. I guess."

Smith gave Dr. Harlow a beaming smile. "Thank you, Doctor! I must go speak to this man's comrades. You can go back to work with your new assistant. She seems so… attentive."

General Smith couldn't tell because of Troy's color-changing lenses, but his eyes darkened with anger. "She is. Nurse Granby does her job well. And only that."

Toni nodded. "Of course, Doctor, I meant no disrespect. Excuse me."

He turned and exited the office, leaving Troy there alone with the dead Waleetr.

***

Three days later, General Dia Harlow and her copilot, Captain Byron Fox, woke up and got ready to run some recon flights over Plato Swamp, which bordered Breger Dunes, for rumored outposts. During their flight, they were fired upon by an embedded company of Waleetr artillery soldiers hiding within a village, surrounded by civilians. Their craft was damaged beyond safe combat operational capacity, so they had to retreat to the maintenance hangar for repairs. Dia was secretly happy, as she hadn't seen her husband in weeks. Sometimes, she felt guilty for her pilots. They were assigned to her unit for six months at a time, and they usually only got to see their families once during that period. Her occasional visits to the rear—and therefore, Troy—were more than they received. She justified this because of her stress and rank. Either way, she was happy to go back and see him.

Dia hadn't slept for three days, so when she arrived, she wanted to go straight to Troy's lab at the hospital. However, a corporal in a ground transport was waiting in the maintenance bay for her. She was taken directly to the FCC to see General Smith.

Exhausted, Dia walked through the hectic first floor. She was still in her flight suit, but there was no mistaking the silver Kalow warrior ribbon in her braid. Therefore, the entire floor was called to attention as she tried to make her way to the stairs quietly. She dismissed them all and called for them to carry on, but it was enough for Smith to notice her arrival.

He stood at the top of the steps as Dia walked up the stairs. She glared at him and said, "What was so urgent that I was brought directly here after landing? I've had a really shitty day, General."

Smith gave her a sympathetic nod. "I understand, General Harlow. I'm glad you're okay. How's your copilot?"

"He's fine," she answered. "Unfortunately, we lost another DREX today. Luckily, the pilots we recovered were uninjured."

"That's good to hear."

"So, Smith, why am I here instead of looking for a shower and a hot meal?"

Toni cleared his throat and gestured toward his office door. Dia walked past him and plopped down in a chair in front of his desk. She couldn't help but notice the poorly cleaned bloodstain on the floor. She thought, *What the hell has he been doing while I've been gone?*

General Smith sat behind his desk and said, "Three days ago, the Waleetrs attacked this facility. That bloodstain you were just examining is from their leader. According to Dr. Harlow, his head injury was too severe, and he wasn't thrilled about having to care for him here at the hospital."

She just stared at him with her wicked, up-turned brown eyes. Even Smith, who was rarely daunted, felt uncomfortable.

He continued, "We interrogated the other two survivors, but they didn't give us any information worth knowing."

Dia was still glaring at him. Finally, she quietly asked, "So they were testing us?"

He nodded. "Yes, that's what we suspect as well. What for, I'm not sure."

"Weakness. And they succeeded in their mission. They know we're at our wit's end, and a small group was able to get past us in our most secure location. What changes in security have you made, General Smith?"

"More guards were posted in the sensitive areas they breeched and anywhere else we can think of. More secure identification procedures. You didn't notice, mainly because you're the most recognized face on the planet right now."

That didn't make Dia feel very good. "They're going to come again, but you won't expect where they come from. These assholes have known too long how to push our buttons, and now they're breaching the rear." Dia stood up to leave, only to turn back and ask, "Why wasn't I told?"

Smith said, "We determined the fighting at the front was intense enough that we should wait until you came in for the command briefing. Unfortunately, you're here early."

Dia wanted to be angry, but she was too exhausted to do anything. She turned to leave again. "Very well. I'll see you in the morning, General."

***

Dia made her way to the hospital building where the living quarters for the doctors were. She went down the surprisingly empty hall to Troy's lab. The door was open, so she knew he had to be in there.

Peeking around the corner, she saw him standing at his lab table, looking into a microscope. His hair was a mess, and he was singing to himself, which told her he was working on something very important.

As she walked in, Troy heard her. He spun around and started to say, "That was fast—"

"Hello, Troy," she said quietly.

Troy said nothing but went and pulled her into a tight embrace. Dia tried to hold him back and say she was dirty, but he didn't care. She relented and buried her face in his chest. They stood quietly, holding each other until Dia heard another person come in behind them.

"Dr. Harlow, they did—oh, hello."

Dia let go of her husband and turned around to see a pretty, blonde Florian nurse. She smiled brightly at Dia. "Hello! You must be General Harlow! Dr. Harlow has told me so much about you."

Dia gave a slight smile and thought, *No, he hasn't.*

Her intuition was screaming at her about what could possibly be going on between those two, but her logic knew better. Dia trusted Troy; she was just tired and hungry. She said, "I'm probably interrupting your work. I'm going to take a shower and try to find some dinner."

The pretty girl said, "I'd be happy to get you some dinner while you get cleaned up, General. I'd be honored!"

Dia wanted to puke, and Troy wanted to faint. He was standing behind Dia, so she missed the alarmed look he sent Maria. Smiling wearily, Dia said, "Thank you, but that won't be—"

Maria interrupted the commanding general of the Florian Army. "No worries! They had *hago* barley soup, homemade bread, and berry cake for dinner. I'll be right back!"

Dia and Troy stood quiet for a moment after Maria ran out the door toward the hospital mess. "Eager, that one," Dia said.

Troy nodded. "Yes. You could say that."

Dia turned and looked hard at her husband's face. "I do need a shower. I'll be back."

Dia and Troy had thought about each other constantly, about how painful it was to be apart, yet now that they were in front of each other, they didn't know what to do.

She walked into the small room she and Troy shared to grab some clean clothes and her shower items. She went down the hall to the doctors' locker room and took her first hot shower in weeks. General Harlow let the water wash the stress of the day away. It seemed like so long since she and Fox were nearly shot down just that morning.

After she was done, Dia returned to the room and was hit by the smell of soup. Her appetite returned after days of not eating well, and she went into the lab. Nobody was there, not even Troy, but the soup was sitting on the table. A pang of jealousy hit Dia, but she pushed it aside. She hadn't had a hot meal in what felt like years, and the bland soup and stale bread were like a four-course meal at the royal palace on Kalow 9.

After Maria brought back Dia's dinner, Troy released her for the night. Troy could see the jealousy on Maria's face. She said, "I felt like because she wasn't here, she didn't really exist. Now she's back. Where do I stand now?"

At that moment, Troy realized Maria had more feelings for him than he did for her. In fact, he had no real feelings for Maria at all. It was horrible of him, but she was just a means to an end, and now Dia was back, whose attention he really desired. What a mess.

He said, "I told you before—this was never for keeps."

"But she'll go back out to the front, won't—"

Troy only stared at her, reaffirming that he didn't desire her affection anymore.

Maria straightened up. "Dr. Harlow. I'll see you in the morning, then?"

Troy nodded. She turned and left the room. He hated himself.

Shaking off that feeling, he decided to hit the showers as well. When he got back to the room, Dia was there, finishing her meal. He went into the lab and sat next to her.

"I'd offer you some soup," she said, "but I was starving and ate it. Bowl and all."

He laughed. "I'm glad you ate so well."

Troy studied her face. Her large, brown eyes were slightly sunk in. It was uncommon for Florians to lose weight, but she had. Dia was still beautiful, but the burden of the war was weighing down on her hard. As if she could read his mind, she said, "We'd both need a vacation to look our best, Dr. Harlow."

He glanced down sheepishly. "It just hurts to see you so drawn, but I guess I feel the same."

The small smile that had formed on her lips faded. "I need to sleep."

He nodded, and they both went to the small room in the back of the lab. As they climbed into bed, Dia turned and embraced Troy tightly and buried her face in his chest. He wrapped his arms around her as she began to weep. She cried for a few minutes until finally, she whispered, "Troy, I'm losing this war. Everyone is looking to me for answers that I don't have. I've never had this happen before."

He didn't know what to say. He held her closer and tried to think of what to do when Troy felt her lips on his neck. He tensed at first, but the feel of her against him quickly turned to desire. He brought her face to his and kissed her deeply. They both reacted desperately to each other and made passionate love. For Dia, it was a much-needed release of stress and fear. For Troy, even with his deep guilt, it reiterated how much he still loved and wanted her. That night, they slept in each other's arms, resting better than they had in months.

Unfortunately, the next day would change their lives forever.

***

When Troy woke up the next morning, he rubbed his eyes and saw Dia standing in front of the mirror on the other side of the room. She was already wearing her dress uniform, save for the outer jacket. She was putting the finishing touches on her makeup and hair when he said, "Early start?"

Startled, she turned back. "Yeah, I need to get as much done while I'm here before the command briefing."

He just stared at her. She put her brush down and sat down on the edge of the bed next to him, so Troy laid his head in her lap. "You aren't losing the war, Dia. They're ahead of us because they know your hands are tied by the fucking chancellor. The tides will turn, and you'll be the one to do it."

Dia ran her hands through his thick, soft hair. "Maybe. But I still feel like such a failure. You shouldn't be so busy treating the citizens and soldiers I can't save."

Troy sat up and pulled her to him. He pressed his forehead against hers. "Never call yourself a failure again. You're not a failure in any way, Dia."

Dia leaned in and kissed him gently on the lips, intending to leave right after, but she couldn't. Troy placed his hand on the back of her neck and deepened their kiss. She grabbed his hair and gasped as he kissed down her neck. Troy was still undressed, so Dia reached under the covers and ran her hand up his thigh. Wrapping his arms around her, he pulled her on top of him. She took her top off as Troy began to undo her belt.

Suddenly, she stopped and pulled back, breathless. "I can't, Troy. I have to go to the FCC."

He pulled her back down and breathed against her neck. "You weren't even supposed to be here today," he said. "Take the day off, stay with me. Please, stay here. I miss you so much."

Dia's heart shattered, listening to Troy plead with her. She wanted to stay and spend the whole day in that little room, in that little bed. But she couldn't; she had to use her time there to get information on the enemy; to get ahead on the front lines and end the war. That way, they could return to their large bedroom and lay in their large, soft bed with the smooth sheets and feather pillows.

She sat back up again and pulled her hand out from under the sheet. "Troy, I want to. I want nothing more than to be with you. Pulling away is killing me. But I have to go to work so we can go home together and make love in our own bed," she said.

Dia could see he was holding back tears. Taking his face in her hands, she whispered desperately, "Troy. Baby, I don't know what to do."

"You need to go to work, my love," he said, attempting to sound strong. "I know you have to; I just miss you."

She ran her hand through his hair again. "Leaving is absolutely painful, but I'm here for a few days at least. I'll be back here tonight."

Troy knew that wasn't going to happen. She usually stayed in the FCC for half of the nights she was in the rear. As desperate as she was to get a handle on the war, she wouldn't be back tonight. He made her promise anyway.

Dia kissed Troy on the forehead and finished getting dressed before leaving his lab for the FCC.

***

Both Troy and Dia had trying days. He had a deluge of patients from a clinic in Ratlebo that was damaged in a skirmish. Dia fought relentlessly over the channels with all of the outlying commanders and the chancellor. They all wanted ground troops, but the chancellor was still being stubborn. A day she'd hoped would be promising turned into more bureaucratic bullshit. If a commanding general wasn't allowed to command, then what good was she?

The sun was getting low on the horizon, and Troy needed a break from everything, especially his melancholy assistant, who was jealous that he'd slept with his wife last night. Troy kept having to tell himself he didn't cheat on Maria with Dia. He didn't understand what his mind was doing anymore. When he needed to get away, Troy would go to the roof of the hospital and watch the sunset. That night, when he got to the top of the steps, he was surprised to find Dia already up there.

He came up beside her. "Well, aren't you a sight for sore eyes."

She smiled at him. The golden light from the setting sun shown on her face and made her peach-porcelain skin glow. Curls that had fallen out of her braid waved gently in the breeze. Troy watched the warm smile on her lips fade and her eyes grew wide. Dia, focusing on something over his shoulder, took a step forward. Troy started to turn as he said, "What is it, my love?"

For the rest of eternity, the following events would be burned in his memory forever. Dia grabbed him by his shirt and pushed him to the roof, screaming, "*Get down!*"

Just as they hit the roof, he felt and heard the impact of a bomb close by. In the sky past Dia's shoulder, three unfamiliar gunships flew over the hospital.

Dia pulled him back to his feet and dragged him toward the stairwell. "Get to the hospital bomb shelter!"

Troy stumbled down the stairs behind her, and as they got to the bottom, a bomb hit the rear of the hospital. They were thrown to the floor by the blast, but Dia was back up immediately. She turned to Troy as his head slowly cleared. He said, "I have to help these people. I'll get to the shelter as soon as I can."

Her eyes met his. "Be careful," she said. "I love you."

Troy watched her run out of a hole in the wall toward the maintenance hangars.

He found Maria, and they worked for hours between bombings to try and treat the injured and evacuate as many people as possible. At one point, Troy himself was injured seriously enough to keep him from being able to help for nearly two hours until he healed. Maria pulled him to a corner of what they thought were once the maintenance hangars and stayed with him. Troy looked past the personal feelings troubling him and made sure to let her know how much he appreciated her efforts.

After an entire night of bombings, the morning showed the extent of the damage to the rearguard for the Florian Army. The FCC and maintenance hangars were utterly destroyed. The only survivors were any Florians and a few Hanner-Florians, many of whom were still trapped in the rubble. Even the bomb shelters completely imploded. The back half of the hospital was gone, and the rest of the structure seemed ready to collapse. Troy and Maria were working there, trying to evacuate as many patients and personnel as possible. The refugee camps were a mess, and many were on fire. The enemy attacked everyone and everything without discrimination.

Troy's thoughts strayed to Dia. She'd gone running to the maintenance hangars when they separated, and he didn't know if she was in the rubble or if she'd been able to get out in her DREX.

In the middle of loading a patient into a transport, a corporal who looked on the edge of collapse found him and said, "Dr. Harlow?"

"Yes? Who's asking?"

"General Smith," he said, "He needs you in the FCC bunker."

"As you can see, I'm needed here," Troy snapped.

"He said you'd say that, so I was told to tell you it's about General Harlow."

The color drained from Troy's already pale face. "What about her?" he asked.

The corporal just stared at the doctor, making Troy's mind race. He turned to Maria. "Please keep helping here as much as you can. I'll be back soon."

She nodded with a genuine sense of sympathy. "Yes, Doctor."

When Troy arrived at the bunker, what he learned nearly brought him to his knees. Dia and her copilot Captain Byron Fox did make it to their barely repaired DREX, and they were one of the few to escape the hangar. They'd gone right to work fighting with the strange ships, which led them all out over the swamp.

None of the Florian Army personnel had known what kind of danger they were in. The enemy was anticipating Rygonian pilots would be sent to fight the gunships after the attack on the rear. The enemy drew the fighters away and pushed evacuation transports out over the swamps, which weren't considered as dangerous as they truly were.

The air battle was intense, but General Dia and a few other DREX managed to destroy the gunships, then escort surviving Rygonian transport craft to safety. A few ships crashed into the water and the commanders in the bunker were working hard to get rescue crews out to the swamp.

After destroying the final enemy gunship, Dia and Byron ran one more recon flight over the swamp, and she said, "Okay, let's Jump back to the rear. I need to see the damage."

Byron said, "Aye, General. Engaging Jump Drive now."

He slid his finger across the control panel, but instead of the drive engaging, the entire craft completely shut down. The DREX went into an immediate nosedive toward the murky water, and before Dia could hit the emergency power, they slammed into the swamp's surface. They were nose-down, hanging in their seats. Byron was starting to show his fear, and General Harlow yelled at him, "Keep it together, Fox, we'll be fine! Put on your emergency life support!"

He stuttered, "What about you, ma'am?"

Dia unbuckled from her seat and fell forward onto the instrument panel. She assessed they were definitely sinking. "I'm going to try to get the emergency power going and deploy the beacon. Now put it on!"

Dia climbed up through the middle of their seats toward the emergency beacon embedded in the roof. If it had engaged when they crashed, like it was supposed to, the red emergency lights would have turned on in the cockpit. She made her way to the control panel and tried to open the door, but it was jammed. Her mind began to race, and her thoughts kept going back to sabotage.

As Dia was working, Fox yelled behind her, "General! Look!"

Dia turned around and stumbled into the back of her seat. Over the top of the headrest and out through the front canopy, she was horrified to see the glass *dissolving*. DREX craft were designed to Jump in space under enormous amounts of pressure. That shouldn't have been possible. She didn't have time to swear when the glass cracked and burst, filling the DREX with murky Pexallun-contaminated water.

***

Troy stood motionless in the bunker, having just watched the footage from the onboard camera that managed to record those last moments in Dia's DREX. General Smith said quietly, "I know that was hard for you to watch, Dr. Harlow, but your wife's wasn't the only ship to hit that swamp, and there are widespread reports that there's some kind of acid-like substance destroying everything, even the ships that survived the impact. It's killing or injuring people, and I need your help to figure out what we're up against."

Troy faintly whispered, "Pexallun."

Smith leaned in and asked, "Pexa-what?"

Troy spoke up. "I think the chemical in the water is Pexallun. It's a crypto substance that I studied in medical school. It was only a myth, but I saw a boy and his mother come into the hospital not long ago with burns and lesions I'd never encountered except in mock-up sketches of Pexallun injuries." Troy turned to Smith. "The problem is, if this is indeed the chemical in question, it's said to…"

"Said to what, Doctor?"

Troy choked out, "It's said Pexallun can permanently injury or even kill Florians. We must find a way to get all of the survivors out of that water immediately. Whoever orchestrated this attack did their research and knew exactly where and when to hit us and with what."

Smith nodded. "If you know roughly what this chemical can do, what do we need in order to get to them?" he asked.

Troy's head was spinning, and he didn't know if he could help. "We need to call Dr. Oscar Strom. He's the best engineer in the galaxy, and he'll know the best way to proceed. As a matter of fact, I'll call him now."

Without waiting for a response, Troy called Oscar, his best friend and Dia's younger brother, on his communicator. He explained what was happening and how they needed to get the survivors, if any, out of the water. Oscar had already started to devise a plan when Troy said, "Oscar, I have to tell you something." He hesitated. "Dia's DREX was one of the crashed ships. She's completely submerged, and we already know the canopy was breached."

The line was quiet for a moment before Oscar asked, "If I can get her out, can you save her life?"

Troy choked again. "I don't know," he admitted. "I think she'll live, but I'm not sure if she'll recover fully. We've never faced this before."

With determination in his voice, Oscar said, "I'll be right there."

***

It took seven days to get to Dia's DREX. It was the last ship to be located. With a bit of trial and error, Oscar was able to rig a hovering platform that could fly out over the water with divers and equipment. He also designed special suits to help protect the divers. A fortunate revelation was the half-life of Pexallun was short, and by the third day, they couldn't detect any more in the water, making recovery much easier. They located each ship and recovered what they could. On the first day, they rescued several civilians from a transport who'd been able to stay dry. Fortunately, they only suffered minor injuries.

On day two, they located the other DREX that crashed into the water and were relieved that the Florian pilot survived with relatively minor Pexallun-related injuries. Unfortunately, his copilot was a mortal Gorman and had been killed instantly when the DREX crashed.

Two more transports and one enemy craft were recovered over the next five days. By that time, even the Hanner-Florians were dead. The total casualties from the Pexallun numbered 218, with one injured and two still unknown.

On the morning of the seventh day, Troy was out on the edge of the swamp, refusing to leave until Dia was found. After the recovery at the hospital wound down, Maria came out to the field to help. Troy tried as hard as he could to ignore her, but her presence was both comforting and vexing.

They were standing next to the platform as it was being readied to head out to where they thought DREX-1 crashed. Maria asked, like she did every hour, "Can I get you anything, Doctor?"

Troy shook his head. "No, thank you," he said. "I don't have much of an appetite for anything." *Except for a forbidden hug I shouldn't even be thinking about*, he thought.

The divers were ready, and the platform went out over the water. Oscar came up next to Troy and placed a cup of strong tea in his hand. "You're a doctor; take care of yourself and drink this."

Troy didn't argue and started drinking the tea. Maria wanted to laugh at the way Dr. Strom spoke to Troy but kept it to herself. She wasn't invested in the sadness of the situation; she had her own agenda. She hoped it involved General Dia Harlow being the first known Florian to die.

It wasn't long after the platform went out that a commotion came from the water. They were too far away to see what was going on, but they speculated that a diver made it to the ship. Troy's communicator chirped; it was the dive commander. Troy put him on speaker. "What did you find?"

"We found DREX-1," the dive commander said. "The ship is in very rough shape, incredibly deteriorated, sir. We're getting ready to go inside to make our recovery."

Troy cleared his throat. "Rescue, you mean."

There was a long pause before the commander said, "Of course, Doctor. Our rescue."

The line went dead, and Troy realized how foolish he sounded. Was it going to be a rescue or a recovery?

They all waited by the side of the water for what seemed like hours when another commotion came down from the dive site, only that time, there was much more desperation. After about ten minutes, the platform came back to the shore at a high rate of speed. When it arrived, Troy didn't even give the craft a moment to stop, instead using his long legs and agile body to leap up.

To his horror, they'd indeed found Dia, and she wasn't in good shape.

Troy had already arranged for a medical DREX to be waiting while survivors were found, so when he grabbed his wife's limp body and jumped off the platform to run toward the ship, everyone knew how dire things were. Oscar and Maria were already on board, and the moment Troy stepped inside, the pilot, Dia's best friend, Colonel Renee Connor, closed the door and engaged the Jump Drive, taking them directly to the landing pad on top of the Baltica City General Hospital.

Troy leaped off the ship, not even knowing what he was going to do and almost ran into his father, Dr. John Harlow. Troy stopped in his tracks. "Dad?"

John Harlow said, "Yep, now let's go. The moment I heard they found the ship, I set up the trauma suite to throw everything we can at her."

Father and son raced through the hospital door and directly to the open suite doors. There was already a team of nurses ready to help as much as they could.

Troy laid Dia's cold body on the Water Table his father had set up. John designed the metal table to treat Florians with external injuries and illnesses. The patient was washed with a constant flow of healing glacier water and medications.

The Pexallun had dissolved all of her clothes and boots, leaving her completely nude. It had also eaten away almost all of her long, curly brown hair. Although Dia's usual smooth peach-porcelain skin remained intact, it was marred with giant, red boils. Troy shined a light into her closed eyes. They were bloodshot and swollen. He began taking accurate vitals; her heart rate was only fifty bpm—typical for a Florian in a survival stasis. Her blood pressure was erratic, which concerned him, but he thought maybe it was because her body was trying to wake back up. She wasn't breathing, which wasn't that troubling, but Troy and John realized she was choking when she began having convulsions.

John turned Dia on her side and tried to purge her throat, but it was full of debris. They were forced to put a hose down her nose and feed water into her airway to unblock it all. John and Troy knew it was an excruciating procedure, but because she couldn't breathe, they couldn't administer pain medication.

After hours of purging her system and flooding her with laxatives and antibiotics, Dia began to stabilize. She was breathing with the help of a tube, but her body was at least trying to take over on its own. With the help of his father, Troy learned how to treat her better with each passing day. Neither of them had ever had a Florian patient present with such horrific injuries. But it was promising that Dia was responding to the treatments and her own body. She was healing, and both doctors were convinced that, although slowly, she'd make a full recovery.

On the fourth day, John was monitoring her vitals when she finally opened her eyes. She tried to speak, but her throat was still too raw. John turned away from the monitors and saw her staring at him. He smiled broadly.

"Hello, dear Dia!" he said as he sat down in a chair at her bedside so he could look closely at her face. Quieter, he told her, "I've never been so scared, kiddo."

Dia couldn't say anything, but a tear ran down her cheek. John dabbed it with a tissue. John and Jeannie adored their daughter-in-law. They'd known Dia since the day she was born and had always considered her a surrogate daughter before Troy and her finally married. When John saw how seriously she was injured, he felt like he was going to lose a piece of himself.

He stood up and said, "I'll go get Troy. He's been anxiously waiting for you to wake up."

John went to Troy's office, where he found his son with his head on the desk, fast asleep. He gently shook his shoulder. "Dia's awake."

Troy sleepily jumped up and practically ran to Dia's room. She was lying on the bed dozing, but when he sat down in the chair, her red, irritated eyes opened. Troy could tell she couldn't see well, so he said, "Hi, my love. Can you see me?"

Dia nodded. She swallowed hard and pointed at her throat. Troy stood up and grabbed a small device bearing a face mask that fit over her mouth and nose. The tank held aerosol formulas of the medications she was being treated with. It kept her from having to swallow, and Florian skin didn't allow for needles. He programmed a medicine that would soothe her throat and nasal passages without pain medication. Troy placed the face mask on her and said, "On three, take as deep a breath as you can."

Dia only managed a shallow breath, but it was enough to administer the medication. Troy had invented the device, along with many other medical advancements. Besides being a brilliant doctor, he was also an avid inventor.

For the next few hours, Dia drifted in and out of sleep. When she was awake, she tried to engage with Troy or John, but she was still far from being fully aware. Troy was just glad she was steadily progressing toward full recovery.

***

Since arriving from the swamp, Maria had continued to follow Troy faithfully. Troy was beginning to suspect Maria wanted Dia to die, and she would be right there to comfort him. He knew it was time to end things once and for all. The day after Dia woke up, Troy requested Maria to be promoted and assigned to a ward of her own choosing. He took her into his office, and as she was going to shut the door, he quietly said, "No, please leave it open."

Troy cleared his throat. "Maria, I think it's time that we put this behind us. I'm a married man, and I want to stay that way. I truly love my wife, and she needs me now more than ever. I've put in for a promotion for you because of the incredible work you did when the hospital was attacked. You'll get to choose whatever unit you want."

"Just not yours."

"Just not mine," he echoed. "I'm sorry for ever allowing this to happen."

Holding back tears, she said, "So am I." Maria grabbed her jacket and was about to leave when she turned around. "You know, I fell in love with you, Troy. Did you have any love for me?"

Maria Granby was beautiful, attentive, willing, and tended to his every want and desire. He swallowed and answered, "I appreciate everything you are and what we shared for that brief moment, but I'm sorry. I can't return your feelings."

She nodded. "Goodbye, Dr. Harlow."

Troy and Maria, as Veronica, would meet again, but the terms would be much different.

***

Dia continued to improve with her treatments and therapy, both physical and psychological. After a month, she left the hospital and continued treatment at home. The Florian Army insisted she take an open-ended leave of absence to be sure to heal completely. Troy thought she'd insist on returning after her physical injuries were fully recovered, but Dia was perfectly happy staying home.

She read a lot of books and began cooking more. She even remodeled their closet, much to Troy's annoyance. However, he was proud of her for planning and working on something constructive.

Dia left their apartment only to go to therapy, work out with Renee, or visit their family. Dia was a larger-than-life figure for the Rygonians, and she was hiding from everyone and everything. Troy and her therapist were concerned, but Dia insisted she just needed time away from reality to get her head on straight.

Within six months, she was in better physical shape than she'd been before the war started. There were absolutely no signs left of the Pexallun's effect on her body.

There had been an emergency election for the commanding general when Dia was placed on her leave of absence. Several brigadier generals came forward to vie for her job. She was happy to back General Toni Smith, who won by a large margin.

One afternoon, ten months into her recovery, Dia was surprised when he showed up at their apartment. "General, how nice of you to visit! What can I do for you?"

Smith looked around the place and was surprised at how small it was. "When they told me you lived on the thirty-eighth floor, I was expecting the south wing," he said. "You have a lovely home, but—"

She laughed and cut him off to say, "You were expecting us to live in the newer part of the city."

He nodded. "Yeah, I did."

"It's small, but Troy and I don't need much. We don't have kids, and half the time, we're working. He's lived here since before we got married, and we never left."

Dia picked up her data pad and opened the blinds on all the floor-to-ceiling windows. The apartment was bathed in warm sunlight, and the view was unobstructed all the way to the mountains and grass plains beyond the city.

Smith smiled. "Yep, I wouldn't move either. Anyway, I came to ask you to do something for me—well, for everyone."

"What is it?"

"As you know, the anniversary of the attack on the FCC and hospital is in two months. The grounds are almost completely returned to a natural state and will be preserved as such. We're dedicating a memorial to those who were lost."

"That sounds wonderful, Toni," Dia said.

He continued, "I want you to do the dedication."

She shook her head. "I don't know... I don't think I can."

He stepped toward her and pleaded, "Dia, your people miss you. Even if you only came back for this, they just want to see you're okay. Most of the pilots in your unit haven't even seen you since the days before your crash. You've always told us we're like a family; your family misses you, General."

Dia swallowed hard, but she'd known this day would come. She stared down at her hands for a long moment, then back up at him. She asked quietly, "Can I talk to Troy and let you know tomorrow?"

Smith gave her his flashiest smile and said, "Of course! Take a couple days if you need to. We just want to know you're still okay, Dia."

"Thank you, Toni."

He gave her a quick hug. "I look forward to hearing from you."

As Smith turned toward the door, it opened, and Troy walked in from work. They nearly ran into each other. Toni clapped his hand down on Troy's shoulder. "Heya, Doc! I stopped by to see the general and now here you are! Bye!"

Smith didn't wait for Troy to respond and walked out of the apartment, whistling.

Dia laughed. "He's so strange sometimes."

Troy nodded and said, "Agreed. Why'd he stop by?"

Dia stopped smiling and said, "He wants me to dedicate the monument at Breger Dunes. He told me how much my people miss me."

Troy and Dia spent the rest of the evening talking about the prospect of her doing the dedication. After much deliberation, she agreed, but only if he, her brothers, and Renee were with her.

***

On the morning of the dedication, Troy found Dia on the small balcony just off their living room. He went out and gently kissed her on the back of the head. "Good morning, my love," he said softly.

She didn't respond and Troy realized she was quietly sobbing. He put his arms around her waist and pulled her to him. Her sobs became harder, and she tried to speak, "I—I ca-can't, Tr-troy."

She turned around and buried herself against him. He held her tight and felt her body rock as she sobbed. He wanted to tell her it was okay and that everything would be all right, but he knew better. Even Troy felt tears fill his eyes, knowing what today was. Finally, he said quietly, "You don't have to go, Dia. Nobody will fault you if you don't."

She was quiet for a moment, then stepped back. Her face was splotchy and tear-stained, and her brown eyes were red from crying. "I have to go. I have to go because they can't. The men and women who lost their lives carrying out my orders can't be there. I have to be there for them."

He kissed her on the forehead. "Well then, let's spend the rest of the time before we go enjoying what we still have because of their sacrifices."

For the rest of the day, Troy and Dia stayed together in their tiny apartment. They laughed, they talked, they ate junk food, they made love—they simply enjoyed each other.

The ceremony was going to start at 4:30 p.m., and Dia's best friend, Renee, was going to pick them up in her DREX and fly them to the site.

Troy was in his dress uniform for the Health and Science Division, and she couldn't help but notice how handsome he was. His dark hair was combed perfectly in a gentle wave on his head. He wasn't wearing his color-changing lenses yet, so his eyes were still dark and mysterious. Troy had a very expressive face, and he was giving her a side smile that she didn't acknowledge right away. He was tall and thin, but the way he moved and carried himself was so smooth and sexy. Watching him, knowing that he was hers, made her feel better.

Dia took a shower and changed into her own dress uniform, including her silver warrior ribbon and Morai dagger. She didn't feel like she deserved to wear any of it, especially the ribbon, but she agreed. Her shoulders no longer bore the three gold stars of the commanding general. Instead, she wore one for a brigadier general, which she was able to retain since it wasn't an elected position. She dried and smoothed the curls on the top of her head and braided her hair with the ribbon. Her name tag and flight wings were pinned above her right breast. She put on her newly shined boots and slid the dagger into the inner part of her left boot; only the very top of the pommel was visible.

She sighed. "I feel horrible for saying this, but I can't wait until this is all over."

Troy kissed her forehead and said, "Neither can I. Come on, Renee will be here soon."

As they walked into the living room, the doorbell rang. Renee and Dia's brothers, Dominic and Oscar, appeared on their living room monitor. Troy opened the door, and Dominic went straight to his sister and gave her a huge hug, picking her up in the process. "How goes it, sis?" he asked.

"It goes, brother, it goes."

As they left the apartment, Dia took a small bundle wrapped in a silk cloth off the kitchen counter. The five companions made their way to the flight deck. Dia was nervous because she hadn't flown since the crash, and now they were going back to the same place. Troy knew he wasn't supposed to while she was in uniform, but he took her hand and squeezed it. He smiled warmly at her. She thanked the stars he was there.

They made their way onto Renee's DREX, where her copilot, Captain James Ramsay, was getting the ship ready to go. Dia shook his hand. "It's good to see you, Captain."

He gave her a modest smile. "It hasn't been the same without you, ma'am."

She smiled; she still longed for the comradery she had with her people. They all sat and strapped into their seats. Renee began preflight checks as James closed the bay door. Dia began to panic internally. She knew they were going to Jump rather than fly, but the vague memories of being trapped, unable to move, in her ship for seven days in that swamp hit her like a brick. Dia grabbed Troy's leg and squeezed so hard he almost cried out in pain.

"It's okay, my love," he said.

Dia nodded. "I know, I'm sorry. It's just—the last time I was in one of these…"

Renee heard her friend struggling and made the Jump almost before any of them knew what happened.

The six of them stepped out of the ship, with Dia coming out last, behind Troy. Several battalions of soldiers were in line at parade rest, but when she stepped out, they were called to attention and saluted her. Thousands of soldiers and pilots were acknowledging her at that moment. It was something she'd taken for granted for so very long, but now it was terrifying.

Dia stepped up next to the elected Commanding General Toni Smith on the podium. He used to really irritate Dia, but he was now a very impressive leader, and she was proud of him.

Despite the thousands of people out on that plain, it was utterly silent. The Breger Dunes and Plato Swamp, especially the locations of the FCC and field hospital, were hallowed battlegrounds. There would never be any land development in that area again. The remains of the destroyed buildings and surrounding camps were gone entirely. It was now just a quiet field on the edge of a sea of grass.

A gentle breeze brushed against Dia's face as she scanned the land around them. The sun would be setting soon in the west and the air was warm and sweet with *ablesun*. She took a deep breath and began the speech she'd been working on for a month.

She talked about the heroes who fought, the innocents who were lost, and the brave doctors and nurses who put the pieces back together. Troy had watched Dia for the past year hide in their home, avoiding what she was meant to do. He was one of the doctors who put her back together, and he'd rather she stayed home and read books and cooked dinner than fly DREX fighters across the galaxy. But that wasn't who she truly was. Dia was a warrior, and seeing her talk to her fellow warriors—each and every one of them was hanging on to her every word—made him so proud of her.

Dia's speech was perfect. Once she finished, General Smith and Dia went to a small table with a silver box. He explained it was a memory totem that would be buried to honor the fallen. Inside the box were different items that families of fallen civilians and soldiers had donated. Dia took the small bundle she brought from the apartment and unwrapped the contents. Everyone watched as she pulled a Morai dagger, one of the highest honors bestowed upon a member of the Rygonian Army, from its sheath. As she gently placed the priceless weapon into the box, she said, "I inter this dagger in honor of Captain Byron Fox. May his soul be at rest."

The whole crowd repeated, "May his soul be at rest."

Dia and Toni finished filling the box and put it in a pre-dug hole. The hole was filled with concrete to deter any thieves. The plaque honoring the battlefield with a list of civilians and hospital personnel lost in the hospital attack was dedicated by Troy. Once the ceremony was complete, there was a reception for all involved. Dia, Troy, and Toni walked among the soldiers and families and talked about the past, the present, and the future. None of those people had seen Dia since the crash, and they knew she'd been seriously injured. Seeing her up and as good as new made the question of when she was returning to work fly off everyone's lips. She'd smile and said she wasn't sure yet, but she hoped it'd be soon. They didn't have to know it was all up to her.

The sun had completely set when the transport crafts to take the troops back to the base began arriving. Dia and her crew were ready to get back to Baltica City, so they returned to Renee's DREX after saying their goodbyes. Troy watched his wife as they got ready to take off. She seemed much less nervous this time. They Jumped back to the hangar and bid Renee and Dia's brothers goodbye. Troy and Dia entered their apartment, and both began to get ready for bed.

Dia took down her hair, removed her makeup, and put on a silk nightgown. Troy was in his office when he saw her standing in the doorway. Her hair was wild, and the white silk nightgown did very little to hide the shape of her body. "Are you almost finished?" she asked.

Troy leaned back and said, "Come here."

Dia slowly walked around the desk, next to his chair. Troy took her hand and pulled her in front of him. He looked into her eyes and said, "I'm so proud of you, Dia. I know you've been scared about today for weeks, but you did so much better than I ever imagined you would."

She whispered, "Thank you for being there. I know you dedicated the hospital plaque, but I'm glad you were there for me, too."

Troy leaned forward and put his arms around her. Dia ran her fingers through his hair, and they stayed like that for a few minutes until Troy stood up. He took her by the hand and said, "Come on, let's go to bed."

They went into their room, where Dia climbed under the covers and watched Troy take off his shirt. In the dim moonlight coming from the window, she could see him effortlessly move about. He finally joined her and pulled her to him. Troy kissed her deeply. Dia rolled herself on top of him and slipped off her gown. Troy smiled at her in the moonlight, knowing her shell was breaking. Dia and Troy spent the next few hours making love. When the moon Erran 1 was high in the sky and spilling pale white light across their bed, they lay in each other's arms. Troy traced his fingers along the outside of Dia's arm while she caressed his chest.

After a long while, Dia said, "Troy, I need to tell you something."

Troy tensed for a moment and looked down at her, even though she was still looking at his chest. "What is it, my love?"

Dia was quiet, like she was scared to speak, until she finally said, "I'm going to go back to work."

A small part of him didn't want her to go, but he knew she needed to. "I'm glad, Dia, I really am. I want you to be happy, and quite frankly, this damn place needs you."

She laughed, and he continued, "But you have to make me one promise."

Dia grew serious. "Of course."

"You still have to make that malson fruitcake at least once a month. That thing is so good."

Dia burst into laughter again. "Deal!"

They exchanged small talk for a few more minutes before Troy finally slipped off to sleep, followed closely by his wife.

That night, all seemed right with the universe.

Until Troy dreamt of Maria for the first time since she vanished from Rygone.

CHAPTER 30
THE CORONIANS LIVE HERE?

R enee Connor and her team Jumped to the outer edge of the Keplen Solar System. She and Dominic reviewed the plans they'd made before leaving and settled on exploring. They decided they'd try looking for Dr. Harlow on the planet Rol first.

The three DREX entered the turbulent atmosphere under cloak. Lieutenant Fox found a safe canyon system they could land in to begin a more thorough search for a viable Coronian outpost.

Once they landed, Renee was concerned about them leaving their ships due to the stormy weather. The atmosphere on Rol was thicker than Rygone but not too much for any of the species on her team to handle. Still, she wanted the weather to be as hospitable as possible before subjecting her crew to the elements.

She pulled up the weather monitoring system on her ship and saw they were right below a significant windstorm that wouldn't dissipate until nightfall, which would be the best time for them to start their ground search. She said over the secure radio, "This storm will be around for a few hours. Eat and rest; we search after nightfall."

"Aye, Colonel," said Captain Dober on DREX-15.

Renee leaned back in her seat and put her foot up on the console, watching the dirt being swirled around her craft by the wind. She tried to ignore Dominic staring at the side of her head, but it became too difficult to act oblivious.

"What?" she asked him.

He gave her a big smile. "We should expand the ship. It's really cramped in here right now."

She looked back out of the front and shook her head. "No, we can't. We need to stay in flight-ready mode in case we have to leave immediately."

Renee could feel the desire of the two other members of her crew wanting the same thing. She could tell they'd never been in serious combat situations. While in enemy territory, DREX ships were not to be expanded out to their more comfortable shelter positions. If there was an emergency, the ship would take longer to get back into combat-ready flight mode.

She explained, "For our safety, you have to stay uncomfortable. If something happens and we have to leave, a DREX can't Jump from an expanded stance, and it takes time to retract. You can get out and stretch in a few hours, Colonel."

Dominic pouted. "It looks like I have to talk to my brother about a design flaw in his precious DREX."

Tugging on a loose thread on her knee, Renee smiled and said, "Trust me, that's the number one complaint he gets from everyone. That and the bathroom."

All three crafts fell quiet. A few team members drifted off to sleep or wrote letters on their data pads. Renee and Dominic continued to stare out the front canopy of their craft.

After a long time, Dominic said quietly, "I've never sat in one of these so long without moving. It gives me the creeps."

Renee looked over at him, curious. "Why?"

Dominic was quiet for a moment. "You remember when Dia crashed in the swamp, right?"

Lieutenant Rock and Sergeant Teller had heard the stories about General Harlow and Lieutenant Byron Fox crashing into Plato Swamp, which had been poisoned with Pexallun, but not from anybody close to them. Now Dia's brother *and* Fox's brother were on this mission.

"Remember, Colonel, Lieutenant Fox's brother was with her and didn't make it," Renee said.

He nodded. "I know. I just think about it a lot. When the glass broke, and the ship filled with water? So creepy."

"Okay, that's enough talking about that."

Just then, Lieutenant Rock pointed out the front screen and asked, "Did anyone else see that?"

Renee and Dominic perked up and looked intently out the glass but didn't see anything. "What did you see, Rock?" she asked.

As if on cue, it seemed like the entire canyon floor began to rise before dropping. All three DREX shook violently, and Renee screamed over the radio, "Jump beyond atmosphere!"

But Renee wasn't aware that DREX-16 had defied her orders and expanded. Therefore, when they tried to Jump, the craft was seriously damaged and barely able to keep altitude in outer space. Renee had them all Jump back onto a different part of the planet to assess DREX-16's damage.

They landed in a plain, but there was bad weather there, too. Renee knew they had no choice but to go outside and assess DREX-16's condition.

She armed herself with a long-range thermal rifle, thermal pistol, and field knife. Sergeant Teller made sure the rest of the team had the best weapons suited to them that she could find. The crew from DREX-14 exited their craft first.

When the ramp lowered, Renee and Dominic were hit with a terrible smell, which wasn't coming from the planet. DREX-16 had landed next to them when they returned to the surface. Much of the expanding mechanism was twisted and torn on one side of the craft. Renee was concerned. She'd seen damage from an expanded Jump hundreds of times, but it was never that bad.

Renee slowly looked up and scanned the surrounding land. As her gaze came back around, it met with Dominic's, and they both realized they were in real trouble. Renee said very quietly, "We need to get the people and whatever gear we can off DREX-16 and get the hell off this planet. Troy Harlow isn't here."

Just then, a loud screech came from behind them. They turned and could see figures moving in the grass toward them, but the wind from the storm was giving the creatures cover. Their shiny ships were like beacons, so she pulled the emergency latch on the ramp of DREX-16 and started yelling orders for everyone to evacuate. The pilot would go on 14 and the copilot on 15. They grabbed a few cases of gear for each ship, and just as they were getting ready to load the other DREX, a creature the size of a small child with long front arms and short legs dropped out of nowhere onto the copilot of DREX-16. The creature bit down on his arm and leaped away before anyone could react. The copilot began screaming, and Lieutenant Fox pulled him into DREX-15. They closed the door, cloaking the craft.

Renee and her team managed to make it into 14 and cloak before hundreds of the creatures descended upon them. Luckily, when a DREX was cloaked, it was completely invisible and untraceable. You could be standing on top of the craft and not know it. They all sat breathlessly in their seats, watching the creatures screech and claw at themselves in confusion.

Lieutenant Fox came over the radio. "Uh, Colonel, we have a problem!"

Renee brought up the feed from DREX-15 on their canopy. She could see the crew trying to subdue the copilot of 16. He seemed to have turned into a rabid animal from the bite. He was attacking and trying to bite the other crew members, and the confined space made it hard for them to stay away.

"Sedate him, Fox!" Renee yelled.

"I have! Six times! I need permission to—"

Dominic cut him off. "It's him or all of you! Use lethal force, damnit!"

Without hesitation, Captain Dober stabbed him in the chest. The copilot from DREX-16 quickly expired and the chaos in 15 calmed.

All nine crew members across both ships were quiet for a moment. Renee tried to collect her thoughts. *This is only the first planet and you've lost a DREX, half your gear, and a crew member. Good job, Renee. Dia would be so proud.*

Dominic said, "Is this what we can expect from the rest of this planet? I can't imagine even the Coronians would be willing to deal with shit like this."

Rock was scanning his data pad, examining readings the ships had taken while being there. "The rest of this planet is worse," he said. "The canyons we were in earlier were probably the best location for a base, but we saw how that went. I agree, Colonel. I don't believe the Coronians are here. And even if they were, I don't think there's enough stability for Dr. Harlow to do any sort of work."

Still fixated on the frenzied animals running around outside their ships, Renee asked, "What's the next planet on the list?"

Dominic looked at the display on the canopy. "Bodeolr. I know there's intelligent life there; it's probably the best choice for Coronians. But it's also dangerous just for that reason."

Renee sat up. "Okay, everyone, get ready to leave. We'll Jump to the outer atmosphere of the planet Bodeolr, where we'll determine the location of our landing."

As her crews were getting strapped into their seats, Renee set up a self-destruct on DREX-16. Hopefully, that would take out a bunch of those creatures in honor of their copilot.

Renee set the coordinates and asked, "Captain Dober, are you ready?"

"Yes, ma'am, waiting on your command."

"Then let's get the fuck out of here."

She slid her hand up the control screen and their DREX Jumped and reappeared in the outer atmosphere of the planet Bodeolr. DREX-15 appeared right next to her, and she turned to Dominic, almost relieved. "Now what?" she asked.

CHAPTER 31
BEACON

S ince his escapade of leading Veronica on and stealing the strand of Hoiltle from her dress, she had surprisingly left him alone. Actually, nobody seemed to be bothering him much, which was deeply concerning. Troy was brought to his lab each morning and he "worked" all day, keeping to himself. Sometimes Veronica would come into the observation area and watch him, but she never said anything, and neither did he.

Troy had successfully created a diversionary system to appear as though he was making progress on the EIP, but nobody had checked it yet. The real work he was doing was using the Hoiltle wire to create a small beacon that could be mounted under his workstation. It would broadcast a signal across at least a few solar systems without, hopefully, being discovered by the Coronians. The signal could only be detected in space by certain radio frequencies that were rarely monitored, except by the Rygonians. All he needed to do was make the signal unique, so if a Rygonian transport or Florian Army DREX were within range, they would know it was him.

At last, Troy finished the beacon but still had no idea what signal he would use. When he was getting ready to be taken back to his cell,

Veronica finally came down from the observation area and approached him. Troy was nervous about how she would react to him, and honestly, to keep her from discovering his side project, he might have to bend to her will. *Please don't let it come to that. Please*, he thought.

Veronica waved off the Coronian guards and said to Troy, "Let's go sit down."

He cleared his throat and nodded.

There was a small table that he used for staging, and they both pulled up chairs across from each other. She stared at him so intensely he had to avert his eyes. Finally, he asked quietly, "What was it you wanted to talk about, Veronica?"

She didn't respond at first, only picked up a piece of wood sitting on the table and drew small circles in a pile of dust. Eventually, she asked, "Troy, have I told you why I'm here?"

Troy was surprised by the question. "No, but I've been wondering why you betrayed your people."

She gave a loud, harsh laugh. "Me, betraying my people? That's funny. How about my people betraying us? The Community Florians."

Troy was confused but curious and asked, "How were the Community Florians betrayed?"

She leaned forward. "Many thousands of years ago, my parents left Baltica City and settled in Ratlebo, thinking they were going to have a simpler life than what they experienced in Baltica. And they did; my parents are still happy in Ratlebo. But when I was born, I wanted to return to the city once I was old enough. But that can't happen, can it, Troy?"

"Baltica City was closed off to new residents almost a million years ago," he said. "Why didn't you go to Baltica North or South? They're beautiful, larger, and much more advanced than Baltica City. And open to anyone who wants to live there."

She stared at him for a long moment, thinking of the perfect words. Finally, she said, "If you were given the chance for a much nicer, larger, and newer home in North or South, would you move out of Baltica City?"

Troy used to live in Baltica South with his second wife. He hated it. But he sure as hell wasn't going to tell Veronica that. Especially since he requested to move back to Baltica City after his divorce, and he was given special privilege because he was a Harlow. "Probably not. I work there. Well, I did, at least."

Shaking her head, she continued, "I would be willing to bet if you worked in North or South, you would still stay in Baltica City. Am I right?"

He crossed his arms in irritation. "What's this about? Why are you upset that you couldn't move into Baltica? It's mostly a sterile, government environment housing the main hospital, parliament, and scientific research facilities. It's also highly guarded; even the residents don't get to move freely, except in the mezzanine."

"You don't get it, Troy; it isn't so much the city but who was grandfathered in to live there. The Stroms, the Harlows, the Smiths. All of the high-ranking Florian families who have, for the most part, controlled our lives since the Second Generation. All of you sit on your high thrones and say you're doing what you can to give every Rygonian a chance at voicing their opinions, but it doesn't make it too far outside of those walls."

That was an ongoing theme on their planet, all the way back to when the First and Second Generations began accepting refugees onto Rygone. She was right that his family, the Stroms, the Smiths, and others influenced the government, medical, and research fields on the planet. But it was the first time Troy had heard of a Florian betraying their people simply because they wanted to live in Baltica City. It didn't add up.

He quietly asked, "What did you want to achieve by living in Baltica City? Were you interested in government service? Or did you just like the view of the Raltain Mountains?"

Troy saw her eyes light up with anger—usually, she would strike him, but she refrained. Instead, she took a deep breath and said, "The government needs new blood. It needs more Community and Hanner-Florians to come in from the outlying areas, run for office, and retake some of the residences in Baltica City. That way, they are just as close as the old blood."

"But they already do come in and run for and win offices! Our last chancellor was a mortal refugee, and she wasn't the first. It isn't going to be handed to you, Veronica." He sighed and asked, "Why do you think the Coronians will get you where you want to be on Rygone? What did you do when you left?"

She shrugged. "I was working with them well before the war, Troy. They were smart and studied the several other past attempts to overthrow the Rygonian government, and knew they had to be patient. The process of weakening parliament was slow but well underway. The leadership here, under Premier Baxelhoff, decided certain Florians needed to be eliminated in order to make a good run at invasion. Your wife was at the top of that list."

Troy furrowed his brow at her and growled, "Eliminate Dia."

"Oh, yes. That powerful, capable, irritating bitch had to go. That's where the war with the Walteers came into play. Coupled with the Pexallun, and even being able to persuade the chancellor to never allow for ground troops to be sent. All orchestrated by the Coronians, with me at the helm. Unfortunately, the hell the Coronians went through to find and use the Pexallun didn't work. She lived."

What she said was painful, but the devastating part was how nonchalant she was about telling him. She was proud of the fact that tens of thousands of Rygonians died at *her* hands. "Do you know how many Rygonians *died* because of you?"

"Many. Now, come on." She grabbed his hand and led him into a hall he hadn't seen before. His mind was racing, wondering where she was taking him and what she had planned, especially after everything she just told him. They stopped in front of a door, which she opened. She stood in the doorway and motioned him in.

Troy cautiously stepped into the room and was surprised by what he saw. It was a small bedroom with a regular bed, complete with a pillow and blankets. There was also a desk that had a lamp, paper, and pens.

Veronica pointed to a door at the back of the room. "That's a private bathroom complete with a shower, soap, towels, fresh clothes, and pajamas. You'll get three meals a day, and it'll be the same as the food I eat. This room is right next to the lab, so you'll be able to go back and forth without needing an escort. You'll still be woken up and expected to maintain the same work schedule, but you can move more freely."

Next, she pointed to the four corners of the room. "You're being watched at every angle; don't pull any shit, and you can stay here rather than that rat hole being scrubbed down by those ever-so-willing Coronian women."

Troy was a bit speechless, but he saw through her shit and said, "Thank you, Veronica. I appreciate your generosity."

She smiled and stepped up to him. She was taller than Dia, but not by much. "Don't get me wrong, Dr. Harlow. After the other day, and now with this, I'm still certain you'll eventually come to me for comfort and love, exactly like you did before. You just haven't accepted it yet."

With that, she turned and left him standing in his new room. A room that scared the shit out of him.

**

The first night Troy got to sleep in a relatively comfortable bed brought him a strange dream.

He was walking on a beach, but it wasn't just any beach. It was the beach Dia married Prince Ben on so many years ago on Kalow 9. There wasn't any ceremony now, but he recognized the sand and water when he saw it. He was wearing a loose white shirt and pants, much like all Kalowians wore. He walked slowly, feeling the warmth of the sun and listening to the waves crash against the shore.

After a long while, Troy spotted what looked like a person walking toward him. As he got closer, he saw it was a woman, but not just any woman. It was Dia. She was dressed in a loose white dress with a black, red, and gold sash tied around her waist. He wanted to walk faster, even run, but he could only move at the same slow pace.

Finally, they were standing in front of each other. Her hair was pinned back at the sides, and the rest of her curls were blowing in the sea breeze. Her face was sad, and her brow was furrowed.

Troy said, "Hello, my love."

"Hello, Troy. Sit down." Dia gestured behind him where a bench had appeared. He sat down, not taking his eyes off of her. She slowly stepped forward and straddled his legs, settling on his lap and bringing her face close to his. Troy was startled, but the feeling was indescribable. He was dreaming, but she felt so real.

He took her face in his hands and asked, "How are you, Dia? How are we here?"

She didn't say anything for a minute. She pressed her forehead against his and traced her fingers along the features of his face. Finally, she said, "Do you remember the last time we were both on this beach at the same time?"

Troy swallowed hard. "Yes. You and Prince Ben's wedding. It was so long ago."

With her forehead still pressed against his, she nodded. "I admit, I miss him sometimes," she said. "That marriage cemented a million-year alliance between Rygone and Kalow 9 that's still strong today. We know everything about each other."

Still confused, Troy asked, "Dia, why are we here?"

She lifted his face, locking her gaze onto his dark eyes. "We're nowhere. This is a dream, but if you truly listen, it is the key."

Troy said, frustrated, "My love, the key to what?"

Dia kissed him long and hard. He wrapped his arms around her and held her as tight as he could, not wanting to let go. She buried her face in the side of his neck and whispered, "I miss you. Find me."

***

Troy startled awake. He sat up for a moment and considered his dream before it could become jumbled in his mind.

He whispered to himself, "If you truly listen, the dream is the key."

Troy began to smile. Hopefully, his camera crew didn't notice.

Kalow 9 and the alliance with the Rygonians was the key.

Troy could broadcast a small portion of the Kalowian anthem on his beacon, and any Rygonian ship in the vicinity would hear it. He just had to hope they understood.

"Thank you, my love. I will find you soon."

CHAPTER 32
TONIGHT'S GOTTA BE THE NIGHT

Heather watched Brody intently as he made different adjustments to his equipment. Since she really didn't understand what he was doing, she looked out the window. They were in the same office that the team ran into when the warehouse collapsed, and she was amazed by the progress they were making outside. She felt guilty about what had happened, but she hadn't chosen to be in that situation, and when she knew there was danger, she got the others to safety. She had a propensity to want to protect others.

What did I do at home? she thought.

Brody said, "Okay, I think I'm ready. I need you to put your hand in this glove, then try to pull the power from this box." He gave her a small, black glove that had the fingers cut out. There were also copper wires poking out of the sides.

Heather was skeptical after the other day. "Are you sure? I don't know if I trust you yet, Brody."

That hurt the tech genius. He said, "I'm trying as best as I can. I realize things are rushed, but we need to get these tests done before Major Mallory decides to send you to some deep, dark government hole."

Heather thought back to the hole she made when she landed and wondered if it would be like that. If so, she didn't want to go. "Okay." Heather put the glove on and placed her hand on the box. She immediately felt the energy reaching out to her. "Now what?" she asked.

Brody asked, "Can you absorb anything you feel?"

Heather pulled the power into her hand, and Brody had to hold in his excitement as she began to glow with green fire. When she realized he was really close to her, she said, "You need to step back."

Dejected, Brody did as she ordered and watched as she slowly pulled all of the electricity from the generator box. Once the box was dead, she asked again, "Now what?"

"Put it back, if you can."

Heather pushed the power back, wondering why they were wasting time on such mundane tasks when she saw it. As the electricity returned to the box, there was still a pale green glow on her hand surrounding the glove. She examined it closely and asked, "Why did it do that?"

Brody, who was visibly excited, said, "That's residue attached to the glove. Can you feel it in your body, like you need to release it?"

Heather realized she didn't. There was definitely energy in the glove, and she felt it in her hand, but she didn't feel the tickling sensation that usually made her need to release it. Somehow, Patterson had managed to stabilize a component of her power with the glove. "How is this possible?"

He said, "I don't quite know yet, but I'm working on—"

Carl hurried in and snapped, "Shut your damn mouth, kid." He stopped in front of Brody and continued, quieter, "Mallory and his cronies are watching this room like a hawk and you're giving them exactly what they want. They're chomping at the bit to take her outta here, now."

"Sorry, boss, it's just exciting for me to work with such… art and beauty."

Heather looked at him inquisitively and asked, "What does that mean?"

He shook his head. "Never mind, can you absorb the power stored in the glove?"

She stretched her hand out, and the glove turned black again as her body began to glow. Heather giggled as she then pushed the energy back into the glove. "This is fun."

Brody and Carl were both intrigued by her actions but concerned as well. The young technologist turned to Carl. "This is just the tip of the iceberg of what I can do, but we need to leave *now*."

Heather stared Carl dead in the eye like the general none of them had any idea she was and said, "I go nowhere until you and I talk, alone."

Patterson's eyes went wide. "I'll go pack my gear. Let me know what's going on later, okay?" He quickly left the room.

Heather and Carl stood in silence for a moment while he examined her gloved hand, which was still glowing green.

Stupidly, Johnson went to touch her hand, but Heather pulled away. "I don't know if that's a good idea. Who knows what Brody's glove could make this power do."

Carl nodded. "Good point; it's fascinating, though." He gestured for her to sit. "Let's talk."

They sat in chairs next to each other at the desk, with Carl eyeing her hand warily. Noticing his apprehension, she pulled the stored power from the glove and began drawing on the desk with the bright white tip of her finger, using it as a wood burner. Johnson watched in awe as she drew the symbol on the back of her neck onto the desk. The power ran out just as she finished, and she sat back, proud of her work.

Carl laughed. "You're an artist."

Heather smiled brightly, and for some reason, Carl was taken aback. He knew she was beautiful, that she was different. She needed his help, and he needed hers. But for some reason, when she smiled that time, it was almost as if she was human and belonged there. He shook off the strange feeling and said, "Okay, here's the deal, love."

"I told you not to call me that. I don't like 'bitch' either."

He rolled his eyes and said, "Saying 'love' is just something I do! Ask Penny! Maybe it's outdated, but it's part of who I am, Heather. I'm sorry."

She shook her head. "It's actually not personal, Carl. It just feels strange for some reason."

He obliged her—this was a whole new place for her and all—and said, "Okay, Heather. We need to get you out of here tonight."

Heather looked around the room and asked, "Aren't you afraid that the people you don't want to hear you are listening to us?"

Carl smirked. "I took care of the monitoring systems for this room a little bit ago. I didn't tell Brody because he would've kept being stupid with you," he said.

The wheels in Heather's mind began to turn. She'd changed immensely from the timid girl found in the impact crater who knew nothing to a cognizant woman who was getting a grasp on her circumstances. "What's in this for you, Carl? What's my value to you, Brody, and Penny?"

"Freedom," Johnson answered.

She shook her head. "You're going to have to do a lot better than that. Freedom for who and from what?"

Carl was impressed and terrified by how quickly she'd become self-aware and learned about her situation. Most of that was his doing, and he was about to release an incredibly dangerous alien into the world. He only hoped he was right.

He said, "All I can say is it would be freedom for us all, and if all goes to plan, freedom for most of the world."

"So, you want me to be your weapon? Just like Mallory wants me to be his weapon?"

"Essentially, yes."

She shrugged. "At least you're honest. Who are we fighting?"

"That, love, remains to be seen," Carl said. "Brody still needs to get you completely ready, but that work can't be done here. The man is a genius, but he needs resources." Johnson, realizing he called her love again, winced. "Sorry."

Heather shrugged.

"Now, will you cooperate and help us break you out of here in a bit?"

"Yes," Heather said. "Even if I didn't care to help you, I want out. I feel like a caged animal. But only on one condition."

Carl didn't like hearing those words come from her lips. If she felt like a caged animal, what would she do with a taste of freedom? *You have to take your chances, man; this may be your only opportunity*, he thought.

He cleared his throat and asked, "What's your condition?"

"I want my rings back. I was wearing two rings when I was brought in, and they're the only connection I have to my former life. I want them back, please."

Johnson nodded. "Deal. I'm going to take you back to your cell now. If you need to rest, do so. The three of us will come get you when we're ready. Also, I need that glove, just in case."

"What will I need to do once you get me?" she asked.

"Blow shit up, I guess."

***

Heather was waiting in her cell, anxiously wondering what would happen next. She was lying on her new bed with her back to the mirror, staring at the wall. How was she supposed to "blow shit up," as Carl said, if she didn't have any energy to do so? She could pull from the lights but that probably wouldn't be enough. Brody, with his seemingly infinite knowledge of what she could do, would hopefully bring something for her to use. The lack of information made her nervous. Maybe leaving with Carl, Penny, and Brody was a bad idea. Why wasn't Helen in on this plan? What would happen to them all if they were caught? Did Carl want her to hurt people when they got on the outside? Would they at least bring her a banana?

Just then, Heather heard a faint tapping on the mirror. She turned over, but, of course, she couldn't see anything. She was on her guard anyway and felt as if their plan was about to take place. The Florian sat up on the bed and looked at herself in the mirror. Her hair was pulled back into a neat braid. She was wearing the same gray top and bottoms they gave her every day. They didn't offer much protection from any outside elements. Her shoes were flimsy canvas pull-on slippers—not very good to run in if need be.

Heather approached the mirror, wondering who was behind it at that very moment.

It turned out to be Major Mallory and Helen.

Mallory said, "She still scares me."

"She should," Helen said. "She should scare us all. Brody Patterson already seems to be working on something to harness her potential, and he isn't on our side. We have to be on the lookout for Dr. Johnson, Patterson, and maybe even Singleton to pull something to get her out of here very soon. That woman, or thing, or alien is dangerous to our existence." She walked up to Mallory and rested her head on his shoulder. "I know you want to use her, but I think we need to destroy her."

Jason Mallory gave a harsh laugh. "Did you see what happened in that warehouse? I doubt there's anything in our arsenal that could hurt that thing."

Heather could hear their conversation and was glad she'd learned the language. She wasn't sure how aware Mallory and Helen were of her newfound knowledge, so she said, "No, Major Mallory, you probably don't have anything that can hurt me."

Mallory's jaw dropped, and Helen gasped. Heather could hear that, too, and just smiled and turned around. As she started to walk back to the bed, she felt power coming from the door. Attracted to the strong tendrils of energy, she went and stood in front of it, apprehensive about touching, even though she knew it had to be Carl, Penny, or Brody. Heather glanced back at the mirror for a moment and made her fateful decision.

She slammed both of her hands against the metal and was instantly flooded with powerful energy. "Stand back!" she yelled and kicked the door, sending it flying into the wall across the hall.

Startled, Brody said, "I was going to unlock the door for you!"

In a low, calm voice, she said, "I was sending a message."

***

Once in the hall, Brody shoved another black box with wires into her hand and said, "Hold this until we make it to Penny and Carl. It should give you the energy you need to, you know, gets us out of here." He pointed to the left. "This way. Guards will come out of the door at the end of the hall, but I don't know how many."

Heather silently took the box. She felt another surge of power that replaced what she used kicking down the door, and for the first time, she realized the energy was euphoric. She smiled and knew she was going to enjoy what she was about to do.

She and Brody made it to the end of the hall just as the door burst open and guards came pouring through. They stopped in front of them, blocking the way. Heather paused nonchalantly and told Brody, "Get behind me."

Brody didn't hesitate one bit and stood behind Heather, trying as hard as possible to use her tiny frame to shield his whole body.

"Please move," Heather said to the guards. "We aren't here to hurt anyone."

The commander snapped, "Ma'am, get back into your cell, or we will be forced to fire on you!"

Heather wanted to laugh in his face, but she realized Brody could get hurt. She raised her left hand, let a gentle stream of green flame pulse toward the commander. "Last chance. Move."

He instinctively raised his weapon, like she knew he would, and she wrapped the flame around the barrel, melting the metal instantly. He dropped what was left and quietly ordered, "Fall back."

All of the guards, either reluctantly or thankfully, fell back into the hall beyond, making way for her and Brody to continue. Once they were through the door, Brody said, "Right."

For the most part, they traveled unimpeded through the rest of the complex until they met up with Penny and Carl. He was ready to go, but she looked apprehensive. She stared at Heather, fully powered, just a few feet away.

Heather could tell she was afraid. "Don't worry, if I don't intend to hurt any of them, I'm not going to hurt you."

That really didn't make Penny feel better, but she gave Heather a hesitant smile.

Carl said to Brody, "We got it. We need to get her changed and going in less than three."

"Good."

Heather was confused as Penny said, "Come with me, do you think you can change your clothes when you're… like that?"

Heather shrugged. "Why am I chang—"

Singleton pulled Heather by her arm into a dark corner in one of the hallways. Penny could feel the warmth coming off her, and it scared her to death, but she knew what they were doing was the right thing. She handed Heather some black clothes and a pair of heavy-duty leather boots. "Put these on right now, don't ask questions."

Heather said, "But wh—"

"Don't ask questions!" Penny growled. She immediately felt bad. "I'm so sorry."

Heather just laughed and pulled off her gray top. Throwing it at Penny, she said, "Hold this."

***

Carl and Brody were amazed that Heather got the new clothes on so fast. She was now wearing a tight, black Lycra shirt and pair of pants that Brody had managed to run thin copper wires throughout, a lot like the glove. It was itchy, but Heather felt more in control of the energy than she ever had.

213

"What is this?" she asked, pinching the material.

He hurriedly said, "I'll explain later. We need to go."

Heather stepped out in front of the other three and asked, "Which way?"

"We need to get across a large gymnasium that leads to a side parking lot," Carl answered. "That's where the van is, and we can get out down the farm access road."

Heather said, "Sounds easy; I bet it isn't. Do you have my rings?"

Carl said, "Fuck no—I mean, I have your rings, but fuck no. The gymnasium is where they're keeping the civilian contractors."

"Shit," Brody breathed.

"What?" Heather asked.

Penny pointed back and said, "They found us. We need to go."

Heather started running toward the gym. She had to go slow in order to keep her companions with her, which was irritating but necessary. They made it to the gym door before the guards got to them, but a shot rang out from behind, hitting the wall just above their heads. Penny screamed, and Brody dropped to the ground. Heather and Carl turned and saw Major Mallory pointing a gun at Penny's head.

"That was a warning shot," he said. "The next one won't miss."

He cocked the hammer and Heather lifted her arm, swinging it in an arc in front of Mallory and his guards. A wall of green flame stretched across the ground and rose fifteen feet in the air, cutting off the guards from their retreat. Heather grabbed Brody. "Get up! We have to go now!"

Carl could hear Mallory and his men trying to get around the wall of flame, and he knew they didn't have much time. He said to Heather, "Open the damn door! We need to get through that gym!"

Heather grabbed the door handle and ripped it from its hinges, throwing it behind them. She realized that even after creating the fire and breaking the handle, she hadn't lost any power. *What the hell did Brody make?* she wondered.

The four companions ran into a hall that led into the large open space of the gym. It was shift change for the workers, so luckily, there weren't many people in the huge room, but there were enough to make Heather nervous about them becoming collateral damage. She urged the others to run as fast as they could, but in her eyes, it was still way too slow. The people stared in shock as Heather lit up the dim room with bright, green light as they ran through the gym.

Another shot rang out, hitting her. She heard Mallory yell, "Get back here or I swear you'll have innocent blood on your hands."

Heather stopped in her tracks but told the rest of them, "Keep running!"

Carl looked back to see her face Mallory. He wondered if all this had been for naught, and he was going to jail for treason, and she would be subjected to an unknown hell.

Heather turned to see the major holding a young woman from one of the crews cleaning the warehouse. She slowly walked toward them, but one of his guards lost his cool and began firing at Heather. All the bullets did was bounce off her chest, legs, stomach—even her head. They didn't so much as slow her down.

That made the rest of the gym come unglued. People went running in every direction, trying to get out of the way of the flaming woman. Finally, Mallory called, "If you take one more step, I'll blow her head off."

Heather replied, "If you even try, I'll burn your dick off. I'm sure Helen would be disappointed." She couldn't believe she just said that. Carl would be proud.

Mallory placed the gun against the woman's head, and Heather immediately shot out a tiny ball of flame that burned his hand just enough to make him drop the weapon, allowing the woman to struggle free.

Heather watched as she ran to the exit before turning her attention back to Mallory. "You're fucking pathetic. Using innocent people's lives as bargaining tools to get what you want. From what I found while researching your world, military commanders are supposed to protect their citizens, not use them as cover."

Mallory clutched his burned hand and breathed, "Fuck you, you wouldn't know shit about being a leader! Collateral damage is a necessity! Kill the one to protect the many!"

Heather shook her head, disappointed. "I have to go. I hope to see you again someday, Mallory. Maybe on different terms."

With that, Heather turned and rushed out the door her companions left through. She spotted Brody behind a tree as he yelled, "Over here!"

Heather turned to run toward him. They'd made it to the parking lot where many of the people who were in the gym were standing, bewildered. Carl and Penny were in a van waiting for her and Brody. As they got there, Heather stopped. "I can't sit in there with all of you like this. Who knows what could happen."

Heather searched around for the safest place to release her energy when Brody said, "Push it into your clothes, like the glove earlier."

Heather did as he said, and to their amazement, her power dissipated and seemed to be stored harmlessly in the black shirt and pants he had made for her. He said, "You now have a battery."

Carl said, "Really neat trick, Brody, now get in the fucking car."

Heather climbed in the front seat, looking around the vehicle, wondering how it worked. Brody and Penny were in the back. He pulled the door closed and cried, "Go!"

Carl hit the gas, and they took off across the parking lot. Heather laughed out loud in spite of herself. He side-eyed her. "You all right, love?"

She said, "Yeah, I like cars! But where are we going?"

Carl smiled and said, "Oh, just a little sanctuary."

CHAPTER 33
CIVIL UNREST

C hancellor Warren Strom was beginning to regret sending his son Dominic to find Troy. Each day that went by, the unrest all over the planet grew. Baltica City had been placed on lockdown, and the only people admitted were residents and employees of the government agencies. John Harlow had even restricted Baltica City General Hospital, the largest on the planet and the entire thirty-seventh floor, to dire emergencies. All other patients were referred to Baltica North or South, and even they were on restrictions, which only made the residents angrier.

The population of Rygone was demanding answers to questions he couldn't answer. Like why the Rygonians weren't actively looking to attack the Coronians for the assault on their people, including the kidnapping of Troy and Dia—since nobody believed Dia hadn't been captured. Due to the unrest and threat to other allies, the supply chains from other planets were being disrupted. Chancellor Strom's teams of ambassadors were working tirelessly, traveling to all their neighbors, trying to keep peace and commerce alive.

Yet, one question kept running through his mind—how had they known?

How did the Coronians know that Troy and Dia were going to be secretly escaping through Summerset Cave? How did they know to plan an attack right at the exit of that cave? The civilian assets were only a few farms and ranches, yet they knew to be there. Warren had his son Oscar combing Troy's close staff to see if there were any possible spies. He had to keep his mind from going back to the possibility that Oscar himself could be the culprit, but he just couldn't believe that. Not because Oscar was his son, but because his disposition was not that of a traitor. Oscar practically worshipped Troy, and they'd been best friends and partners since Oscar finished his engineering doctorate. No, it had to be someone else on Troy's team, one of his nurses or scientists.

Warren had practically barricaded himself in his office, trying to think of what to do, when a knock came at his door. "Can it wait?" he called.

His assistant Raquel answered, "It's Lady Strom. She's been trying to get in touch with you, Chancellor."

Warren didn't even want to talk to his wife because he felt like he was letting her down, too. He said, "Very well, put her through."

There was a small ping, and a screen appeared on the wall in front of him. His wife's face was long and sad. Her shiny, black hair, usually arranged in a lovely updo or a simple braid, was just brushed down at the sides. She must've known his thoughts, like she usually did, because she said, "Warren, honey, I know I'm not even on your list of people you want to deal with, but I have a problem I must see you about. Immediately."

Warren sighed tiredly. "Can't we talk about it now?"

Her face became stern, and he knew what that meant. He said, resigned, "Meet me on the fortieth floor, by the pilot's lounge."

She nodded. "I'll be there in fifteen minutes. Love you."

Warren nodded and said in a distant voice, "Love you, too."

He gave another big sigh and slowly stood up to grab his jacket. The weather had started to turn cold. He looked out his office window at the Raltain Mountains; the peaks were covered in a thick layer of snow that had fallen last night. *Oh, to be lost in those mountains right now*, he thought.

He walked out of his office and scanned the parliament floor for any issues before turning to Raquel. "I'm meeting Lady Strom for a few minutes; I should be back soon."

Raquel nodded. "Very good, Chancellor."

Warren liked Raquel; she was a Hanner-Florian who had the rare characteristic of looking physically like her non-Florian parent. Raquel's mother was a Jorderston refugee; therefore, Raquel was very tall with large, golden eyes and pastel-pink hair. Her skin color was different shades of creams, tans, and browns swirled together in elaborate designs. She'd worked for Warren since the end of the Breger Dunes War. Raquel was one of Dia's pilots who'd been injured and had to be medically discharged. She received total disability but had still wanted to work in some capacity. Dia recommended Raquel to him, and it'd gone well ever since.

The chancellor put on his jacket, which was plain blue denim, over his black uniform shirt. He made his way up to the fortieth floor via the back stairs and found his wife standing outside the pilot's lounge with, to his surprise, General Toni Smith. He approached and said, "Pam, General. What's going on?"

Pamela studied her husband with sadness. They hadn't been getting along well for the past few weeks over differences with the people, and it was wearing on him. Actually, it was wearing on them all. Pam said, "Chancellor, General Smith has something very interesting for you to look at."

Smith took out his data pad and opened a file with a video of the hall outside Troy's office. He explained, "Since Dr. Harlow's disappearance, his office door has been accessed four times. Three of those were by Dr. Strom, your son, but we know for a fact that Oscar had permission to access Harlow's office, no matter what. It also went the other way around. Your son had access to Dr. Harlow's access badge, which is not the issue."

"Then what is?"

General Smith started the video, which showed a man walking up the hallway toward Troy's door. He was young and had wavy, black hair and a fair face. He peered around, placed the badge on the keypad, and opened the door. The video changed to Troy's office. The young man looked at the camera so directly they could see his odd blue-violet eyes. He sat down at Troy's desk, used the badge to open the top drawer, and he removed a small, worn envelope before closing everything back up and leaving.

Confused, Warren said, "What does this have to do with anything? It was a piece of paper."

"Right, a particular piece of paper," Smith explained. "When we served in the war, Dr. Harlow and I periodically met in my office for different reasons. Toward the end of the conflict, he always had one of those envelopes in his pocket. His assistant at the time gave them to him for something or other. Anyway, if you zoom in on the paper..." He zoomed in. "Those are her initials. Maria Elizabeth Granby."

Strom remembered the name. Troy put her in for a promotion after the war for exemplary service, and she'd been transferred to a new unit. Only, she disappeared before she ever made it there. There was an extensive investigation, but she'd vanished without a trace.

"Maybe he kept it as a souvenir because she disappeared. Troy can be weird that way," Warren suggested.

Pam shot her husband a look. "But why would the boy want to get it after Troy has been gone this long? And we need to find out from Oscar how this boy got the badge."

Strom tried to put it all together in his head, but he couldn't.

Smith must have noticed. "This is a long shot, but about five years ago, on an outpost in the middle of the Keplen System, a deep space DREX team thought they spotted Maria Granby with a team of female Coronian soldiers. Pictures were taken, and we took it all straight to the chancellor at the time, but we were shot down. We were told the pictures weren't good enough, even though they were clear as day. And that Granby, a Florian, would never betray her people."

Warren stared at Smith for a moment. "Karakas actually said that?"

Smith nodded and continued, "Chancellor, we need to investigate this boy and find out what his connection to that letter is. This was three days ago, so who knows if it still exists."

"Good work, General," Warren said. "Have someone you trust absolutely work on this for you. The more you're involved, the more suspicion you'll draw. And forward me a copy of that video."

Smith nodded again and turned to walk away, but he paused and looked back after a few steps. "You know, Dia and I butted heads more than we got along throughout our time working together. But she was always there for me when it counted. She's my friend, and I want to find her as much as anyone." He turned and quickly walked away.

His words brought a tear to Pam's eye. "This just keeps getting more and more convoluted. How're we going to stop our world from unraveling, Warren?"

Warren watched as Smith disappeared down the stairs and said, "We're going to start with that letter and that boy. We need to talk to Oscar right now."

***

The chancellor went straight to Research and Development and directly into Oscar's lab. His son glanced up from his microscope and asked, "Chancellor, what can I do for you?"

Warren closed the door behind him. "Where's the access badge to Troy's office?" When Oscar swallowed hard and choked on his words, just like he did as a kid, he added, "I don't care that you have it. I want to make sure you *still* have it."

Oscar reluctantly went to his desk, opened his top drawer with his own badge, and took Troy's out. "What's this about?" he asked.

"Have you ever let anyone know that you have it or use it?"

"Hell no! This was a pact between Troy and—"

Warren stopped him. "Isn't there a way to attach your badge to a data pad and bring up its history?"

Oscar nodded and put Troy's badge into the slot on his data pad, revealing the last recorded time stamps were over three weeks prior.

"Three weeks ago. Would that be you?"

Oscar nodded again.

"How easy is it to remake one of these? Who would have access to be able to do something like that?"

"I mean, usually security does it, but if need be, one can be made in here. It only takes a minute or so as long as the information in the system is correct, and Troy always made sure everything was up to date for himself," Oscar explained.

Taking over the data pad, Warren accessed the video Smith sent him. "Watch this. It happened three days ago."

Oscar watched the whole video and muttered, "What the hell was Tristen doing?"

Warren raised an eyebrow at his son. "You know that boy?"

"Yeah, Tristen. He's a floating lab tech between Troy's team and mine. He's worked here for over twelve years, Dad."

The chancellor said, "I want you to find him and bring him to my office—quietly—in an hour. And make sure he has the badge and that letter."

Oscar swallowed and asked, "Dad, do you think he's the spy?"

"He's our biggest lead, and we need a win to get the growing civil unrest in check."

"Noted. We'll be there in an hour."

But they weren't there in an hour. Tristen was no longer on Rygone.

CHAPTER 34
SONGS OF A DISTANT MEMORY

C olonel Renee Conner was growing increasingly frustrated with their search of the Keplen System. Rol cost her a ship, gear, and a pilot. Bodeolr had been their biggest prospect, and it turned out to be a barren wasteland with absolutely no intelligent life. They'd landed on one of the moons of Bodeolr and were regrouping, trying to decide their next course of action.

"What are the three remaining planets?" she asked quietly.

High Colonel Strom pulled up the map and displayed it on both of the DREX canopy screens. He said, "Pletor and Domdoele are the two remaining planets. Darsayn isn't appearing on the map right now, so who knows where it's moved to."

Renee thought about the characteristics of both planets. Neither seemed like they could be viable places for whatever work the Coronians wanted Troy to do. She sat back and closed her eyes, trying to think. After a few minutes, a strange melody started playing in the cabin. "Can you please turn that off?"

Dominic leaned forward. "I'm not playing it. Look." He pointed to a small spot on the map. "It seems to be coming from there. It sounds familiar, doesn't it?"

The crew members from both DREX listened to the faint melody that had a few notes, stopped, then repeated. Dominic's face went white. "Holy shit," he said. "That's the first part of the Kalowian anthem!"

After listening closely, they all agreed. Lieutenant Fox said, "What does that mean, Colonel?"

Renee said, "Well, the Coronians hate the Kalowians as much as they hate us. They wouldn't be playing this for fun. Either it's a trap—"

"Or it's Troy," Dominic finished.

Renee closed her eyes and tried to get her mind around what the next step needed to be. She said, "Dominic, I think we need to investigate no matter what. We're out here for Troy and know the risks."

Everyone said, "Agreed."

That made Renee smile. Her people believed in her—for now, at least. All she had to do was keep from killing or hurting any more of them.

Dominic plotted a course to where the transmission was coming from and entered it into the computer for both DREX. Renee said, "We need to make three short Jumps to get the lay of the area before approaching what I'm going to assume is Darsayn. Stay cloaked no matter what. It makes Jumping slower, but we aren't in a hurry."

Captain Dober said, "Aye, ma'am. Just give me the signal."

Renee made sure all her calculations were correct and took a deep breath. This was the biggest assignment of her career, and there was so much resting on its success. Dominic touched her hand and she looked at him. "It's okay. You got this, Conner," he told her.

She nodded. "Let's Jump."

***

The two craft stopped closer to the planet than they wanted, and Renee realized why. It was indeed Darsayn, and the planet had moved in the middle of the Jump. She said, "We need to make this in only one more Jump, or we risk losing them."

"Aye," Dober said.

This time, they landed just above the atmosphere, which was closer than she wanted to be. She thought about Jumping back, only to realize the melody was much stronger. Dominic was able to pinpoint the location on the ground where it was coming from. "Dober," she said, "monitor our surroundings and keep me informed of any approaching enemy craft. We're close enough that they'll find us soon."

"Aye."

"Does he say anything else?" Dominic whispered.

"Yes," Dober said.

Renee said, "Come on, concentrate." She brought up a topographical map of the location of the signal. "Lots of desert, lots of sand. No buildings."

Dominic zoomed in on the area and pointed to a settlement resembling a small village. "There."

Rock said, "That has to be a lookout station. The Coronians are said to have bases like that all over the planets they're known to occupy.

It makes sense that Darsayn is where they made a base. What better place to settle than on a planet that moves erratically? Renee thought. "Great. Can we determine if the signal is coming from that village?" She asked.

Dominic pinpointed the exact location. It was three tols north, which was all sand. "Troy is deep underground," he realized.

Renee swore under her breath. "That means we have to go through the village; there has to be an access point there," she said. "Let's land, get our shit together, cloak the ships, and rescue Troy."

CHAPTER 35
SURPRISES OF VARIOUS NATURES

A dust storm had kicked up in the vicinity of the village and made for perfect landing cover. Renee had no idea if the Coronians had detected their arrival yet, but she was sure if they had, they probably would've been attacked by now. They waited in the cloaked ships until the storm passed. By then, it was twilight, and Renee and Dominic felt it was the best time to go.

They all outfitted themselves with gear and weapons. Dominic scanned the ground and was able to determine the layout of the complex. "Well, it's pretty fucking big. I still have a lock on the signal; we just have to hope Troy is close to it. And that this isn't a trap."

Renee said, "Either way, it's time to go."

The team consisted of Dominic as the lead and Renee as the second. Rock would guide them, Sergeant Teller was responsible for the special weapons, and Fox and Dober were there for additional support.

Rock stepped next to Dominic by a rocky outcropping that overlooked the village, though it wasn't more than an outpost guarded by two Coronian male beasts. He said, "That small building to the right is going to be the access to the underground complex. However, there's no way of knowing how many enemies we'll encounter once we get down there."

Renee clapped him on the back. "I know! Isn't it great?"

Dominic said, "Renee, Dober, take out the beast closest to us. Fox, you and I will take the one closest to the access point. On my mark."

The team got ready and awaited Dominic's instruction. He dropped his hand and they moved out as one. Renee and Dober were able to get to their target before he even knew what hit him. The small, alabaster-skinned Florian woman dispatched the huge, boar-like Coronian beast with ease. The same went for Dominic and Fox on their target. Renee whispered to the team, "Search the bodies for any sort of access badges or identification. Other than that, let's move."

Each guard had an access key that could operate the lift down into the complex, but the problem was it was thumbprint activated. "Well, Fox," Dominic said, "you get to cut their hands off. Enjoy."

Fox's face went a touch pale, so Renee took out her field knife and removed the hands herself. The team was amazed at how nonchalant she was about it. She didn't care; they had a job to do. She passed one of the hands to Dominic, who was a bit queasy himself, and said, "Let's go."

Renee placed the thumb from the severed hand on the screen and waited with bated breath to see if it worked. Luckily, it did. She stored her nasty prize in her side pocket and stepped into the lift, where she noticed the camera, and while she was sure she'd been seen, she put the Coronian's glove over the lens anyway. She waved them all into the lift and glanced at the control panel. Dominic knew Coronian, so he was able to determine there were ten levels based on the control panel. They'd no idea what level the signal originated from, so they had to brainstorm.

Rock hit level three and Renee glared at him. "What the hell, Rock! Why did you do that?"

He pointed to the symbol next to the number. "Dr. Harlow is a scientist, right? That looks like a beaker to me," he said.

Renee's expression was one of wonder and disdain. "I hope you're right."

***

Troy was sitting at his little desk, writing a formula for absolutely nothing. He preferred his cell to this room because now she watched his every move. The anxiety of being stalked by someone you despised but who had an obsession for you was immense. If he made it out of there, he was going to write a book. Or maybe not. He didn't know; he couldn't think!

Only three days ago, he'd finished his beacon and put it under the lip of the desk. So far, nobody was suspicious, but he was taking a big risk for a very slim chance at reward.

Finally growing bored with trying to appear busy, he stood up and turned toward his bed. The doctor heard a commotion in the hall, but when he went to open the door to investigate, it was locked. He heard several guards loudly rush past. Troy stood there for a moment and had a funny feeling that maybe his beacon worked. He laughed to himself and laid down.

***

Rock was off by a floor, but luckily the number they landed on had a large opening that looked down into a vast lab. The guards had detected their presence the moment they stepped off the lift, but they were ready. The team stayed around Rock as he kept scanning for the signal now that they were in the facility. "The signal is coming from the other side of the lab, on the floor below us," he said. "There's a flight of stairs right past all of the guards over there."

Renee didn't appreciate his humor, but Dominic did. Dominic said, "Take cover against the wall; we'll head to the stairs. I need you to find me the exact door so I can—"

Dominic was shot in the face from a different direction. He wasn't hurt, but it was enough to distract the team. Renee stepped out and nearly had a stroke. Walking toward her in all her blonde-haired, blue-eyed splendor was Maria *fucking* Granby.

Renee saw red. She nearly forgot everything about their mission and was taken back to the Breger Dunes. Maria gave her a sinister grin. "You're the cunt's best friend, right?"

Renee smiled back. "Nope. I'm the general's best friend."

Coronians and Rygonians alike watched as two beautiful Florian women set to beating the living shit out of each other. Unfortunately for Maria, Renee was much better at it. After a few punches, Renee lunged at Maria and knocked her off balance, sending them both over the railing into the lab below. The confusion caused by the women allowed Dominic to go to the lab level and search for Troy. He asked Rock, "Where's the signal?"

"Directly below us."

Dominic nodded. "Keep the guards at bay. Let the ladies fight; they're a good distraction and shouldn't be able to hurt each other. I'm getting Troy."

***

Troy heard the commotion in the lab and got to his feet. He stared at his door, wondering what was happening. Suddenly, the lights went out, plunging him into darkness. He heard someone pounding on the doors yelling, but he couldn't make out what was being said. Finally, they pounded on his door, "Troy! Dr. Troy Harlow, are you in there?"

Troy froze. Was that… Dominic Strom?

When he heard the person move on, he came to his senses and lunged for the door, yelling, "Dominic, it's Troy! I'm here!"

The banging stopped, and after a moment, his door flew open. Low and behold, High Colonel Dominic Strom was standing there. Dirty, sweaty, and beautiful.

Neither man cared about their contentious relationship as they embraced. Dominic squeezed his wayward brother-in-law. "Holy shit, we found you!"

"You found me," Troy breathed out.

Dominic pulled back. "Come on. We need to gather the team and get out of here."

Troy fell in behind Dominic and asked, "Team? Who?"

"Renee and a few others. Come on. We need to get Renee off that bitch Maria."

Troy ran into the lab behind Dominic and saw Colonel Renee Conner squaring off with Maria. It was plain to see Maria was losing. She turned and saw them, and Maria yelled, "No! You can't have him back!"

Dominic glanced at Troy and asked, "You wanna stay?"

Troy panicked and cried, "No! Why would you think that?!"

While Maria was distracted by the prospect of losing Troy, Renee grabbed her by the shirt and yanked her off balance. "I have a gift for you, traitor," she hissed into Maria's ear. "Suck on this, bitch."

She reached into her side pocket and pulled out the severed Coronian hand. Rearing back, she smacked Maria with it as hard as she could, knocking her out cold.

Now that the Florian traitor was incapacitated, Rock and Renee tried to drag her with them. She needed to face the consequences of her actions and answer for the pain she caused the citizens of Rygone. Unfortunately, fighting their way out was far more difficult than breaking in. They were set upon by dozens of Coronian guards, advancing from every direction. Seeing that rescuing Troy was more important to the mission than Maria, they left her behind.

Dominic was surprised at how proficient Troy was with a thermal pistol, especially in pajamas and slippers. Unfortunately, Sergeant Teller was wounded, and she tried to get them to leave without her. Dominic put her over his shoulder and said, "We have the best doctor in the galaxy. You just need to make it to the ship."

The rest of the team made it relatively unscathed, to Renee's surprise. She ordered them all onto the ships, and Troy went to work assessing Teller's injuries. Renee looked at him out of the corner of her eye; she was so glad they'd found him. She also wanted to know the deal with Maria Granby, but that was for a calmer time.

Once they were all set, both DREX Jumped back to Rygone. They came out about five hundred feet from the landing platform, and Renee requested permission to land. Several of the flight crews on the deck watched with curiosity as the two DREX approached, scuffed up as if they'd been in a battle. Renee and Dober docked their ships, and they all sat quietly for a moment. Renee looked back at Troy, who seemed like he was a million miles away.

He turned to her, almost devastatingly hopeful, and tears filled her eyes. "We haven't found her yet," she said.

Troy cleared his throat and nodded. "I need to get Sergeant Teller to the hospital."

With that, everyone came back to themselves and began disembarking from the ships. As they stepped out, a crowd gathered around the DREX and their beleaguered, battle-weary crews. Troy stepped off last, carrying Teller, and nervously started walking toward the gathered people. Two medics from the emergency room came on a ground transport and took Teller from Troy and sped her away to the hospital.

They were left standing there, awkwardly staring at the crowd, not knowing what was going to happen. Then, a few people in the back began to clap. It became contagious and soon, there was thunderous applause. Troy stepped back and made sure the crew that rescued him from his own personal hell were acknowledged.

Renee drew up alongside Troy. "You and I need to talk, Troy. I need to know exactly what happened to Dia."

He nodded. "I'll tell you everything, I swear. I'm done with secrets."

From the back, Troy heard a familiar voice cry his name and spotted a small woman making her way through the crowd. His mother came bursting through and practically jumped into his arms. Troy gave her a big, long hug as the cheers went up again. For the moment, the unrest on Rygone was held at bay.

That night, Troy stayed with his parents. Luckily, his father respected that Troy didn't want to talk about six months of torture and terror at the hands of a traitorous bitch.

He took a long shower and scrubbed as many of the memories off his body as he could. He had to think of the perfect way to thank his rescuers. He had to think about what he would say to the chancellor and Lady Strom about both Dia and his actions. He had to talk to Oscar about so many things. He had so much to do.

But he didn't care about any of it. He was home, and Dia wasn't.

CHAPTER 36
COMFORTS OF HOME

T hey were still driving when Heather asked, "Where are we going? Is it far? I need a snack; all that work made me hungry."

Carl couldn't help but think she sounded like a seven-year-old kid on a long car ride, but she kind of was. "Does anyone have a snack for Miss Stone?"

Brody said, "No, but I wish I did. I haven't eaten in a while."

"Me neither, but a cheeseburger would be nice," Penny said.

"Cheeseburger," Heather repeated. "I read about those. Can we get one, Carl?"

Brody snickered. "Yeah, Dad, can we get McDonald's? Heather's never had a Happy Meal!"

Heather laughed. "I want a Happy Meal. And a cheeseburger. Please, Dad?"

Johnson rolled his eyes. "Y'all are going to get us caught! Let me get farther down the highway; then we'll stop."

Brody and Penny cheered, and Heather joined in. Carl thought, *What a group to maybe save the fuckin' world.*

When he knew they were within ten miles of their safe house, he pulled off the highway and found his "children" a McDonald's. Heather was amazed by the drive-thru and how Carl talking into a box got them food. Wonderful.

Her Happy Meal consisted of a cheeseburger, French fries, and apple slices. Plus, Carl splurged and got her a large Coke. Heather loved the Coke. She drank it almost in one gulp. She loved the cheeseburger and apples, but the best part was the French fries. Heather ate them slowly to savor the salt and crispiness. She decided to wait and open the toy until they got to their new home.

Carl pulled off the road onto a tree-lined driveway that was about a quarter-mile long. It opened up to a large, manicured lawn and a beautiful white mansion.

Gaping, Brody said, "Did you say this was some kind of sanctuary?"

Carl nodded. "Yeah, you could say that." He turned to Heather and said, "Come on, it's been a long night, especially for you."

It was pretty late at night and the moon was high in the sky, making the white house gleam eerily. "How many people live here?" Heather asked.

Carl smiled. "Just us. Let's go see your room, shall we, love?"

She smiled back. "Okay."

The companions left the car and walked up the path to the large, ornate front door. Heather watched as Carl entered a code into a security pin pad. She heard a metallic clang, and he opened the door. They stepped into the vast foyer. She looked around in amazement. "I thought this world was all dirt and government buildings, but McDonald's and this house are nice."

Penny stifled a laugh. She had to remember Heather was just beginning to experience their world. She was excited to help her explore and learn new things. And, of course, do whatever Carl needed her for.

Heather was tired. "Where's my room?"

Johnson gestured toward a large curving staircase. "Follow me. All of you."

They all followed him up onto a landing that had two wings splitting in opposite directions. They walked down one side until Carl stopped and said, "Brody, your room is here."

Patterson opened the door into a huge bedroom with a king-sized bed, a sixty-five-inch flat-screen TV, and its own bathroom with a steam shower. "Awesome!" he yelled.

Carl pointed down the hall to a set of double doors. "That's my room if you need anything."

Brody said, "I'd be mad, but I'm good. Goodnight, everybody." He went into his room and closed the door.

They walked back to the landing and went down the other hall. "Penny," Carl said, "I hope you aren't—"

Singleton saw that her room mirrored Brody's and said, "This is bigger than my apartment. I'm good, too."

Carl walked with Heather down to the double doors in that wing, mirroring his room's, and he opened them both. She walked past him, shocked by what she saw. The room was large, big enough for all four of them to live in comfortably. The bed was tall, giant, and looked comfortable. There was a fantastic bathroom with a steam shower and spa tub. A large projector television on the wall and several different electronics boxes were sending out feelers to be absorbed, though she ignored them. She noticed a sliding glass door on the far side of the room and wondered where it led. Heather looked back at Carl. "I can't stay in here. Aren't there more rooms like Brody and Penny's?"

Carl put his hands behind his back. "Yes, there are. But why when you can enjoy this instead?"

Heather trailed her eyes over the room, feeling so small.

"Okay," she said to him. "Thank you."

There was a large skylight in the ceiling that filled the room with dim moonlight. Heather saw Carl differently at that moment. His rough features and tough exterior were softened. He had a warm smile on his face and almost seemed happy. He nodded. "There are some comfortable clothes in the dressers. I'm not sure what size they are, but they're new and nice."

He gestured toward the sliding glass door. "Come here for a moment."

Heather followed him out onto a beautiful, glassed-in porch. It was full of flowering plants, benches, and bubbling fountains filled with colorful fish. The scent of flowers and the sound of the bubbling water were intoxicating. She got lightheaded for a moment and tripped, giggling. She straightened up and found Carl was smiling at her.

"Are you all right, love?" he asked.

She nodded, still giggling. "I feel like I just had whiskey!"

Carl narrowed his eyes. "When did you have whiskey?" he asked.

She brushed an errant curl out of her eye. "At the crash site. Maeve gave it to me." Heather grew serious. "I wonder what happened to her."

Unfortunately, Carl hadn't heard anything about the woman who tried to take Heather in before Mallory got his hands on her. He had to admit; he was glad she was captured by the dickhead in that respect. "I'm not sure, love. Now, let me show you something."

They walked through the finely manicured plants and small pools of water until they arrived at another sliding glass door. "This is my room. If you need anything, you can go through the house or come this way. It doesn't matter to me."

"Oh, okay. That's pretty neat."

Carl smiled again. "I hope you don't mind me saying, but you were amazing in the facility, and just in the past few hours, you've blossomed even more. Are you sure you aren't from around here?"

"You probably know that better than I do."

Carl chuckled. "Maybe. Well, we both should get to bed. Good night, lo—Heather."

"You can say it. I don't mind anymore."

Heather turned to go back to her room when Carl stopped her. "Oh! I almost forgot." He reached into his pocket, "Your rings."

Heather came back and Carl put the two black rings made from silver, gold, and something nobody could identify into her hand. She smiled genuinely. "Thank you, Carl. Getting these back means so much to me."

"And you trusting me enough to take such a huge risk means a lot to me."

Heather stared at him for a moment, then, without thinking, gently kissed him on the cheek. She stepped back and said, "Good night, Carl."

Johnson watched as she shuffled back toward her room and stood there contemplating what just happened. He shook his head and said to himself, *Don't start to like her. You've said it time and again!*

But Carl couldn't help it. Heather was growing on him, fast.

CHAPTER 37
THE MANSION

T he next morning, Carl woke up early to make coffee in the expansive kitchen on the main level. He thought about the events that had happened over the past couple of weeks, from the moment he got the call about the meteor impact in Kentucky.

Johnson had monitored the news and police coverage at the site for anything unusual, like his benefactor always instructed. When he found out a woman was rescued from the bottom of the crater days after impact, he became intrigued. When he first heard of her attack on the camp, he knew he needed to act. He flew straight to Kentucky once she was in custody. His position with the International Space Coalition got him higher priority access to Heather than even Major Mallory. Unfortunately, that wasn't without the stipulation that Carl had to examine her at Mallory's facility. If he couldn't get her to the level the ISC wanted, the major and the army would get unimpeded control over her.

That was the closest Carl had been to a legitimate target since starting with the ISC ten years ago. He'd contacted Dr. Helen Grace, Penny Singleton, and Brody Patterson, as they were close to the facility, and while he'd worked with them in the past on different projects, they didn't know the extent of the work he was doing, either in the past or present.

Carl would never forget when he finally made it into the facility and saw her for the first time. At first, he'd been skeptical that such a tiny woman could do so much damage, but he'd learned over the years that size didn't always matter. She was covered in mud and sweat, and her clothes were singed from being shot with bullets and grenades. She was unconscious but would periodically stir and mumble, scaring everyone working with her.

Carl was fortunate that Mallory's facility was only a three-hour drive from the mansion, so they were able to get to safety easily enough, but he knew Jason was on the hunt. Another thing in Carl's favor was nobody wanted Heather's existence to become more than a few conspiracy theories and grainy cell phone videos. Therefore, the major wasn't going to call in a huge search party. As long as they stayed on the property, nobody would find them.

He was staring out the large kitchen window when he was startled by a voice behind him.

"That coffee smells wonderful."

Carl spun around to find Heather on the other side of the center island. Her hair was wet, and she was wearing a pair of satin pajamas. "Good morning," he said. "How did you sleep?"

"I didn't. I think the bed was too comfortable. Plus, there was a thunderstorm in the distance, and it made me nervous."

Carl could understand that. They should all be nervous around her and thunderstorms. He would talk to Brody to see if he could do something to help her with the attraction to lightning.

He turned around, opened a cabinet, and took out two coffee cups. Pouring for them both, he asked, "Would you like cream and sugar? I know you didn't get it at the facility, but this is a more civilized place."

Heather took in the gigantic kitchen. There were countless cabinets filled with things she could never imagine. There was what she thought was called a refrigerator, stocked with food she was excited to try. Across the large walkway from the kitchen was a large room with two couches and several chairs, all facing a large fireplace with a TV bigger than the one in her room. Past the kitchen was another room that was curved and had a huge, long table with at least twenty chairs. Floor-to-ceiling windows looked out over a beautiful grassy garden with manicured trees and a swimming pool.

Finally, she said, "Hopefully, the more civilized accommodations match the more civilized company."

Johnson smiled. "It does, love." He opened the refrigerator to get out the creamer, allowing her to see all of the wonderful food.

She walked around and stood next to him. "This is amazing; there's so much to eat!"

Laughing, he said, "What would you like for breakfast?"

She shrugged and reminded him, "All I know are pancakes, sausage, and orange juice. Surprise me, I guess."

"Have a seat, and I'll make you a nice 'Carl special' for breakfast."

From behind them, Brody said, "I hope that goes for all of us."

Carl and Heather turned. Both Brody and Penny were there, looking fresh from the sleep they enjoyed in their new beds. "Fine, but you have to help," he said before turning to Heather. "Not you. You relax and watch. We don't need you blowing up the stove."

Everyone laughed except Heather, who rolled her eyes with a huff. She took her coffee and sat down at the island to watch her companions cook scrambled eggs, bacon, toast, and hash browns. Penny found apple juice in the fridge, so they had that as well.

Once breakfast was ready, Carl said, "Everyone make a plate. Let's go into the curved room and discuss what happens next."

Heather filled her plate first and sat down at the long table in the curved room, reveling in the garden's beauty. The house was so splendid; it felt too good to be true. After everyone was seated and eating, Carl said, "Okay, now let me start by saying this house and the surrounding land are a dark site, meaning we're completely invisible to anyone who wants to find us. No satellites, no radio waves. It's an open field and forest to anyone who looks.

Surprised, Brody said, "That's nearly impossible these days, how is—"

Johnson stopped him and said, "Quiet. You can ask questions when I'm finished."

Patterson, dejected, poked at his food. "Fine."

Carl told them about the International Space Coalition and how they'd set up this place for research and experimentation for any possible alien assets that came to Earth. Heather paused from shoveling eggs into her mouth when she realized all eyes were on her.

"What?" she asked.

Carl then went on to say that none of them were allowed to leave. He explained that he was working with the coalition to find and protect any extraordinary people or aliens who came into his custody. Heather was the first asset he knew of in the group's history to have such power, so it was their job to make sure she was kept safe.

Heather, with bacon in her mouth, said, "But you told me I would be a weapon. You didn't bring me here just to be kept safe. You brought me here for a purpose, your purpose."

"Yes, I did. There's a significant threat to the planet that has been known to the coalition for some time now. We're afraid they're going to make a move to attack or damage Earth, and we're afraid that we, namely you, are our only hope."

It was quiet for a moment before all three started talking at once, asking him various questions.

Penny asked, "What role will I play? How extensive is this threat?"

"This sounds like some *Men in Black* level shit," Brody said. "How can the four of us defeat a secret, global threat, especially when I know you aren't going to tell us anything else? If you want my help, I need a lab and equipment."

"I'm glad you're putting this all on us. When are we starting the training? By the way, I love bacon," Heather said.

Carl waited for them to fall silent before speaking. "Penny, you'll continue to monitor Heather's health during training and testing. Brody, you'll figure it out, and you're correct, I ain't telling you shit. I'll show you your workspace; you have unlimited resources for helping our friend control her incredible gifts. Heather, we start right after breakfast—and I'm glad you like bacon."

After that, they were all quiet until they finished eating. Carl said, "Get dressed for a long day. Meet down here in the kitchen in half an hour."

They all got up, and Brody said to Heather, "When you come down, please bring the clothes you wore last night with you. There's a lot I still need to do."

She nodded and walked back down the pathway to the stairs. Instead of following the other two, she watched as Carl went back into the kitchen. He turned, saw her staring at him, and waved her over. She reentered the kitchen and stood in front of him, quiet.

"There's a lot at stake," Carl said, "and I wouldn't have broken you out of Mallory's place if I didn't think you were up to the task."

"What task, though? You want me to train so I can help you defeat a threat, yet you won't tell me what that threat is. I think I deserve to know."

He knew she was right, but he needed to wait a little longer to tell her. He needed to get his benefactor up to speed first. "I promise I'll tell you soon," he said.

She gave a slight nod, turned around, and walked away without another word.

***

When they all met later, Carl took them to a large, heavy door in the living room. He placed a plastic card against a pad on the wall, and there was a click, unlocking the door.

They entered a hallway that looked nothing like the rest of the house. It was all white, and the lights were so strong, Heather automatically sent feelers out to them, which she ignored.

When they got to the end of the hall, the team stepped into a vast room filled with various equipment, servers, and lab gear. The far wall was lined with shelves covered with different materials and medical supplies that Brody and Penny could use to perform their jobs. The PA-C and technologist walked into the room with pure excitement, eagerly taking in the sights. They immediately started setting up their workstations and inventorying what they had.

Heather said to Carl in awe, "I've no idea what all of this is, but it looks amazing."

He chuckled. "It's a playground for minds that are incredible at what they do." He turned to her and added quietly, "There isn't anything else you can do today, so I'll show you the rest of the house."

"Okay."

Johnson took Heather around the rest of the mansion. He showed her the living room and went through the cabinets and pantry, showing her all the food and anything else she might want. She was glad to see they had whiskey. He also led her to the backyard and took her to the end of the ornate garden. The view was an expansive field.

"This is where you and Brody will do most of your work," Carl explained.

"It's big."

"After what I've seen you do, it needs to be big."

Heather kicked a small rock on the ground. Carl could tell she wanted to say something but was hesitating. "What is it, love?" he asked.

Her gaze drifted across the field again. "I'm sorry about last night on the porch. I shouldn't have kissed your cheek."

Carl didn't know what to think at first, since he'd thoroughly enjoyed the gesture. He said, "It's perfectly all right. If I weren't okay with it, I would've told you."

She nodded. "I know, but I've been reading so much material about personal space and how you should always ask permission before touching someone, and I didn't think. I'm sorry."

Carl wanted to laugh and hug her for the innocence she was showing, but in retrospect, maybe she needed to heed those lessons. He couldn't imagine how hard it must be for her to learn so much about a strange, complicated place. "I agree with your readings, and I give you permission from now on."

She turned and gave him a sly smile. "Okay, deal," she said. "I guess I give you permission as well."

Carl was a little surprised by her candor, and he knew he shouldn't even allow this conversation to continue, but she was becoming intoxicating to him. He knew he needed to distance himself from the team for the next few weeks, especially her. He smiled. "Let's finish the tour."

He showed her the rest of the mansion's compound. The garage had four different vehicles to be used for whatever they needed. He showed her the lower-level bedrooms—twenty-two throughout the house, twenty of which were exactly like Patterson and Singleton's, and the other two were theirs. After a few hours, Carl said, "I'm going to go check on Brody and Penny. You can do whatever you please."

She nodded and watched as Carl walked away. One of the books she'd read was what the humans called a romance novel. It was about two people who were put into a compromising position and fell in love. The description of sex was interesting and made her curious to a fault as she later found Pornhub on the internet. The images of human sex were even more fascinating. She wondered if there was someone in her past life whom she loved and had sex with. Carl was kind, funny, and seemed to legitimately care for her, and she couldn't help but be attracted to him.

Yet, something in the back of her mind nagged at her to not act on her developing feelings.

***

That night, Heather finally fell asleep in her big, comfortable bed. She slipped into a dream.

She opened her eyes and was back in the room where the man in the bed turned to the yellow-haired volunteer from the Red Cross. She was standing this time, facing the window. It was daytime, and she could see beautiful, snowcapped mountains in the distance. She enjoyed the view for a while before she heard someone speak behind her.

"Dia."

Heather turned around but didn't see anyone at first, so she said, "Hello? Is someone there?"

Out of a dark corner in the back of the room, a man stepped into the light. He was tall and thin with dark-brown hair. He wore what looked like some kind of uniform with a gray, form-fitted jacket with a blue stripe going from his right shoulder to his left hip. He wore black trousers and black boots. His skin was pale, smooth, and radiant in the light coming through the window. But what caught her attention the most were his large eyes; they were such a dark brown that they almost seemed black. Heather was in awe of how incredibly handsome he was.

He stared at her with confusion at first, as if he didn't know who she was. They both slowly walked toward each other, and as he got closer to her, his face filled with anguish. He began speaking to her, but she couldn't understand him. She strained to recognize his voice and language, but neither rang a bell.

She stepped closer to him and asked, "Do we know each other?"

But he just stared at her with more sadness and fear on his face. She knew he couldn't understand her either. He reached out and took her left hand and raised it to his face. He pressed his cheek against her fingers. His skin was warm and soft. He then spun the ring on her middle finger, prompting Heather to glance down at his left hand, but he wore no rings. She tilted her head back up to his face and uselessly said, "I think we know each other, but I don't remember you. I really wish I did. I wish I remembered this lovely place."

He let go of her hand as a tear ran down his cheek. He kissed her on the forehead and said something else so quietly she could barely hear it, but she made out the word Troy. He took a large step back, and just like that, Heather woke up. She sat up in her bed and tried to run the dream through her mind, but the memory of it faded fast. The room, the mountains, his handsome face, and dark eyes. Troy.

By the end of that day, Heather didn't remember any of it.

CHAPTER 38
FACING THE MUSIC

Troy had been home for two days and could no longer hide in his parents' home from all of the people and responsibilities that awaited him. He had Dominic escort him back to his apartment to get ready to face the music. First, he'd meet with the chancellor to explain himself. Second, he'd find Renee to tell her the secrets he'd kept for so long.

When he got home, he stood in front of the door reluctantly, not wanting to go back to the life he left without Dia by his side. Everything was going to change now.

Dominic quietly asked, "Do you want me to go in with you?"

Troy shook his head. "No, I'll be okay."

Dominic nodded and put a hand on Troy's shoulder. "I hated you for leaving with her like this. I want to know the reason someday. That being said, I'm glad you're back. I know we all have a long road ahead of us."

"That's the nicest thing you've ever said to me."

"Don't get used to it. I'll be back in a little while to pick you up for your meeting with Dad." Dominic turned to leave, but Troy stopped him.

"Dominic, thank you. Thank you for finding me and bringing me home. There's no way to repay you for what you and your team did for me."

"I was the muscle; Renee was the brains. Make sure you thank them all."

Troy nodded. "I plan to. I'll see you soon."

He went into his empty apartment and closed the door, standing in the dark. He sighed and turned on the kitchen light, cringing at how sterile it all looked. There was no fruit on the counter, no tea glasses in the sink. Dia's work data pad wasn't sitting on the edge of the table, about to fall off. But their other personal effects were still in place. Pictures, art, furniture. It was all spotless because his mother had been coming in every other day and cleaning, just in case they came home. Troy lost it and fell to his knees, finally breaking down into a hard cry. He sat on his heels with his head against the clean floor for ten minutes, sobbing uncontrollably. Between losing his wife, being captured and tortured by his former mistress, and the looming prospect of having to explain to everyone Dia loved what had happened, Troy was an absolute mess.

He eventually pulled himself together and sat up. He was supposed to meet with Chancellor Strom in twenty minutes. Standing, he rushed into his bedroom and took out clean clothes he couldn't believe were still there. It was as if they'd never left.

Troy splashed some water on his face and tried to smooth his hair into something presentable. He shaved off the beard he'd grown on Darsayn, but his hair was still long and unruly. He'd take care of that after his meeting with the chancellor if he didn't get thrown into the Ice Lake for treason.

Dominic soon arrived on a transport and whisked Troy away to the Command Center. Residents were out, cheering as they watched him go by. Troy felt like a fool, but Dominic told him to smile and wave anyway. Just having Troy back was already helping to quell the civil unrest. When they arrived, Troy was able to see down into the mezzanine and was horrified by the murals. "What the hell?"

Dominic laughed and explained, "Requested by the people, man. They didn't have any hope you'd come back."

Troy said, "Well, since I'm here at least, they can paint over mine."

"Fat chance. Now let's get this shit over with."

Troy nodded as they entered the Command Center. As they walked toward the chancellor's office, the floor with the operations crew stopped and stared. Dominic loudly said, "You've seen him before. Be happy he's back and get to work."

Troy wanted to smile at the irony of having the one person in Dia's family who didn't really like him standing up for him, but he decided to keep it to himself. When they reached the door of the chancellor's office, Dominic didn't even get to knock before Troy heard Warren Strom yell, "It's open, damnit!"

Dominic glanced at his brother-in-law. "Good luck, dude."

Troy swallowed hard and nodded. He opened the door and saw Warren sitting behind his desk, reading his data pad. "Sit, Dr. Harlow."

Troy quietly sat down and stared at Warren. The chancellor kept working for a few minutes, making Troy sit in uncomfortable silence. He finally set the data pad down, and to Troy's surprise, Warren had tears in his eyes. He cleared his throat. "First of all, I just want to say I'm glad you're home. I'm glad the mission was successful. We need you for what's to come." He wiped away a tear with a tissue. "That being said, what the *fuck* did you do to my daughter?"

Troy swallowed hard and tried to remember everything he'd planned to say. "As I know you're aware of, Dia was bonded with the EIP Oscar and I were working on. A few weeks before we attempted to leave, we were trying to find out what she could do with it in both practical and defense applications. Unfortunately, a horrible accident occurred, and the true nature of the EIP came to light. We knew we had to get as far away from Rygone as possible."

Warren stared at Troy for a moment. "Why didn't you tell anyone?" he asked, "You're both high-ranking government officials and *faked* documents to flee. That's treason, Troy."

The doctor nodded. "I'm aware of that, and I'm fully prepared to take responsibility for my actions because… because in the end, I achieved my goal. Dia is out of our enemies reach."

Warren raised his eyebrows. "What the hell does that mean, Troy?"

Troy looked Warren Strom, chancellor of Rygone and father to his beloved wife, in the eyes and asked, "Did you ever meet Daniel Williams?"

Warren thought for a moment. "Yeah, he worked as a freelancer for Oscar a while ago. What's he got to do with this?"

Troy said quietly. "He was working with Dia and me. There was a freak accident, and Dia killed him. Not survival stasis, not injured, she unintentionally *murdered* him." He cleared his throat. "Dia bonded with the EIP, and the EIP is capable of killing us, killing Florians."

Warren Strom stared at his son-in-law in disbelief. "Show me proof, Dr. Harlow."

***

After he told the chancellor about the accident with Daniel Williams, Troy took him to see the proof he kept. Back when it happened, he and Dia hadn't known what to do, so Troy put the young Florian's body in cryostasis in his lab. Luckily, nobody had discovered anything, and Daniel was still there. Troy brought Daniel out of cryo and showed not only the chancellor but also Oscar, Dominic, Renee Conner, and Troy's own father that Daniel could not be revived no matter what they did. He was the first known Florian, beyond a shadow of a doubt, to *die*.

Renee said to Troy, "Is this what you meant by no more secrets?"

He glared at her and said to everyone, "Dia and I knew that if our enemies found out about what she could do, they'd stop at nothing to get their hands on her and find a way to eliminate our kind. We thought if we told anyone, even those close to us, we'd put all of us at risk, so we fled. Unfortunately, the Coronians knew. They knew everything, and I still don't know how. We should thank the wishes that they only got me instead of her or both of us. There's no way to replicate what happened to Dia, so there was no way to reproduce it for them. Trust me, they tried."

It was quiet for a moment as they processed his words before Renee asked, "What about Maria Granby?"

Troy's glance was pleading, but there was no way to take back what she said. "I had no idea, but it turns out when Maria Granby disappeared after the Breger Dunes War, she didn't just fall off the map; she went back to her benefactors, the Coronians. The Pexallun, the attacks on the rear, everything was being fed to the Coronians by her. She even arranged to have Dia's DREX sabotaged while it was being repaired for battle damage." Troy looked down at his hands and said, "She was very proud to tell me all of this."

Warren carefully considered everything Troy had told them so far, trying to form a plan of action. "We must find Dia before they do.

Obviously, the Coronians are smart and crafty enough to turn their enemies to their will. They have to know she's out there somewhere." He turned to Renee and Dominic and continued, "I need you both to work on something to find her."

They nodded and were about to leave when Strom yelled, "Wait!" He pointed to all of them. "I can't express how critical it is that none of you breathes a word of this to *anyone*! It's for all of our sakes." With that, he left, with Dominic and Renee on his heels.

Troy and Oscar watched in silence as John took a scalpel from a drawer in the table. He made an incision down Daniel William's forearm, visibly saddened when it penetrated his skin. He addressed his son, "I'll be back in a little while to perform an autopsy on this body."

Oscar was left with Troy and the body of Daniel Williams. He quietly asked, "Why didn't you tell me, Troy?"

"I couldn't risk anyone else's safety, even yours. Especially yours. But now, that's all in the past. We need to find out who told the Coronians about Dia and the EIP. I don't think they knew about this, but they knew enough."

Oscar surveyed his best friend and said, "You look like you've actually aged. What the hell did they do to you?"

Tortured me with the biggest mistake I've ever made, he thought.

Troy just shook his head and answered, "Too much to talk about right now. I just want to go home and try to sleep."

CHAPTER 39
FLASHPOINT

T he next few months at the mansion were productive and rather enjoyable for Heather. When she landed on Earth, she knew how to use her powers, but only to a certain extent. She knew instinctive rules, but she and Brody were working very well to develop her abilities both with and without the suit he was making for her.

One day, while he was having her tell him everything she knew about her powers, he asked, "What about a live being? Can you pull the energy from a living thing?"

"I think I can, but I won't."

Brody shrugged. "Why not? I've seen you pull energy from an object and push it back in. Why can't you do that with a living being?"

Heather glared at him. "Because I don't want to take the chance. I'm not doing all of this so I can outright kill someone or something. I just feel that's what would happen."

Brody wouldn't let the topic die. "But what if we try with a mouse or a fish?"

Heather said, "Come on, no. I don't want to hurt anything like that."

From behind them, she heard Carl, who they hadn't seen in almost a week, say, "I've always wondered that myself. I know you don't want to hurt anything, but wouldn't you like to know for certain what happens instead of only trusting your instincts?"

Penny, who'd also just joined them, added, "I'd hate for you to hurt something, but if anything ever happens in the field, it'd be good for me to know what to expect if a person is injured."

Heather sighed and reluctantly said, "Fine. What animal are you going to make me kill?"

Brody walked over to a cage in the corner. "This is a common field mouse. And I don't think you'll kill it."

He placed the mouse in a plastic dish on top of a machine that could monitor its vitals. To Heather, he said, "Draw just a little of its power, and if its vitals drop, push it back."

Heather was apprehensive, but their logic did make sense. She hesitantly hovered her hand over the mouse and concentrated on the electric pulses that each cell of its body let off. She had worked on learning how to focus on certain parts of an energy source, so she paid particular attention to the electrical pulses made by the mouse's leg muscles. But nothing happened.

"What's wrong?" Brody asked.

"I dunno. I can feel the energy in the mouse's body, but I can't draw it out. Maybe this won't work."

Carl asked, "What if you touch it?"

Heather shot him an irritated glance. "Fine."

She reached down with her finger and gently placed the tip against the mouse's back leg. She felt the tiny bit of energy transfer into her hand, and she could see that the mouse was having difficulty walking, so she pulled back. The mouse's vitals were going crazy, probably due to the pain. Heather pressed her finger back against the creature's leg and tried to push the energy back into the mouse's body, but no matter what she did, it wouldn't go. After about a minute of struggling, the mouse's heart gave out, and it died.

Heather looked at her hand and felt the minuscule bit of energy, the last of the mouse's life force flowing in her veins. Tears filled her eyes, and she choked out, "I told you, I can't put it back, and now it's dead. What am I supposed to do with this energy? Blow something up?"

Heather slammed her hand down on one of the pads Brody had set up for her to release excess stored energy and pushed the mouse's life into it. She stormed out of the lab.

"I'll go talk to her," Patterson said.

"No," Carl said. "Leave her be. She'll be okay by tomorrow."

***

Carl was right. The next day, Heather and Brody discussed what had happened. He started by saying, "I'm sorry I pushed you yesterday. You've always been reluctant about life energy. I should've listened."

She nodded. "I needed to confirm it anyway; I just didn't want to. Now let's get this suit finished. I think Carl is up to more than he's telling us, and I want to be ready."

"I like your way of thinking. I finally have the full suit prototype complete. I think today's the perfect day to test it out."

Heather became concerned. "Brody, it's supposed to storm all day. I'm not good around lightning, remember?"

He smirked and asked, "Don't you trust me, Heather?"

She shook her head. "No. I don't. But I'll oblige you this time."

Brody went to the back of the room and came back with a long gray box. He set it down on the table in front of Heather. "Open it."

She glanced from the box to his face, then pulled the top off. Inside was a long, bright-green suit made out of thin but super-strong fabric. It was made with a synthetic thread—designed by Brody himself—and woven with copper wire. Heather ran her fingers over the material. The box also contained more clothes like the black shirt and pants he had her wear on the night they escaped. There was a special pair of medium-weight leather boots lined with copper wire and heavy-duty rubber soles. What surprised her was how light they were. She asked Brody, "I guess it's time to try this on?"

He just smiled and nodded.

***

Heather left the bathroom and stepped back into the lab. This time, all three of her teammates were waiting, and they all stared at her in awe. Penny said, "Oh my God, you look incredible."

Brody walked up to her and made a few adjustments to how the suit sat on certain parts of her body. "How does it all feel? Is it uncomfortable? Are the boots too heavy?" he asked.

"It feels great, almost as if I'm not wearing anything at all. I'm interested to see how it feels with power."

"So am I," Carl said.

***

They all went out to the curved room. Heather could see a thunderstorm in the distance, heading toward them. Despite her apprehensions, she'd told Brody she'd take a chance.

Brody instructed her, "Go to the end of the garden. Stop when you get to the beginning of the field."

She nodded and stepped outside. Her hair was pulled back into a ponytail, blowing in the growing wind. Carl couldn't help but feel concerned for her safety.

Johnson, Penny, and Brody stayed in the curved room where they were safe but could still see Heather. She walked out to the edge of the garden in her new suit and watched the storm approach. The closer it got, the faster the lighting moved toward her. She could feel the electricity buzzing all around her, but instead of fear, she felt elated. Heather reached her hand to the sky, and she was immediately hit with a bolt. The power was extremely painful for the briefest moment, but it quickly passed into the suit and was stored for use later. Suddenly, the storm unleashed its full fury onto her—rain, wind, lightning, and thunder.

The rest of the team watched in horror and awe at the scene at the edge of the garden. "Is she really going to be okay?" Carl asked Brody.

"Of course. Penny and I have tested her abilities and limitations for weeks now. She's going to be just fine."

Penny stepped back from the window, which was shaking from the power of the storm. Suddenly, everything went quiet. Penny's eyes widened, and she pointed out at Heather. "Look."

They all turned their eyes to the end of the garden. The storm was gone entirely except for the wet grass and a light breeze. Heather was still standing in the same place, facing away from them. She wasn't glowing; her appearance was precisely as it had been when she walked out there. Carl turned to Brody. "We saw her get hit dozens of times. Did she release it all already?"

He smiled. "No, she stored it in the suit. It works. *It fucking works!*"

Brody started jumping up and down like a child celebrating while Penny and Carl walked outside. Heather turned around, and they saw that her eyes were bright, but nothing else was different. No green flame, no yellow mist, no flowing blonde hair, just emerald eyes.

Brody ran past them and got to Heather first. He asked excitedly, "So, how do you feel? Was it bad? What do I need to change? When do—"

Heather stopped him and said quietly, "It was incredible. I didn't just absorb the lightning but the entire storm. It was as if it came to me and—and…"

Carl pressed, "And what?"

"And gave itself to me. It's hard to explain."

"That's weird," Penny said. "Anyway, how do you feel?"

"Fine. I don't feel any different than I do when I discharge. How much power did I absorb?" Heather asked.

"Well, a thundercloud usually holds about a billion volts of electricity, so I'm going to assume that much. Or more, who knows," Brody said.

Carl made a skeptical face. "How the hell is there that much power stored in the suit?"

"The power is still all in our friend here, but the suit stabilized it," Brody explained.

Heather cleared her throat. "What if I have to pee, like, right now?"

He laughed. "Not a problem. The suit has an energy dissipater built-in, like the pads in the lab. I can't guarantee that an entire thunderstorm—"

Heather turned away from them all, and the air grew heavier. Time seemed to slow as she took one hand and slammed it into the ground and stretched the other out in front of her. She erupted in green flame, and two huge beams of green and yellow light burst from her hands, one into the ground, the other parallel above it. One beam raced across the field and the other under the earth until Heather had released all of her stored energy. She stood up and surveyed the massive crack in the field that was ten feet deep and half a mile long. Heather smiled at Brody. "That works, too."

The rest of the team looked at the damage in shock as Heather walked past them back into the house. She really did have to pee.

***

That evening, they were all in the curved room playing poker. Since it had been almost a week since any of them had seen Carl, he was the focus of their conversation.

"You look tired, Carl," Penny said. "Where have you been?"

"You keep preaching to us not to leave the mansion, but you're gone all the time," Brody added. "What's her name?"

Heather asked, "Aren't we having pie for dessert? Brody, what do you mean by what's her name?"

Carl hung his head. "You three are truly like children, aren't you?"

Heather put her foot up on the table. "I've never been around children, so I wouldn't know."

He laughed despite himself. "That makes you the worst one, love. Anyway, our benefactor has me running some recon on our friends at the Kentucky facility. Strangely, Mallory never came after us when we fled. I think they were anticipating it. But they haven't been even coming close to finding this site, so I just need to keep an eye out for those cocksuckers."

Heather, dead serious, asked, "Are they really cocksuckers? Because I hav—"

"No!" Penny interrupted. "It's a figure of speech, which he should *not* be using in front of a child."

Heather smirked. "I'm willing to bet I'm *way* older than all of you."

They all nodded in agreement. Heather turned in her chair and asked, "Now, who's getting the pie?"

***

Over the next few days, Brody and Heather worked together to get the bugs and limitations out of her suit. By the time they felt comfortable for a real test, Heather could attract, store, release, and instantly dissipate power. He'd changed the way the suit held energy so that if she needed to take it off for some reason, it could store a certain amount without needing her body to keep it stable. He changed it from a one-piece jumpsuit to a two-piece shirt and trousers that could seal together when both were being worn. This allowed her to use the bathroom without taking the suit off, a very high priority on her list of wants.

During the test, she went into the middle of the field and worked with different types of energy. She perfected different techniques to help those in need and be the weapon they wanted her to become.

The last problem that Penny and Brody were trying to solve was that when Heather used her powers with the suit on, the moment she took it off, she was left exhausted, dehydrated, and in desperate need of sustenance. Penny was beginning to wonder if they were actually hurting her, but both Brody and Heather assured her she was okay. Heather would insist, "I just need something to eat or drink that will bring me back to life faster. Gatorade and a granola bar aren't cutting it. But other than that, I feel fine."

Singleton and Patterson went to work on creating a drink high in electrolytes and calories that she could keep on her in the shell of her suit. But Penny didn't think it'd be enough. She pulled Brody aside one day and said, "I know you love this project, and both you and Heather are excited about your progress, but I'm very worried about how much of her own energy this suit takes. If Heather is that important to Carl and our so-called benefactor, we need to address this issue *now*."

Most of the time, Brody would brush her off as if she didn't know what she was talking about, but after seeing Heather in action and how hard it was for her to recover, he knew she was right. "We need to work on this together. You have the medical knowledge, and I have the tech know-how. It needs to go beyond just a drink because there may come a time when she won't be able to get to her drink."

Penny smiled sincerely. "Thank you, Brody." Before walking away, she asked, "Have you had a good time here? I mean, other than the exhausting work?"

He nodded. "Yeah, I never thought I'd get the chance to do something like this, so it's been cool. The company ain't bad either."

Penny nodded back and left. She smiled in spite of herself and couldn't help but think about Brody for the rest of the day.

***

The next day, Patterson called everyone into the living room after breakfast and said, "I have an announcement to make."

They all stared at him with anticipation as he turned on the television and started a video that documented Heather's progress from the moment she landed to what she could do now. They watched her become an incredible force to be reckoned with. And they each had different opinions:

Penny smiled and thought, *She's going to be able to help so many people!*

Brody thought, *I'm going to be rich and famous. I've created the world's first bona fide superhero!*

I hope this is what Roger wants, Carl thought.

Heather, though, thought, *I'm scared of myself.*

She said, "What's this about? Why did you want us to see all of this?"

Brody turned to them and said, "Heather, you're ready. Ready for whatever we've been brought here for and not told shit about. If you want to be a weapon, you can be a weapon. If you want to be a protector, you can do that as well." He puffed up his chest and gestured grandly at her with his hand. "I present to you: Heather Stone, the superhero... Flashpoint!"

"Oh! Like an Avenger!" Heather said excitedly.

Brody shook his head. "No, they're fictional, so they're only in comic books and movies. Besides, that'd be a copyright infringement."

Dejected, Heather said, "Oh. What's a copyright infringement?"

CHAPTER 40
TROY'S DILEMMA

T roy sat on the couch in his living room, staring at Renee's face as she processed what he'd just told her. He went to spin the rings on his left hand and cringed, forgetting they were still in the Coronians' possession.

Finally, she asked, "Did she know? Did Dia know before you escaped?"

Troy nodded. "Dia has known for some time. About twenty years after the war, an anonymous source sent her a video I didn't know existed. Those were not good times for almost a year, but she forgave me in the end."

Renee thought back to the hell that was the Breger Dunes and remembered the horrible chaos the war put them all through. Maybe Troy most of all because he and his staff had to put the citizens and soldiers back together with limited resources and support. But she didn't think it was an excuse for him to fuck his assistant. She sighed. "Damnit, Troy, you guys weren't supposed to succumb to the Florian Curse."

The Florian Curse was a made-up problem that plagued full Florian relationships. When someone was with the same person for eternity, adultery was almost guaranteed. Many couples entered into open marriages on purpose in hopes that it would make their union happier; more often than not, that wound up making things worse. Troy and Dia were always held to a sometimes-unattainable higher standard, but they managed to stay faithful to each other after almost eight hundred thousand years. Until Maria Granby, that was.

He looked blankly out the sliding glass door toward the Raltains. "That time was just unprecedented. I expected Dia to be back with me in the rear, not to put herself in harm's way. Then she took over flight operations without even telling me. Do I have the right to be angry at her? I don't know; she did it to try and turn the tide of the war. For some reason, it hurt worse than usual to be left behind by her. I took it personally when I shouldn't have." His eyes narrowed. "And then that manipulative bitch came into my service, and she knew how to push already tentative buttons until I broke down and made one of the biggest mistakes of my life. Am I asking for forgiveness or sympathy? Am I making a valid excuse? No, I'm just telling you the way I felt. I'm telling you the truth."

Renee stared at him, considering his words. She adored Troy because she knew he was probably the only man in the galaxy who could handle Dia's complex personality. However, he had strayed and put a lot of people in danger by doing so. "Thank you for telling me all of that. I know it must've been hard." She cleared her throat and continued, "And while you were in captivity?"

"Absolutely not. There was one time I pretended to want her, only to get close enough to steal a piece of Hoiltle out of the dress she was wearing, but I insulted her and got punched. That strand of metal is how I was able to build the beacon which led you to me. Other than that, I endured horrible torture rather than make that mistake again."

Renee could tell by his sincerity that he was telling the truth. She sat back in her chair and asked, "So, now what? How do we find her? *Can* we find her? There have been rescue teams combing the galaxy searching for her, but to no avail."

Troy shrugged. "I have no idea. The problem is, unlike me, she has no memory of this place. Who or even what she is—it's all gone. A few years ago, threats were made against us that made me afraid that if Dia were captured, she'd be forced to tell our enemies everything she knew about the EIP, even before she was bonded to it. So, I had rings made with Sonadem, gold and silver that looked exactly like ours. That way, I would be able to grab her hand and hopefully pull her memories into my rings."

Renee just blinked at him for a moment before saying, "I've never heard of anything like that." She saw his rings were gone on his left hand. "So, the flaw in all of this is if your rings were stolen by a completely traitorous cunt, then Dia will never get her memories back, am I right?"

"You are. It's been a shitty fifty years," he said.

"You're not wrong, Harlow. What the hell do we do? Do we just let her go?" she asked sadly.

Troy shook his head. "Nobody here is just going to let her go—not her family, her soldiers, me, or you. Right?"

"Right. What now?"

"Now, we monitor the galaxy as best as we can for signs of the EIP. From what I could tell, there's nothing like it throughout at least this galaxy," he said with an air of determination.

Renee checked her communicator. "You need to start getting ready for your homecoming gala," she said. "You can't face your fans with your hair looking like a coffer rat's nest, Harlow."

Troy chuckled. His meeting with Renee had gone better than he expected.

***

A few hours later, after much-needed grooming, Troy was met at his front door by a transport that took him to the Command Center where his family, Dia's family, Renee, and General Toni Smith were waiting for him. He felt strange dressed in his formal uniform, but it was what his father and the chancellor wanted.

They all went down to the mezzanine, which was filled with delighted citizens. Troy walked around and said hello to everyone. Young women practically threw themselves at him, expecting him to accept that his wife was never coming back.

Troy stopped for a moment and gazed at the murals on the courtyard wall. He admired Dia's for a long while, in awe at how detailed it was. He wasn't thrilled about his, not when he felt he didn't deserve it. Besides, he was home, so it wasn't needed anymore.

Troy gave a speech about how wonderful it was to be back. About how courageous the rescue team that found him was, especially Sergeant Teller, who was healing well from her injuries.

After the ceremony, a large banquet was held in his honor that made him feel even more ashamed.

When the event was finally over, the transport took him back to his apartment. Renee rode with him, and as they stopped in front of his door, she said, "You did good today, Harlow. I know it wasn't easy. But I do have a question."

"What is it?'

"Now that you're home, what're you going to do?"

He thought for a moment before answering, "I'll go back to work as a doctor again. At least, in between heading up the team that I'm going to assemble to find her. You're my commander, Conner."

She smiled. "Good answer." Once Troy disembarked, she told the driver to go, and he watched as her pitch-black braid blew in the breeze as they drove away.

***

Troy aimlessly walked around his apartment before his exhaustion finally drove him to go to bed. As he lay there, glaring out the window, he ran his hand over where Dia should've been. He pulled her pillow toward him, hoping it would smell of the kata orchid shampoo she always used, but it just smelled clean. Troy sighed and finally gave in to sleep. He slipped into a dream.

He was standing in their bedroom, in the far corner. It was daytime, so the room was bathed in light, except where he was. There was a figure standing in front of the window. He recognized the long curly hair, pulled into a ponytail high on her head. She wore a strange green-and-yellow suit with black leather boots.

"Dia," he said.

She turned around, and he was taken aback by her eyes glowing emerald-green but no other signs of the EIP. She didn't seem to see him, as she said in a strange language, "Hello? Is anyone there?"

Troy stepped into the light, and she slowly walked toward him but didn't seem to know who he was. As Troy approached her, he could tell she wasn't the same person he knew as his wife. He asked her, "Where are you, Dia? Are you safe? Help me find you."

She didn't seem to understand their language anymore. She said something he couldn't comprehend. "Do I know you?"

Wherever she was, she seemed to be doing well; she looked happy and appeared to be working with her abilities. Despite all of that, he reached out and took her left hand, pressing it against his face. The feel of her extra-warm skin was intoxicating. He couldn't help but notice she wore her rings, just like she did at home. It comforted him. He spun the ring on her middle finger like she always used to do. She said something else, but the strange words were lost on him.

He let go of her hand and kissed her smooth forehead. Leaning down, he said, "Dia, I'll stop at nothing to find you. If you ever see me, my name is Troy."

Troy stepped back from her and opened his eyes. It was morning in their bedroom.

And Dia was still gone.

CHAPTER 41
CARL'S DILEMMA

C arl and his team's benefactor, Roger Miller, stood in the secret garage control room that the rest of the team had no idea existed. They were watching a video of Heather dismantling a car with precision cuts of green flame. "So, what do you think?" Carl asked, turning to him. "She's come a long way in a relatively short amount of time."

Roger stared at the tiny woman with curly hair doing tasks that defied explanation. He said, "If we ever find our enemy, she'll be the perfect weapon, even if she doesn't want to be."

Johnson studied the screen and said, "It isn't that she doesn't want to be. She's resigned herself to being used as a weapon. She just wants to make any sort of attack or defense be as lethal to the enemy and as safe to the citizens as possible."

"She could achieve that best if she would just take the enemy's life energy. We could end this all very easily."

Carl remembered how upset Heather was about killing the mouse. He could only imagine how devastated she would be if it were a human or these Coronian things Roger was tracking. "She can only do that by touching her, uh, victim. Good luck forcing her to do that, Roger."

Miller continued, "That doesn't matter right now. She's exactly what we've been searching for. Our efforts over the past ten years have paid off, Dr. Johnson. You and your team have done well."

Roger was never one to give him enough information about their mission, but he paid exceptionally well, so Carl didn't ask questions. Johnson looked at the screen and watched as Heather used her energy to unscrew a tiny bolt out of a part on the car. What she'd been able to learn was astounding, which was one of the reasons why he was so concerned, other than the fact that he had become hopelessly attached to her.

Miller could see what Carl was thinking on his face. "You'll do neither of you any favors if you continue to develop feelings for her. I understand—she's beautiful, powerful, mysterious. But also dangerous, volatile, and we have no idea where she's from. Someone of her caliber is probably being sought out by her own kind, Dr. Johnson."

"You don't think I haven't thought of that? I hope each and every day that we're well hidden from more than just Mallory at this compound. What now?" Heather was exceptional, and he was sure someone out there wanted her back.

"Keep letting her work, and do *not* let her leave this facility until I say so." Roger said, "I haven't heard from our foe on this planet for some time now, and I don't want them to find out about our advantage until it's too late for them. Now, I need to go back to my part of this program." He leveled a serious look at Carl. "Remember, no favors."

Carl nodded, and Roger turned and walked out the door.

Back on the screen, he saw she'd found a bunny in the garden and was sitting on the ground, playing with it.

He smiled and shook his head; she truly was extraordinary.

***

That night, as Carl was getting ready for bed, he walked out onto the garden porch and took in the fragrance of the flowers. He sat down on a bench close to his door and heard a familiar sound. Gentle footsteps approached him. Heather came around a fountain and saw him sitting there. Her damp hair was down, and she was wearing a soft cotton robe and slippers. She asked quietly, "Can I join you?"

He smiled at her. "Of course, love."

Heather sat down beside him. They were quiet for some time, listening to the evening sounds of nature. Finally, Carl reached up and placed his hand on her opposite cheek. She rested her head against his shoulder. After a few moments, he said, "You know, Roger thinks I'm not doing us any favors by getting close to you."

Heather didn't say anything, just moved her head closer to his neck. Carl took a deep breath and asked, "Do you think he's right?"

"Is spending time together sitting on a porch and enjoying each other's company a bad thing?" Heather replied. "Or does he believe it's more than that?"

She lifted her head so they could look into each other's eyes. Carl leaned in, and they shared a long, passionate kiss. He pulled back and pressed his forehead against hers. "You know it's much more than that, love," he whispered.

EPILOGUE

Roger had sat by for the past several months, holding his tongue about their new friend.

When Carl contacted him after getting her to the mansion, it was the first time he'd seen her face, and he'd nearly had a heart attack. Somehow, someway, General Dia Harlow had landed on Earth with some mysterious power that Florians weren't known to possess. And she had no idea who she was or where she was from.

Dailings and Rygonians weren't enemies, but they weren't allies, either. Planet Zole was within the same quadrant as Rygone, but they usually had nothing to do with each other. He was sure that would change soon now that they shared a common enemy. Coronians.

Roger had heard about the Coronians turning citizens of their enemies against their home worlds, and he knew that even the mighty Rygonians had a Florian traitor. Nobody was perfect.

He was aware of a unit of female Coronians working on Earth, planning to use this planet as a waystation for attacks on other systems in the area. Earth was closer to Zole than he'd expected, so he was assigned to watch out for movement against the humans. And now, he finally had the tool he needed to make an actual difference. He just hoped Carl didn't ruin everything.

General Dia Harlow had a powerful family and a loyal husband back home. They were all known throughout that quadrant and much of the galaxy as a force to be reckoned with. Carl and Heather—or Dia—were walking a knife's edge that could come back and destroy their tentative advantage against the Coronians. He hoped he could stop them in time.

Roger rewatched a video where Heather absorbed an entire thunderstorm and said to himself, "No wonder they call her Flashpoint."

AUTHOR BIO

Kelly Pardue was born in Colorado Springs, Colorado. She and her husband met in the army, had two kids, and now live in Mesa, Arizona. Any scenes she's written that involve the acquiring and detaining of aliens in mysterious government compounds have no relation to her time in the military. This is a work of fiction, imagination, and not at all of personal experience, of course. Kelly dreamed of being an author her whole life, and those dreams finally came true thanks to hip surgery, of all things. In need of something to do during her recovery, she began writing *Flashpoint*, the first installment of the Regarding Florians series.

After dipping her toes in the mystery and crime genres and toying with fantasy, she discovered sci-fi was her true calling. She also found inspiration in works like *Westworld* and *Shadow and Bone*. Outside of extraterrestrial imaginings, Kelly loves her family and cats, believes donuts are the superior pastry, and admits to singing horribly while driving. *Flashpoint* may be Kelly's first book, but it's not going to be her last. And she won't even need more hip surgery to keep writing!